Also by Paul Bryers

Coming First
The Adultery Department
In a Pig's Ear
The Prayer of the Bone
The Used Women's Book Club

For Younger Readers
The Mysteries of the Septagram:
Kobal
Avatar
Abyss
Spooked: The Haunting of Kit Connelly

ritten as Seth Hunter and Available from McBooks Press

The Nathan Peake Series
The Time of Terror
The Tide of War
The Price of Glory
The Winds of Folly
The Flag of Freedom
The Spoils of Conquest
The Sea of Silence
Trafalgar: The Fog of War

The Vatican C

W

THE VATICAN CANDIDATE
A Harper & Blake Mystery

PAUL BRYERS

McBooks
Press

Essex, Connecticut

McBooks Press

An imprint of Globe Pequot, the trade division of
The Rowman & Littlefield Publishing Group, Inc.
4501 Forbes Blvd., Ste. 200
Lanham, MD 20706
www.rowman.com

Distributed by NATIONAL BOOK NETWORK

British Library Cataloguing in Publication Information available

Library of Congress Cataloging-in-Publication Data
Names: Bryers, Paul, author.
Title: The Vatican candidate : a Harper & Blake mystery / Paul Bryers.
Description: Essex, Connecticut : McBooks Press, [2023]
Identifiers: LCCN 2022034714 (print) | LCCN 2022034715 (ebook) | ISBN 9781493067206
   (cloth ; alk. paper) | ISBN 9781493071784 (epub)
Subjects: LCGFT: Detective and mystery fiction. | Novels.
Classification: LCC PR6052.R94 V33 2023 (print) | LCC PR6052.R94 (ebook) | DDC
   823/.914—dc23/eng/20220721
LC record available at https://lccn.loc.gov/2022034714
LC ebook record available at https://lccn.loc.gov/2022034715

∞™ The paper used in this publication meets the minimum requirements of American National
Standard for Information Sciences—Permanence of Paper for Printed Library Materials, ANSI/
NISO Z39.48-1992.

History is a nightmare from which I am trying to awake.
—Stephen Dedalus, *Ulysses*

Contents

CHAPTER ONE

The Old Priest

Trapani, Sicily—September 2018

THE OLD PRIEST SAT IN HIS CANVAS CHAIR IN THE SHADE OF THE OLIVE trees and watched the sun go down, sliding off the back of the hills to the sea. It was his favourite time of day. Magic hour, the filmmakers called it, when the world is bathed in a greenish-golden light just before it fades into dusk. This is what Eden must have looked like, he thought, when they looked back for the last time. He had always had a fancy for the movies—the 'fillims' he called them in English. In another life, he might have been a director.

From somewhere across the valley he heard a dog bark; it usually happened around this time of day. Same dog, same bark. And then he saw them coming back from the fields, exchanging banter as if they hadn't a care in the world, and of course they hadn't, even after working all day in the hot sun. So full of life and so impossibly young. They might have missed him sitting there in the shade of the olive trees if he hadn't called out to them. *Back already? You've hardly been gone an hour.* And the familiar refrain: *Hard day, Father? Got the supper on? Got the drinks ready?*

The gurgle of plumbing as they showered for Vespers, the clatter of saucepans and cutlery from the kitchen. He watched the shadows lengthening, reaching up the hillside towards him. The sky changing from rose red to magenta and then violet. The first marauding bat flitting above the new bell tower with its bright, beckoning light—its beacon, its holy star.

There had been a monastery here at the time of the Normans. You could still see the stones in the fields, covered with beards of lichen and a sprinkling of purple saffron at this time of year. Lizards live there now, goats browse where the chapel once stood, the bells clinking about their necks as if in mockery of the ancient rituals. Matins, Laud, Vespers, Compline . . . The old priest sees them still, the ghostly figures shuffling through the vanished cloisters. Forgotten lives ruled by prayer, the goats watching with their sly, satanic eyes. Ring it again, see how they run, these holy mice.

He has become irreverent with age, sitting in his canvas chair, in the shade of the olive trees.

There are even older remains down in the valley. For many years people have been scratching among the poor earth and the stones, finding bits and pieces of Roman pottery, the ruins of an old villa, a temple to the god Jupiter, a mosque from when the Saracens were here, an early Christian chapel . . .

There is no end of gods, he'd say to vex the young ones, if you keep looking for them.

'Are you not feeling the cold, Father, now the sun has gone?'

One of the new students from Ireland, her fair skin pleasantly freckled from working in the fields, and her red hair bound in a scarf. There had been several Irish girls of late, a recent influx which the priest welcomed. He had learned English as a young man, though it was a long time since he'd had to use it.

He thought he would stay out here just a little longer, he said, just to see the bats coming out. He said it to tease her, for they thought he was in the first stage of dementia, and he knew she would repeat it—*he's staying outside for the bats to come out.*

He would be in for the blessing, he said.

'Well, then, shall I bring you out a nice cup of tea? Or are you holding out for something stronger as it is a Friday?'

He hated to be fussed over, but he made an exception for the Irish girls. He said a cup of tea would be very welcome, thank you, sister. He'd share a bottle of wine with Father Norbert later—*as it is a Friday.* Father Norbert had just come to join them from Austria, to convalesce after surgery. 'He'll be company for you, Father,' they had said. *Die Alte Herren*, the two old men telling their stories over a bottle of wine.

2

So the young girl left him alone among the olive trees to watch the bats come out, as the dusk settled across the land. He loved this country, this new *Heimat* of his, so *Gemütlich* with the old farmhouses and their terra-cotta roofs, not so different from those he had known as a child in the South Tyrol. The disused wells with the glint of water at the bottom, the old iron ploughs rusting in the fields, the donkeys and the horses in their paddocks. And the old men, sitting on their benches in the village squares, waiting companionably to die. It was a good place for an old man to die.

Ironic, really, all those years he had feared Death would take him unawares, lurking in ambush on the road ahead—during some youthful indiscretion, or engaged in some act of pious deception, and all the while Death was traipsing along behind, patiently following, catching up little by little, year by year. And now here he was, a presence at his side, like some ageless altar boy with a face like a smirking gargoyle. Save that he was not smirking, nor gleeful. Just a little bored, perhaps? Indifferent? Counting the hours until it was over. He had been waiting a long time now.

Then he saw the headlights. A car—two cars—coming up the track towards them and travelling fast enough to stir up a great cloud of dust. Who could it be? They were not expecting visitors as far as he was aware, though it was possible, of course, that he had been told and forgotten. He could remember stuff that had happened three-quarters of a century ago with a clarity that astonished people, but he'd forget what someone had told him in the last few minutes, or perhaps it was just that he did not hear them properly. No, he did not know what kind of cars they were, but he had noticed that they were both black. Yes, they might have been SUVs. He knew what an SUV was. Two black SUVs then, travelling fast, up the hill towards him and swinging into the parking space as if they owned the place, and maybe they did. *Prominente*, he thought. Maybe the Holy Father himself, come to see what mischief they were up to in their remote mountain retreat, what plots they were hatching.

Everything happened so fast after that, it was all confused in his head, like time itself. Confused and distorted, displaced. A series of images, past and present, all jumbled up, like the pieces of a jigsaw there was no sorting out, no making sense of. The men with no faces, just black ski masks with slits for eyes, and guns in their hands. He saw the young Irish girl coming back with his tea and opened his mouth to shout a warning but no words came. He remembered the look on her face and the way she fell, the cup flying from her hands. And then they went inside, and he heard the sound of explosions and saw the flash of fire in the windows. And he thought he heard shouting and screaming but that might have been part of the jumble in his head, the old nightmares mixed up with the new. Then they were driving away, down the hill towards Trapani and the sea.

It could not have taken more than a few minutes. They did not see him there in the shadows. He was not hiding, he told them later, but he found he could not move or shout out, neither a prayer nor a curse. The doctors said he had suffered a mild stroke. But he was shamed that he had sat there, helpless in the dark during the slaughter of the innocents while he, who alone was guilty, sat silent and unseen in his director's chair among the olive trees.

CHAPTER TWO

The Alien

New York, two weeks later

'HAVE YOU EVER SEEN THE ALIEN?'

'The alien?' The merest flicker of a warning light, not yet urgent.

'I mean the movie,' he said. His smile hovered on embarrassed. 'I know it must be long before your time.'

Hannah had thought this was what he meant, but it was as well to be sure. The interview, up to now, had gone reasonably well, she thought, and a lot better than she had expected. They had been through her resumé and there had been no apparent problems, not even with the acting. They had talked about her interest in history, her command of the German language, her work as a television researcher, and playing Hedda Gabler off-Broadway. This was the first venture into what you might call uncertain territory.

Doctor Michael Blake was an Englishman and a historian— a *serious* historian, Hannah's friend Emily had been keen to assure her, despite his recent celebrity. He wrote best-selling but *serious* histories, he had written and presented a major TV series for BBC and PBS on the history of burlesque ('which despite its title was very political'—Emily), and he had recently been appointed Visiting Professor in European History at Columbia and needed a researcher to help him with his next book. Emily, who worked in the same department, had put Hannah up for it. It would make a change, she said, from 'the usual crap,' by which Hannah assumed she meant most of her working life since she had left Vassar. And quite a bit of her non-working life, too.

Emily had briefed her on Doctor Blake, but she had said nothing about an interest in movies. Or aliens.

Hannah was nodding coolly, restraining her enthusiasm. 'I've seen it a couple of times,' she said. 'We did it at drama school. In the screen acting course. In fact, I've seen all six of them.'

He looked surprised. 'All six? All six what?'

'Of the *Alien* franchise. I did my first year submission on Ripley.'

'Ripley?' Maybe it was dawning on him that this was a mistake, but it hadn't dawned on Hannah, yet.

'Lieutenant First Class Ellen Ripley. The Sigourney Weaver character. Seminal female lead. I love that movie and it doesn't even pass the Bechdel test.'

'I'm sorry?'

She was surprised he was not familiar with the Bechdel test but not averse to filling the gap in his knowledge.

'One, it has to have at least two women in it; two, who talk to each other; three, about something other than a man.' She smiled as if this was a joke.

'Ah.'

It was then that Hannah should have stopped, or maybe a little earlier. But she didn't.

'I went on and on and on,' she told Emily later when they met for the post-mortem at a bar in Brooklyn. 'I could hear myself, but I couldn't stop. I was like, "You do know the part was originally written for a man?" And he's going, "No, I didn't know that actually."' She exaggerated the English accent. 'He must have been feeling under the desk for the panic button.'

'But—' Emily was shaking her head and staring at Hannah as if she shouldn't be allowed out without her mummy, or at least some responsible adult. 'How did you get talking about the Alien in the first place?'

'Alien,' Hannah corrected her. 'There's no *The* in the title.'

'Don't go there,' said Emily warningly.

'He asked me about it.'

'*Why?*' It came out as a wail. Emily was well acquainted with Hannah's obsession with the movies; once upon a time she had shared it and tried to compete, but she had retired defeated some years ago.

'Well, that's the problem.' Hannah sighed. 'It was nothing to do with the movie. Well, it was, but only as an analogy. What he didn't count on was having some idiot going on for half an hour about Sigourney Weaver's portrayal of Lieutenant First Class Ellen Ripley and her importance as a role model for generations of young female actors.'

'Oh God.' Emily put her head in her hands.

Hannah looked contrite. 'I must have been more nervous than I thought.'

Hannah hated job interviews. The pressure to impress, the clumsy attempts to catch you out, the bullshit, the front. Most of all she hated being judged. Judged and found wanting. She'd had enough of that with acting. She was too old for it. All those countless auditions when you know they made up their mind within seconds of you walking through the door, and you're prattling on regardless, and really, there should be a trapdoor, like on the old stages, and it opens up and you fall through. The firecracker and the red smoke an optional extra.

Hannah took another long sip of Aperol spritz, through the straw. It was sweet and sticky. For some reason, probably many reasons, when she was depressed or had experienced a setback in her emotional or professional life, she thought sweet and sticky would help. It never did.

'Anyway, what do you mean an analogy?' Emily demanded.

'What?'

'You said, he meant it as an analogy. An analogy for what?'

'Oh yeah. He got around to that in the end. When I let him get a word in. An analogy for Fascism. The way it keeps coming back. You know. *Transmogrifying.* Like a Xenomorph.'

'A what?'

'That's what the alien is, Emily,' Hannah explained with a hint of irritation. 'A Xenomorph. A facehugger, a chestbreaker . . .'

'If you don't stop I'm going to pour this drink over your head, and it would be a waste.'

'No, you need to know this.' There wasn't much in the glass. 'It's the Enemy, the mortal foe of humankind. But there's always someone or some secret sect plotting to keep it alive, nurture it, protect it, thinking they can use it, like its energy, its power, its capacity for unleashing mayhem, for their own purposes. So at the end, when you think it's dead—you've killed it, blown it the fuck into space, poured kerosene on it outside a bunker in Berlin and set it alight—it always manages to plant its seed in something, or someone, so it can come back in some other form for some future generation to deal with. Like us.'

Emily stared at her for a moment, like if she'd had the alien at her disposal Hannah would have been dead meat—a mess of blood and entrails on the floor of the bar.

'Is this him or you?'

'This is him. That's why he asked me about *Alien*. Poor guy.' Her lips began to twitch as she saw the funny side. She bit on the bottom one, but it came out in her voice. 'He was looking at me like a deer caught in the headlights. Or maybe after you hit it.'

'It's not funny, Hannah.'

'No. No, it's not funny.' Hannah pulled herself together.

'I put you up for this job.'

'Yes.'

'Is that what you were wearing?'

Hannah looked down. She was wearing jeans, boots, black puffer jacket over a black T-shirt. Nothing out of the ordinary.

'Why? What's wrong with it?'

Emily shook her head like she didn't know where to start. 'Well, speaking personally, for a job interview, in academia, I'm not talking television here, I might have gone for something a bit more mature, a bit more sophisticated? Same again?'

'No, I'll have a hemlock. Plenty of ice.'

She had a dry martini, the same as Emily. In pursuit of maturity and sophistication.

'So is this what his new book's about?' Emily asked. 'Fascism, and how it keeps coming back.'

'I guess so. Something like that. He didn't actually say much about his new book. Something about Zero Hour, the summer of forty-five.

That's 1945,' Hannah added helpfully. 'But he didn't go into the details. I expect he thought I was a waste of space the moment I walked through the door, and he saw what I was wearing.'

'Oh well, you can always go back to television. Or acting.'

'Thanks.'

The trouble was, she had really wanted this job. It felt like it was right for her. Even if she didn't know much about it. It was set in Berlin and Rome, two of her favourite places in the world. Her grandmother had lived in both when she was young and Hannah had joined her there many times, in her imagination. Berlin, certainly. Nineteen-thirties Berlin. She had transmogrified.

And then there was him. The man she'd just mugged with the iconic feminist heroine. He hadn't been at all what she had expected, even after checking him out on Google. He looked younger than in his photograph—and less nerdy. If she hadn't known he was thirty-five, she would have put him in his mid-twenties, and he had a smile that was like the sun coming out and made him look even younger. She might have been expected to hate that, but she didn't. And she'd liked what he had to say, when she gave him half a chance.

He was a man on a mission, Emily had said. *He might come over all sweet and cuddly and good-natured, but there's an anger in him. That's why he wants people to know about history. He doesn't think it will help—but he can't help himself. He's obsessed.* And then, pure Emily: *Maybe I should try it, he makes shitloads more than I do.*

Hannah had only managed to read one of his books before the interview and even then she'd skimmed through most of it, feeling ashamed she hadn't given it the time and thought it deserved. It was about homosexuality in the Weimar Republic of the 1920s, and then later, after the Nazis came to power. It was called *The Pink Triangle* after the badge homosexuals had been forced to wear in the concentration camps. In one of the interviews she had read, he had talked about making his own pink triangle and wearing it to school as a protest against the bullying he'd suffered for being gay. The head teacher had made him take it off, but the bullying had stopped. She supposed there was a lot of courage in a gesture like that, anger too. But she'd read another piece that accused him of making it up, that you'd never have been bullied for something like that, not in the school Michael Blake had been to, not at the time he had been there.

Her martini was nearly finished. She was drinking too fast. It felt like it was going to be one of those nights. Her phone went. It was on the table in front of her. She looked at it warily, thinking it was going to be Tony. Again. Her very much ex-boyfriend, except that he didn't seem to know what *ex* meant. Tony was becoming a serious pain. Then she sat up straight and nearly knocked over what was left of her drink.

'Shit. It's him.'

The conversation was brief. Hannah didn't say much. She was conscious of Emily's eyes on her. She wished it was not so noisy. She wished she wasn't in a bar. But it didn't matter, it really didn't matter.

'Oh fuck,' she said, when it ended. 'I've got the job.'

CHAPTER THREE

Mystic, Connecticut

'YOU KNOW MY GRANDMOTHER?' HANNAH SAID THOUGHTFULLY.

Her mother's attention remained firmly fixed on the illustration she was working on. A woodland scene, with chipmunks.

'Your *grandmother*?' As if struggling to remember where she had heard the word before. But Hannah was familiar with her mother's various forms of evasion. Ducking and diving was as much an art form to her as any of her more professional accomplishments.

"Your *mother*, Mother. My grandmother. Gabriele. She was in Rome for a while, wasn't she? During World War Two.'

The brush poised in midair. The chipmunks cowered in the doorway of their little log cabin, their expressions—apprehensive. But then they were destined to feature in a book by Ruth Ryder. Why would they not be?

'Oh, we're back there, are we? God, I don't know. Was she? Why do you want to know, anyway?'

'Just something I was reading, for the new job. About Italy.'

A few swift, bold strokes. The sky turned darker.

'Dad said she was sent there when she was in her early teens,' Hannah persisted. 'When things first started getting difficult, you know, in Berlin.'

'Well, if your father told you, I'm sure it must be true.'

Most of what Hannah had learned about her mother's family came from her father, and that was little enough. According to him, Ruth's grandparents had lived in a small town in the Spessart—a region of forest and hills that sprawled over large parts of Hesse and Bavaria and was famous for its folktales. Hannah could remember her father telling her that the seven dwarves in Snow White were really miners from the Spessart who were small and stunted because of their work in the diamond mines. He had also told her—though this might have been when she was a little older—that most of her mother's family had died in Nazi concentration camps during World War Two. Hannah had never succeeded in discussing this, or any other aspect of her family history, with her mother. Any attempt to do so was rebuffed, with attitude.

'History is a virus,' she had said, when Hannah first expressed an interest in the subject. 'It kills people.'

In Ruth's mirror of life, history was the story not of progress but of human misery, pain, cruelty, and injustice, and its study implied an unhealthy obsession with all four.

Hannah crossed to the window. The long lawn sloped down to the harbour. Leaves were falling. Otherwise it was so still, so devoid of life and movement, it could have been a painting. It contained no objects of interest to Hannah other than the image of escape presented by a distant boat.

In its heyday Mystic had been a major seaport, one of the biggest in New England; now its income came mainly from tourism and the people who retired here. The whole town was a kind of museum: the largest maritime museum in the world, according to its website. Her mother had moved here a year ago when she and Hannah's father split up. Hannah had no idea why she had chosen Mystic. For the peace and quiet? Friends? One friend in particular?

Useless to speculate. Even more useless to ask.

Ruth used her maiden name for writing and not many people knew Hannah was her daughter, but those who did sometimes asked her: 'What's your mother really like?'

And Hannah would shrug and reply: 'I don't know. She's a writer.'

Hannah loved her mother—as she frequently assured herself, even in the wake of one of their not infrequent rows. She admired her many qualities. She was proud of her talent, her success, and her independent spirit. But as a mother . . .

From an early age, Hannah had thought of her in the same light as the mother in 'Little Red Riding Hood,' whose motives in sending her young daughter into the forest were at best ambiguous, at worst homicidal, motivated by jealousy and rage. And as for her writing, Hannah had often remarked that every Ruth Ryder book for the younger reader should carry a warning similar to those displayed on cigarette packets.

This Book Can Seriously Damage Your Children's Health.

'Mother, you cannot possibly give this book to a child,' Hannah had once admonished her, when she was herself not much more than twelve. It was a story based loosely on that of the Three Little Pigs, except that in this case the pigs were three schoolfriends, and two of them came to an especially grisly end. And the one that survived was, in Hannah's opinion, more of a psycho than their killer.

Her mother described it as character-forming.

'It teaches kids to look out for themselves,' she would say. 'Besides, I don't really write for children.'

The first book Hannah could remember her mother giving her when she learned to read was *Cold Comfort Farm*, by Stella Gibbons, a satirical story of English countryfolk based on *Wuthering Heights*. It was not—of course—a children's book, but Hannah had identified with the heroine, Flora Poste, and had striven to be more like her. She wasn't sure she had entirely succeeded in this, but the capable, self-sufficient, down-to-earth Flora was still a role model she aspired to, which was very likely why her mother had given her the book in the first place.

'I think I'll go for a run,' said Hannah. 'Before it gets dark.'

'Wrap up warm,' said her mother. 'It's colder than you think in Mystic.'

It sounded like something the White Witch might have said, before she lets the wolves out.

Hannah ran along the side of the river towards the harbour. Her mother had been right about the cold. It brought tears to the eyes. She could feel them freezing on her cheeks. The few people she encountered on her progress through the town looked at her as if she was mad. Sobbing her heart out as she pounded the lonely streets.

But Hannah Harper never cried.

Generations of New England ancestors had maintained a stoic Christian fortitude in the face of misfortune ever since the French and Indian War, and as for the Jewish side of the family, well, they had done enough weeping to turn the rivers of Babylon brackish, as her mother said, and look where it had gotten them.

Ever since she was a small child, Hannah had learned to put a brave face on adversity. Looking up for sympathy after some minor, or even major, mishap, she would invariably encounter a stern parental frown or vigorous shake of the head and learn to control the trembling upper lip, to dam the threatened tears. Thus had she endured cuts, grazes, falls from innumerable bicycles and trees, a broken wrist (in a skiing accident), a sprained ankle (in a soccer game), the casual disappointments of life and love, and even her parents' divorce without a single public display of emotion.

They were, after all, character forming.

By the time Hannah reached the harbour she knew why she hated running. Every breath scoured her lungs with grit, her legs toiled through soft sand. A mutinous voice in her head urged her to divert into the nearest coffeehouse. But she had entered for the New York half-marathon and she intended to do it in less than two hours. She set herself a target. The end of the street. Now the next street. Now the river.

There was barely a gap in the long line of boats moored along the quayside. A fishing boat went out, its wake spreading down the line of moorings, setting each boat off in a jiggling dance. The seagulls perched on the mooring poles viewed the running figure with silent contempt. But suddenly she felt better. She had achieved a rhythm, mental and physical. It always happened, if she went on long enough. This crossing of the pain barrier. She was really moving now.

Stretching out. Letting her legs do the work. A sleek predator, racing across the tundra, a wolf running down its prey. Pity there wasn't anyone to see her, they'd have been impressed. She reckoned she was the fastest thing on two legs in Mystic. Average age, seventy-five.

As she settled into her stride she let her mind wander, as it often did when she was running, off on a track of its own. She thought about Michael Blake and his preoccupation with the Nazis. Was it really because he genuinely thought history was about to repeat itself, as Emily had told her, or was he was just capitalising on people's fascination, and fear? Perhaps now she was working with him she'd find out.

When she reached home, her mother was cooking supper.

Hannah sniffed appreciatively. The run had put her in a better mood, a conciliatory mood. 'Something smells good. What is it?'

'Fish stew,' said her mother.

Hannah waited. Her mother loved cooking. It was one of the things she couldn't resist talking about. One of the few things.

'It's called *Cacciucco*. A fisherman's dish from Liguria.' A long beat, but she couldn't stop herself. 'They use all the stuff left in the bottom of the net. All the fish that aren't worth selling. You're supposed to put a stone in it, too.'

Hannah thought about this without coming to any helpful conclusion. 'Why?'

Her mother shrugged. 'You just are. I suppose because there were always a few stones in the bottom of the net, from the seabed.'

Hannah peered into the pot. It didn't look like stuff that wasn't worth selling. There was lots of white fish, octopus, squid . . . No stones. But she would chew very carefully, all the same. Breaking a tooth while eating one of her mother's stews could be thought of as character forming. Learning a useful lesson.

'Anything I can do?'

'You can pour me a glass of wine. There's a Muscadet in the fridge.'

Hannah poured two large glasses and they sat in what might have been a companionable silence, if one of them wasn't her mother. But that wasn't fair. *Don't be clever, Hannah.*

'I spoke to Dad yesterday,' she said, after a short silence. 'On the phone.' As opposed to a text, or an email, which was their usual method of communicating.

'Oh yes? How is he?' With apparent indifference. They'd only been married for thirty years.

'Okay. Busy.' Hannah's father owned a boatyard in Black Rock. He built small sailing boats to a traditional design, out of wood. He'd had a bad time of it lately, but things were picking up, he said. If you could believe him. He was an optimist. Before he built boats he was a fisherman. He was a big, calm, unhurried man. Lived simply but well. He had a new lady friend, a good ten years younger than himself, but Hannah wouldn't tell her mother that. No point. It wasn't another woman that had come between them, or another man. They had different ways of explaining it, but basically it was as if they had suddenly realised how totally unsuited they were—in every way imaginable. It was a miracle to Hannah that they'd ever got it together in the first place, let alone stayed together for thirty-odd years.

'You should phone him,' Hannah said. 'Ask him yourself.'

Ruth said nothing. Just kept stirring the pot.

'Do you ever miss Black Rock?' Hannah asked her.

'What?' As in *are you serious?* 'Why should I?'

'Well, you lived there long enough.'

A dismissive shrug, but for once she felt compelled to enlarge on it. 'It was a base. I could get on with stuff. And it was close to New York. I needed the contacts in those days. You were happy enough there. And your father certainly was.'

She made this sound like a criticism. Of both of them.

Hannah's father had been born in Black Rock and never really moved away, not for any length of time. Her mother had arrived there when she was in her mid-thirties. She had left England after art school and lived in several different cities in Europe and then in the States, working bars and restaurants, while she tried to make a living as an artist. She had come up from New York to do the illustrations for a book about a mermaid and a fisherman, met Hannah's father and married him.

When Hannah told this story to friends they thought it was romantic. In fact, as far as Hannah was concerned, it was astonishing. Possibly there was a clue in the book, which was eventually published under the title *Mermaids Can't Run.*

In *Mermaids Can't Run*, which was Ruth Ryder's first commercial success, a mermaid falls in love with a fisherman and they have a child—a beautiful little girl. But the mermaid cannot really live out of water. She feels she can't breathe. Finally, when her daughter is three years old, she tells the fisherman she has to go back to the sea. She says she'll come back when the child is seven.

On her seventh birthday, the little girl waits and waits but her mother doesn't come back. That night the child goes down to the sea and the next morning her distraught father finds her clothes neatly folded at the water's edge. But her body is never discovered, and a few weeks later he is out fishing when he sees two mermaids swimming under his boat. They are his missing wife and child.

This was one of Ruth's happier endings.

'Oh come on, Mother, you must have been happy there, at least some of the time.' It wasn't so much a statement as a question, or a plea.

'Life isn't about being happy, Hannah.'

Oh, good. Glad we cleared that one up, then.

'Have you ever been happy, Mother?'

She was pushing it now. Goading. Why did she do that? Her mother did not answer, but she gave Hannah a look as if to say, *You want a fight? I hope you've been in training since the last time.*

'What about when you were a little girl?' Hannah persisted. 'In England? Were you happy then?'

Stupid question, but the response was unusually phlegmatic, almost benign for her mother.

'Not particularly. Sometimes I was, sometimes I wasn't. Like most kids.'

Hannah sometimes pictured the young Ruth Ryder as one of those kids in a Roald Dahl story whose parents are wiped out on the first page—or even before the story starts—killed by rhinos in Africa, or in a plane accident, or a car crash. Ruth was just two years old when her parents had their own car crash, in the English county of Hampshire, where they were staying with her father's family. They had died instantly. Ruth should have been with them, but she'd had a bad cold and had been left with her grandparents. She spent the next sixteen years with them, apart from when she was sent away to school. They had taught her a little verse, to help her speak English the way they thought it should be spoken. *In Hertford, Hereford, and Hampshire, hurricanes hardly ever happen.* But they had happened to Ruth.

'Do you ever think about your parents?' Hannah asked, taking a chance on the almost-benign mood continuing.

'Why would I? I can't even remember them.'

'But—don't you ever feel sad about that?' No comment. 'Didn't your grandparents ever talk about them?'

Hannah was seriously pushing her luck here. Ruth had fallen out with her grandparents shortly before leaving England—needless to say, Hannah had no idea why. She'd had nothing to do with them since. She never even spoke about them if she could help it.

'Their only son died in a car crash,' Ruth said. 'Maybe they were a bit upset.'

'Even so—you'd have thought . . .'

'What?' The tone was a sharp warning.

'That it would have cropped up—in conversation. I mean, you'd think they'd talk to you about your own mother and father . . .'

'Why should they? They were English, Hannah. They don't talk about stuff like that. They just get on with things. Anyway, what is this?' The clouds swirled, the storm was about to break. 'Is this why you came home—to interrogate me about our family history? Is this research for the new job or something?'

'No, Mother.' But it was true of course, at least partly. 'It's just that, this guy I'm working with . . .' Hannah had told her mother about the new job when they spoke on the phone before she left Brooklyn, but Ruth hadn't shown much interest. It was History. 'He asked me about being Jewish. You know, whether it would make a difference to how I felt about—what we're working on, and I thought, I don't *know* how I feel.'

'Oh God, are we going there again?' Hannah's mother had been brought up to have a firm sense of Jewish identity and the Jewish religion, and she had rejected both. Or so she said, whenever Hannah had raised the subject. Hannah had been brought up to have neither.

'If you're curious about being Jewish, go and read a book about it,' she said now. 'Go and find a rabbi. Go and join a synagogue. But don't ask me about it. All right?'

'Okay, okay. Sorry I asked.' Hannah had been home three hours and already she was sounding like a sulky teenager. This was not uncommon.

Her phone went. It was Blake. She was so startled by the coincidence she took it right there in the kitchen, in front of her mother, though she never liked her mother to know too much about her personal life—or her work. She supposed they were the same in that respect.

'Everything okay?' she said brightly.

She thought he might have changed his mind about her, or found some discrepancy in her resumé. Maybe he'd discovered the real reason she'd quit the job in television.

But it wasn't that. Something had come up, he said. It would mean arranging a trip to Berlin. For both of them.

'Wow,' she said. She was still in teenage mode.

'Is that a problem for you?' he said.

'Not at all,' she said. 'I love Berlin.'

As if she flew there for long weekends. Hannah thought she saw her mother's cheeks bulge as if she was pretending to be sick into the *Cacciucco*, but she probably imagined it.

Instead of meeting at the Uni, Blake wondered if she would mind coming out to his place on Long Island first thing Monday morning and they could talk about it.

'Great,' she said. But she wondered why they could not talk about it in his study at Columbia.

'Sorry to ring you with work. It was just—I think we've had a bit of a breakthrough.' He sounded excited. She could see his face with that boyish grin. She felt happy for him, and herself. She thought she might have made the right decision, for once.

'Great,' she said. She wished she could stop saying *great*, but she still didn't know what it was they were working on, exactly. Maybe she'd find out on Monday.

'I'll email the directions,' he said. 'Enjoy the rest of your weekend.'

CHAPTER FOUR

The Murder Factory

HANNAH CAUGHT THE SEVEN O'CLOCK FERRY FROM NEW LONDON. IT took ninety minutes to cross the Sound and it would take about the same to drive to Blake's place, but despite the early start and the best part of two days with her mother, she felt good—better than she had in months.

The only cloud on her horizon was yet another email from Tony. A rambling piece of nonsense accusing her of having sex with him to further her career, such as it was, and dumping him when he was no longer of use to her. If this kind of thing went on she'd have to do something about it. But not today. Today she felt liberated. Renewed. She was enjoying the drive. She had a ten-year-old Beetle convertible which she hardly ever used and she was tempted to let the roof down, but there was still a bite in the air, and sometimes it got stuck. She was dressed more or less as she had been for the interview. Emily had clearly been wrong about her appearance, she thought with satisfaction. But she had determined on a change of manner. She was going to go for the serious, thoughtful approach. She planned on doing a lot of listening. She was not going to talk much. She was certainly not going to talk about movies.

She had now read two more of his books, or at least most of them. One was called *Bonds of Blood* and it was about the German officers and officials who had planned to assassinate Adolf Hitler in 1944. Her only previous knowledge of the story came from the movie *Valkyrie* starring Tom Cruise as Count Claus von Stauffenberg, who had tried to blow up Hitler and most of the General Staff with a bomb hidden in his brief-case. Hitler's survival had led to the collapse of the coup and in the days and weeks that followed the SS had indulged in a bloodbath of reprisals, rounding up thousands of people who could be even vaguely associated with the conspirators. It was their final act of vengeance on the German officer caste—Prussian aristocrats, professional soldiers, men who had always despised the SS as brainless thugs and jumped-up nobodies until another jumped-up nobody gave them a uniform and a cause. Blake's book had focussed on the feud between these two groups, the old order and the new—and in such a way that you found yourself drawing parallels between similar conflicts in the modern world.

The other book was in many ways more powerful and certainly more original. It was called *The Murder Factory* and it was the story of Mauthausen concentration camp in Austria, known to its inmates as *Morthausen*—the Murder House. Blake's book was not so much about the living conditions inside the camp—it was more about the work that went on in and around it, and in the ring of satellite camps of which it was the centre, especially Ebensee, where they sent thousands of prisoners to dig tunnels in the mountains of the Salzkammergut for the weapons factories the Nazis were building deep underground.

Mauthausen, it appeared, was the hub of a vast industrial complex. The factory system taken to its hellish, brutal extreme. Large global companies, even small local contractors, men who had supported the Nazis with funds since the early thirties, were now getting their payback. Mauthausen was the centrepiece of a system that supplied them with government contracts and labour. The workers did not have to be paid, or clothed, housed, or fed. The SS took care of all of that. They could be worked twelve hours a day, seven days a week, and if they died, you just asked the SS for more. They were literally worked to death.

Michael Blake maintained that despite their later denials, many people had known perfectly well what was happening in the camps and had profited hugely from it. And he backed his claim with evidence. He named individual companies, and the individuals who ran them, and in the last chapter he listed those that were still operating today— the carmakers, the chemical firms, the banks and finance houses, the drug companies and arms manufacturers—the commercial, financial, and industrial core of the modern Europe.

There was anger in the writing, as Emily had said, but what came across to Hannah was more a sense of cold, almost brutal detachment. Blake was like the mythical being her father referred to as the Recording Angel—'the man clothed in linen, who had the writing case at his side,' so that what he observed would never be forgotten or overlooked. *This is what happened. Don't look away. This is what these people did, and they'll do it again if we let them.* But alongside this, or intercut with it, was a much more human voice that Hannah found particularly moving and that stopped the reader from sinking into absolute despair. So that among the recording of horrors almost beyond imagining, there would be stories about the triumph of the human spirit, such as the one about a group of prisoners who 'bought' a boat—a fantasy sailing boat—in which they were going to sail the world together when the war ended. It was an entirely imaginary boat, but they owned shares in it, just as you might own shares in a dream, and they would trade these shares on an improvised stock market. When their spirits were low, men would offer their shares to other prisoners for an extra piece of bread, or a spoonful of soup, and buy them back when they were feeling more hopeful. On the darkest days only the most optimistic would buy into the dream at such a price, and yet it was this optimism, more than the bread and soup, that kept them going when so many lost the will to live.

Stories like this made Hannah warm towards the man she was travelling to meet and with whom she would soon be working, and to feel that at long last she was going to be working on something of value.

She turned off Route 25 at Riverhead and switched on the radio, and caught the end of a news bulletin which informed her that the Pope had arrived in New York to address the UN on climate change. She switched to a music channel instead.

She reached the outskirts of Westhampton just before ten and followed the directions she had been given along the coast road until she saw the mailbox. She turned onto the track and followed it between sand dunes for a few hundred yards to the house. It was not as grand as she had expected, but it was the perfect location for someone who liked seclusion and a sea view. Certainly, it was a great place to work.

Hannah rang the bell twice but there was no response. Perhaps he'd gone for a walk along the beach, she thought, or a run. He looked like he kept fit. She went round the back. Steps led up to a deck with several wicker chairs and a table with a book on it, opened and laid face down as if someone had just been interrupted in reading. There was a sailboat in the distance, a squabbling mob of seagulls at the water's edge— but no Doctor Blake, no one else either. The creak of a door alerted her, and she turned with a half-smile expecting to see him standing there. The door swung in the breeze. She mounted the steps and crossed the deck, pausing to glance at the title of the book, *Alien, the Archive: The Ultimate Guide to the Classic Movies*. She smiled. Was this her doing? Both book and table were covered with a light dusting of sand.

'Doctor Blake?' Hannah stepped through the door. He had told her to call him Michael, but it did not come readily to her—not yet. It took a moment for her eyes to adjust to the change of light, and then she saw the body hanging from the ceiling.

CHAPTER FIVE

Post-Mortem

SHE ASSEMBLED THE PIECES OVER THE NEXT FEW DAYS, FROM THE scraps of information the police fed her and from what was reported in the media—and what had lodged itself in the darkest part of her brain before she fled.

The naked body, turning slightly on the rope, as if moved by the draught from the open doors, and the two black holes where the eyes should have been. And the other one, in a sitting position on the floor, back to the wall, legs stretched out in front of him, his chin on his chest. He might have been asleep if it weren't for the blood.

She had driven back to the road before she phoned the police, but she couldn't remember much about how she got there. She sat there waiting for them, the car doors locked, the engine running. Even later, when they interviewed her, she had trouble putting the facts together, explaining them in a sequential order. They told her a lot more than she could tell them about the inside of the house, but then they'd spent a lot more time in there than she had.

They told her that the man on the floor was Michael Blake and that his throat had been cut. One slash from left to right with a straight razor, found lying at his side. The other one—the one hanging from the stairs, not the ceiling as she had thought—was the man he shared the house with, a man called Bernard Freude. There were extensive burns to his face and genitals. Caused by a barbecue lighter, the police said. They asked her if she thought Doctor Blake was the kind of man who could have done that. She said that had not been her impression when she met him, but you didn't really think things like that, did you, when someone was interviewing you for a job. They looked at her as if she was being sarcastic, but she wasn't. She was in shock.

Her mother came to pick her up, but Hannah insisted on following her in the VW. Otherwise she thought she might never see it again. When they got back to the house her mother poured a large Scotch for them both and made some soup. Hannah drank the Scotch but took only a few mouthfuls of soup before it made her sick. Her mother didn't ask too many questions, but she let Hannah do as much talking as she wanted for a change. She even phoned Hannah's father and he came up from Black Rock. He arrived just as it was getting dark, and they sat there, the three of them, in the kitchen. It was the first time her parents had met since the divorce, Hannah thought. Ruth asked him if he wanted to stay the night.

He said he'd stay in a hotel in Mystic.

'Don't be ridiculous,' said Ruth. 'There are four empty bedrooms.'

Hannah suppressed a wince. Her father lived in a room above a boathouse.

'You don't have to stay anywhere,' she said. 'I'm okay, honestly.'

But he held on to her a while before he left. His eyes were moist. Maybe the ban on crying was down to her mother, all along. Maybe his new woman had told him it was all right to cry.

Hannah watched him drive away and felt terrible. It felt like she'd rejected him. She slept badly. There were the inevitable nightmares, but they were not of the scene in the beach house; they were more like the ones she'd had as a child. Finally, she took a pill and woke up in bright sunlight, her mother at the door with a breakfast tray. Coffee, juice, bowl of cereal, toast, and marmalade in a little bowl.

All it took was a murder.

She spent the day moping about the house and making loads of phone calls. She spoke to Emily of course. She had just been interviewed by the police.

'They think he killed Bernie and then himself,' she told Hannah. Her tone indicated disbelief. 'They said there'd been "tensions" between them. They said they had statements from their friends. I don't know who *they* were.'

Hannah wondered why the police were talking so freely to Emily and not to her.

'You knew this guy?' she said. 'Bernie.'

'I'd met him. He was an art dealer. Lovely man.'

'Do *you* think he could have done it?' Hannah asked. 'Doctor Blake, I mean.'

'Don't be ridiculous, Hannah. They just don't want to look for the real killers.'

Hannah thought about this. 'So, who do you think they should be looking for?' she asked.

'I don't know. I'm not a detective. But there are some obvious suspects. Homophobes. Trolls. Neo-Fascists who didn't like his books. He got a lot of hate mail. I told the police, you should look at his Twitter account. But they don't want to know.'

'Why wouldn't they want to know?'

'To make life easier for them, Hannah. God! Like it's an open-and-shut case.'

There was a silence and Hannah thought she might be crying. She was wondering what else to say when her mother shouted that her father was on the landline. It went on like this for days.

The strange thing was Tony didn't call. Didn't even text. She had a new stalker instead. The detective lieutenant from the Suffolk County Police Department. Lieutenant Kewbank. Call me Stan, he told her. He phoned Hannah constantly and called at the house, to see how she was. Hannah told him what Emily had told her about the hate mail.

'We've looked into that,' he said.

'And?'

'Well, where would you start?'

It seemed an odd question to ask, if you were a detective.

'We've gone through his emails, Facebook, Twitter, Instagram, Tumblr . . .' So much for Emily. 'He knew how to stir the shit, I'll say that for him.'

'So he had a lot of enemies?'

'You could say that but, you know, these people, they don't usually kill people. Not like this, anyway.'

Hannah thought about this. There were several movies dealing with this very subject, but she was trying to stay off movies.

'So you reckon it was the boyfriend?'

'Did I say that? I'm keeping an open mind. What do you think?'

But then her mother came in and threw him out. Hannah had never known her mother so protective. It was like she was on guard duty. But then one evening, a few days after the event, she said she was thinking of going out, would Hannah mind?

Hannah said she wouldn't mind at all. She asked her where she was going.

'Just to see a friend.' She sounded defensive, but then after a moment she added: 'Someone local. I won't be long.'

A friend? So her mother had friends. Locally. Hannah knew next to nothing about her mother's life since she had moved to Mystic. Maybe for some time before that. She had never mentioned any new friends— or even neighbours for that matter—and no one ever called at the house.

Hannah watched carefully to see what she was wearing when she left. But it was just jeans and a sweater, like she always wore. Maybe not the oldest jeans. And she wore boots. With heels. Even a touch of makeup. Lipstick certainly.

'You look nice,' Hannah said, eyeing her shrewdly.

'I won't be late back,' Ruth said.

Had to be a lover. Why not? She was still a good-looking woman. She looked a good bit younger than her age. Even so, Hannah wasn't happy about it. Male or female? she wondered.

This was ridiculous. Also pathetic. She stared moodily out the window, towards the river. There was still some light left in the sky. She thought she might go for a run.

It was dark by the time she arrived back at the house. She dropped her keys and her phone on the kitchen table and drank some water from the fridge. It was seven o'clock. Very quiet. She was soaked in sweat— it had been an especially punishing run. She decided to take a bath instead of the usual shower.

She put in lots of her mother's expensive bath gel and lay there among the bubbles with the water up to her chin and her eyes closed.

It felt good. She did not often take a bath. She felt almost relaxed for the first time since her drive to Westhampton.

Then she heard something, like someone moving around downstairs. A door opening maybe.

'Mother!' Hannah shouted. 'Is that you?'

She had left the bathroom door slightly ajar. She held herself very still, listening for sounds of movement. But there was nothing. Then what could have been a creaking stair.

She climbed quickly out of the bath and pushed the door shut, sliding the little bolt at the top. It didn't look as if it would keep anyone out for more than half a second. She opened the window. It was at the side of the house looking out on the neighbours, just beyond the hedge. Hannah had never met them but she knew they were an elderly couple, with a dog. She looked down. It was a long drop to the ground but there was a drain she thought she might be able to reach.

But this was ridiculous. This was Mystic, Connecticut.

Even so . . .

Where was her phone? She must have left it on the kitchen table. Why had she not brought it into the bathroom with her? She looked around for something she could use as a weapon. Nothing obvious. She looked in the bathroom cabinet. The usual stuff. Lotions, toothpaste, medication, plasters . . . And a small pair of surgical scissors. She was starting to feel cold with the window open but she didn't want to close it. She clenched her fist round the scissors and crossed to the door again and pressed her ear against the thin wooden panelling.

The door burst inward with a violence that threw her back against the edge of the bathtub and into the water. She caught a glimpse of a large figure in black wearing a black mask or hood. Then she was drowning, hands on her shoulders pressing her down. She kicked and clawed without noticeable effect. Then suddenly the pressure eased and she thrust her head up out of the water, gasping for air.

A masked face inches from her own. A black woollen ski mask. Holes for the eyes, a slit for the mouth. The lips moved.

'Hannah? Hannah, right? You know what I mean?'

Hannah opened her mouth, not to answer, but to scream or bite, she hadn't made up her mind which. It didn't matter either way. Her head was back under the water and this time she knew it was for good. But even as she was drowning she felt something hard pressing into her buttocks, and some remaining clarity of thought told her it was the scissors. She groped for them with her right hand and wrapped her fist around them and lashed out, out and up.

The hands left her shoulders. She surfaced again. Her assailant was holding his chest, just below the armpit, and she could see the blood spurting out through his fingers. Then she rose up out of the water and stabbed him again in the middle of his black mask with all the force that fear and fury could give her.

Chapter Six

Home with Mother

There was no way, Hannah had frequently assured her friends, that she could ever live with her mother. No imaginable circumstance could make her subject herself to that level of emotional tyranny combined with a sardonic indifference. This was probably unfair, and even at the time she could imagine quite a few circumstances, but they all involved her mother being in need of the care and attention, not Hannah.

She had been here for over three weeks now. In that time the fall had turned to winter. There had even been some snow—a few thin patches were still scattered about the lawn and the forecast was for more at the weekend. Hannah paid close attention to the weather forecast. It seemed to be one of the few external events that could engage her at the moment. That and the Pope's tour of the United States.

Hannah did not know why the Pope's tour interested her, but it did. Not very much, but enough to watch its progress on television and to listen, albeit vaguely, to debates on the Pope's politics and his attitudes on issues like abortion, and sexual abuse, and immigration, and climate change, and even married priests, an issue that had not troubled Hannah a great deal in the past. There was something going on here that Hannah did not entirely understand, but that had obviously caused a great deal of division, not only among Catholics, but among many people of other religions, and even nonbelievers. Was the Pope a Communist, as some said he was? And did it matter? She tried to engage her mother on the subject, without great expectation, which was just as well.

'Frankly,' said her mother, 'I don't give a damn.'

Her mother thought that people who engaged with religion, even as a subject worthy of debate, were 'nuts.' The only time Hannah had heard her laugh out loud, at least in recent years, was when they were watching *A Serious Man* by the Coen brothers and the main protagonist asks his rabbi what does Yahwah want of him?

'It's not just about religion, though, is it?' Hannah persisted, but received a look that discouraged further discussion.

But for the most part Ruth was unusually conciliatory, and astonishingly attentive. She took to making large quantities of soup which she stocked in containers in the fridge as if she contemplated opening a soup kitchen for the needy of Mystic. Once, for the first time in Hannah's memory, she even made chicken soup with barley. It was a little late in the day, Hannah thought, for her to start being a Jewish mother. She almost said this, but it would have been unnecessarily provocative. Also, ungracious.

Hannah took the coffee she had just made over to the large picture window at the end of the kitchen and stood there looking out over the lawn to the river. It was a depressingly familiar view. It seemed to Hannah that she had spent far too much of her recent life looking at it. This time there was a man in it. A man with a dog. One of the security guards her mother had hired. There would be another out front. Until yesterday there had also been a police car, but the police had decided twenty-four-hour protection was no longer necessary, not from them at any rate, not if Hannah's mother could afford her own.

For the first few days there had been a number of media vehicles. Not quite a media circus, but getting there. The story of the woman in the bath attacked by a mysterious masked assailant and then stabbing him with a pair of scissors before making her escape '*naked and spattered with blood*' had been covered by every TV channel and newspaper in New England, and possibly across the nation. Mystic had never known anything like it, even in its wilder days as a whaling port. But neither Hannah nor her mother had been willing to give an interview on the subject, or indeed any other, and before long they'd all packed up and moved on.

As for her assailant, he too had declined to be interviewed. The police had found a trail of bloodstains from the bathroom to the outside of the house, where he was presumed to have left his car, and there the trail ended. They thought he had probably had an accomplice, they told Hannah. As for the motivation, they confided that they were pursuing several lines of enquiry, though none of them seemed to include the possibility of a link to the killings on Long Island. Neither Hannah's role as Blake's researcher nor her discovery of the bodies had been made public, they pointed out. So unless she was personally acquainted with the killer, how would he know who Hannah was and that she was currently staying with her mother in Mystic, Connecticut?

Hannah had no answer to that.

So, the favourite theory was a burglary gone wrong, they implied. The intruder had been diverted from his primary purpose of theft by the chance discovery of a naked woman in a bath. It was not entirely incomprehensible. Only a few things had been taken—Hannah's laptop, her phone, a few pieces of her mother's jewellery—but the police reckoned that this was because of Hannah's dramatic escape and their own pressing need to quit the premises.

But then she had been asked if she knew of anyone who might want to hurt her, or at least frighten her, and with the greatest reluctance, and only because she felt she had to, she told them about Tony.

Tony had been a director at the last production company she had worked for and they'd had an affair. This was not unusual in the television industry. Nor was it unusual that at least one of those involved was married. The trouble, from Hannah's point of view, was that Tony turned out to be a lot more married than she had thought he was. She had known he had a wife and two young children, but he had told her that his wife was 'cold' and that the marriage was effectively over; they were only staying together until the kids were a little older. He had a small apartment in the Bronx where he lived alone most of the time, visiting his family in New Jersey only at the weekends. But when Hannah really started thinking about this, and had discussions on the subject with her friend Emily, she was as much appalled by herself as by him. Probably more so. She did not ask him to leave his wife; she told him the affair was over. But Tony did not want it to be over, and he was very persistent.

Hannah told the police about the texts and emails, first appealing, then abusive; the messages on social media, the confrontations in bars and restaurants . . .

'So he was stalking you,' they said.

She supposed you could call it that.

What else would you call it? they wanted to know.

So they took him in for questioning. He had an alibi and there was no forensic evidence linking him to the crime, but now they had a plausible motive and a suspect, they were reluctant to let it, or him, go. The discovery that he was of Italian origin and lived in New Jersey was the clincher so far as they were concerned. It was quite possible that he had put someone else up to it, they said. This would explain why the assailant had said 'Hannah, right?' when he was holding her down in the bath—he had wanted to make sure he'd got the right person, and not another family member, or an unfortunate house guest. It could also explain the theft of her phone and laptop with the evidence of Tony's abusive texts and emails.

Hannah was not convinced. Tony might be stupid, but he was not *that* stupid. Sending her abusive texts was one thing—sending a pair of heavies to her mother's house to scare her half to death was probably above his pay grade. Nor, to be fair, was it in his nature, so far as she could say.

But then, as Emily never ceased to remind her, she was a poor judge of character.

She felt obliged to inform her mother of the police suspicions— and the reason for them. After all, she was paying for the protection. Inevitably this led to further interrogation, and Hannah had been forced to reveal the full facts about Tony's family circumstances.

'Just don't tell Dad,' she said.

Her father was descended from New England Puritan stock and though he claimed not to be religious, he maintained a strict moral code. He would have been deeply disappointed in her. In truth, she was deeply disappointed in herself.

'Why would I tell your father?' her mother said with a touch of the old Ruth. 'You're not a child. You make your own choices, even if they're the wrong ones. So long as you're prepared to take the consequences.'

All things considered Hannah would rather have had a blazing row. It stirred up all the murky waters of shame and self-reproach she had felt in the immediate aftermath of the affair.

And then there were the nightmares. Some of them new. The naked body dangling from a rope, the face with empty eyes, the sitting figure in the pool of blood—these were from the house on Long Island. The hooded man and the attempted drowning—these were from her mother's house in Mystic. But they were intercut with the other stuff—the vintage stuff going back to her childhood. Nightmares of frightened people being rounded up by men with guns, violent, shouting men in uniform with barking dogs, while she, Hannah, hid under a bed. Hannah knew this came from the Spielberg movie *Schindler's List*. She had been in her early teens when she first saw it and did not know as much about the Holocaust as she did now, but she had immediately associated the little girl in red with her grandmother, Gabriele. But in the new version, the girl was Hannah. Hannah had *become* Gabriele.

Hannah knew that this was almost certainly the result of her recent experiences, but it turned her interest in Gabriele, the lost grandmother, into something of an obsession. She needed to know what had happened to her as child and adult. She wanted to know what it was like for her in Germany in the 1930s, and then in Italy during the war years. She wanted to know about the fatal accident in Hampshire, where hurricanes hardly ever happened.

She did what research she could on a spare laptop of her mother's, wondering why it had taken her so long. She looked for her under her grandmother's maiden name—Fabel—and then under her married name—Ryder. There were plenty of people with both names, but none of them could be linked even remotely with her own grandparents. And there was nothing about the car accident in 1956. Not in Hampshire. Or Hertford or Hereford. Or anywhere else in the British Isles.

The nightmares continued.

The doctors said she was suffering from post-traumatic stress disorder. She was prescribed paroxetine in the short term and counselling over a longer period. Hannah took the pills but not the counselling and continued to mooch around her mother's house, feeling more and more depressed and worthless. It did not help that she had no job to go back to, or anything useful or challenging to work on. The day after the police left she told her mother she was going back to Brooklyn. She couldn't stay under guard for the rest of her life, she said. In fact, she thought she would feel safer in her apartment in Brooklyn than in her mother's house in Mystic, even without the security guards. It was five floors up and harder to break into. She might even be able to go to the bathroom without fear of someone crashing through the door and trying to drown her. Besides, she had to find another job or she'd go mental.

Her mother offered to pay for security, but Hannah turned that down, too. She was inclined to think that the police had been right in their original assumption that the house had been targeted by burglars because of her mother's status as a writer and artist who had made loads of money. There had even been a recent profile of her in *Vanity Fair*, with pictures of her home in Connecticut which Ruth had reluctantly consented to after pressure from her publicists.

So back to Brooklyn she went.

She shared the apartment with two other women, both in television, but when she arrived back they were out. She had not told them she was coming. This now seemed remiss of her—she might at least have sent a text—but much of her thinking of late was remiss, it now seemed to Hannah, as Emily had been trying to tell her for some years. She did not think things through. She got an idea into her head and declined to examine it for flaws or possible consequences. This was depressing. So was the apartment. It seemed colder than she remembered it, and unwelcoming. She felt like a ghost returning to her past, and the past no longer wanting her. She was unpacking the overnight bag she had taken to her mother's—all of four weeks ago—when her phone went. It was Emily.

'I'm with Michael's brother,' she said. 'He wants to meet you.'

CHAPTER SEVEN

Voice from the Dead

THEY MET IN THE BAR ACROSS THE STREET FROM THE APARTMENT. Hannah felt she needed people about, though in fact there were only two of them besides the bartender, neither of whom looked as if they would be much good in a fight, or even as a witness. She doubted if Emily had checked if he really was Michael Blake's brother. There was a vague resemblance, but he was older, darker, and he had a beard. There was nothing of the engaging, boyish look of Michael Blake, none of the warmth. Eyes like a cold blue sky in Mystic.

'I'm sorry to have to ask,' she said, 'but do you have any ID?'

He didn't seem to mind, or if he did, he didn't show it. He reached into the inside pocket of his jacket and produced a passport which he slid across the table towards her. Burgundy-coloured and stamped with a golden harp and the words *Eire* and *Ireland*. The harp was reassuring. She turned to the relevant page. Aiden Barry Blake. A photograph that more or less approximated to the person sitting opposite her. Born Belfast, 1983. Occupation: public relations consultant. An address in France, nowhere she knew. Under next of kin it had the name Michael Blake, with a contact number.

'I'm sorry,' she said again, sliding it back across the table. 'Recent events have not inclined me to be over-trustful.' She did not normally talk like this, or act like it, but normality had undergone a serious readjustment in her mind. A degree of caution seemed advisable. She was wondering how much he knew already. Emily had probably told him what had happened while she was staying with her mother in Mystic.

Along with every other detail of her life over the past twenty years. It was strange, in fact, that she was not here with him. Had he told her he wanted to see Hannah alone?

'I'm very sorry about your brother,' Hannah said.

A curt nod. 'I hear you were the one who found him,' he said. 'Do you feel up to telling me about it?'

She spared him as much detail as she could, but it was still bad enough. His face betrayed no emotion.

'I'm sorry,' she said again. 'I wish I could have done something for him, but . . .'

'I think it was probably a bit late for that,' he said. This was unnecessary but she made allowances.

'Have the police told you anything? she asked him. 'About what they think happened?'

'They think he hanged his partner from the stairwell and used a blowtorch on his face—and his balls. Not necessarily in that order. Then cut his throat. His own throat. They think he did that last.'

The brutal tone was almost certainly a way of protecting himself, but it shocked her all the same. 'They told you that?'

'Not in those exact words but enough for me to fill in the blanks.'

'But why would they think he would *do* that.' Anything she said was going to sound crass, but she had to do better than this. 'I mean, they must have some—something to . . .' Her voice trailed off.

'You think? Well, I could be prejudiced, but it's not my experience of the police. I suppose it depends what country you're in.'

She wondered how much experience of the police he had as a public relations consultant, and where.

'Did you know his—' What was she to call him—partner, lover, friend? 'The man he was with?'

'No.'

She waited for him to say something else, but he didn't.

'It doesn't make any sense,' she said, still struggling.

'Apparently there's forensic evidence,' he said, 'which they weren't prepared to share with me.'

They sat in silence for a moment. He had bought her a beer when she came in, but she had hardly touched it until now. She wondered what else he wanted from her.

'I heard that you had a break-in,' he said.

She looked at him. 'Did Emily tell you?'

He didn't reply. 'What did the police make of that?'

'What do you mean?'

'Are they working on any theories? Lines of inquiry?'

'They seem to think it might have been a friend of mine.' She realised how ridiculous that must sound. 'Well, not a friend, as such. An ex-boyfriend.'

He watched her as if he was a policeman, waiting for a confession. She wondered if that is what he was. A policeman. She was pretty sure he was not a public relations consultant. 'Is that what *you* think?'

'I don't know what to think. I mean, I know it wasn't my ex-boyfriend who tried to drown me in the bath but—whoever it was, he knew my name.'

'He knew your *name?*'

She told him what she had told the police.

'*Hannah, right?*' he repeated. '*You know what I mean?* What does that mean?'

'I don't know. I don't know for sure if that's what he said. My ears were full of water, I'd been held under it for long enough. I was scared I was going to die.'

'But how would he know your name?'

She was about to say *I don't know* again, a bit more forcefully, but she reminded herself he had just lost his brother, he was grieving. 'He could have got it from my phone,' she said. 'I'd left it in the kitchen. Or from Tony—which is what the police seem to think.'

'But they don't think it had anything to do with Michael?'

'No. But—they haven't exactly confided in me.'

'Why do you think that is?'

'Well, why would they? Whatever happened in that house, it was a while before I got there. The night before, they think. I mean, I'm not a witness or anything. Besides—' She repeated what the police had told her about keeping her name confidential.

'But they took your laptop. And your phone.'

'Well—burglars do—take things like that.'

'With all the notes Michael sent you?'

Emily must have told him that. She was convinced the two crimes had to be linked. Something to do with Blake's work. But Emily was like that. She scorned conspiracist theory, but anything that touched her personally, it was a conspiracy.

Hannah was shaking her head. 'Honestly, they weren't something you'd kill for. It was all history.'

'Was it?' He looked at her in that way again. 'He pissed a lot of people off, Michael, with his fucking history. There was a bit too much of the here and now about it for some people's liking.'

He picked up his beer and drank like there was something he had to drown.

'Another?' he said, setting down the empty glass. She shook her head; she had barely touched her own.

'Mind if I do?'

She didn't but she wondered how long this would go on for.

'What exactly was it you were working on?' he said when he came back from the bar.

She really didn't want to go into that now. It was too complicated. Besides, she was more than a little hazy on the detail, and it was bound to lead to other questions she probably couldn't answer. 'He didn't—we hadn't really discussed it properly, but it was about Year Zero.' Blank stare. 'The end of World War Two?'

He had probably heard of World War Two.

But it wasn't just an ending, not the way Michael Blake had put it—it was a new beginning. The beginning of everything that had happened since. Hannah was trying to remember exactly what he had said to her during the interview. And what she had read of his notes before her laptop was stolen.

'He wanted to follow up on some of the people who lived through all this,' she said. 'Like a time-slice of history. The summer of forty-five. Soldiers, journalists and photographers, victims of the concentration camps, but mostly Nazis. But—' she hesitated, because she didn't know how to put it—'I think he was kind of groping for an idea, or that he had it in his head, but he hadn't properly worked it out yet.'

She judged from his face that she was not explaining this very well, but that was because she did not properly understand it herself.

'So he called you at the weekend, wanting you to work with him at his home on Long Island. Did he say on what, exactly?'

'No. He just said something had come up. That we might have to go to Berlin. I was meant to be arranging it.'

'But you don't know what it was,' he pressed her, 'this thing that had "come up"?'

'No.'

'Would you be interested in finding out?'

'Me?'

He shrugged. 'Why not? You were doing the research.'

But she wasn't, she wanted to say, she hadn't even started. She didn't know why she couldn't say that. He had taken an iPad out of the shoulder bag he had on the floor at his feet. She sat looking at him as he switched it on, wondering where they were going with this. Could she say she had to be somewhere else?

'These are Michael's emails,' he said, turning the pad round to face her.

She gazed at the list. There was nothing that seemed especially significant to her, but she was having trouble taking them in. 'How did you get these?' she said.

Again, no answer. Somehow she didn't expect it. 'Anything strike you as odd about them?'

She tried to focus. 'No. Not without reading them.'

'That's all there is,' he said. 'Eleven emails. All since he died. Not much more in his Junk mail, and the Deleted folder is empty.'

She didn't get it.

'Well, wouldn't you have expected a few more than that?'

'Maybe he deleted them after he read them. Or moved them to another folder.'

'There is no other folder. Nothing with anything in it. And as I said, the Deleted folder is empty.' She could hear a hint of irritation in his voice. More than a hint. Or maybe it was frustration.

'Maybe he deleted that, too,' she said.

He was shaking his head. 'He wasn't that organised, not the Michael I knew. Anyway, look at the ones that are there.'

'You want me to go through them? Now?'

'It won't take long,' he said.

She suppressed a sigh. Most of them were faculty notices, nothing of significance. A couple from students, again saying nothing very much. One was a receipt for $25 from something called the US National Archives and Records Administration—'for the reproduction of inboard Federal passenger arrival records for ships and airplanes 1941-1950.' That might be related to his research for the book, but it wasn't exactly earth-shattering. And there was another from the National Archives in London that read: 'Thank you for your recent enquiry, but while the NA holds records for Germany and Austria, the records of the Allied Commission for Italy were deposited with the Historical Records Section, A60, Department of Army, Washington DC. Copies of a selection of the papers appear among War Office records WO204/9742-WO204/10089 which may be viewed on application online.'

Aiden wanted to know if it meant anything to her. It didn't. But it hardly seemed to be that important.

The only one of any real interest was from a Doctor Irma Ulbrecht, assistant curator of something called the Schutzstaffel Museum in Berlin: 'Hi Mikey—I am so glad you are coming to Berlin. I hope this means you are on the right track at last. I have something to show you that you will not find on the internet. Also, I think I know what Hanna took with her, when she left Berlin.'

It was signed Irma, with two kisses.

'Hanna,' he said. 'Is that you?'

Hannah shook her head. It was the German spelling, she said. But who did she mean?

'Sounds like Mike and this Irma woman were fairly close,' he said. 'Mikey. I've never known anyone else call him that. And the Schutzstaffel Museum in Berlin, do you know what that is?'

She didn't.

'I looked it up,' he said. 'It's a warning museum exposing the crimes of the SS, with a library and an archive.'

He found the website on Google and turned the iPad again so she could see it.

'Between 1933 and 1945,' Hannah read, 'the central institutions responsible for Nazi persecution and terror—the secret state police, their house prison, and the leadership of the SS—were located in the centre of Berlin. There is no other place in the world where terror and murder were planned and organised on the same vast scale.'

They checked on Doctor Irma Ulbrecht but there was not much on her, other than that she had been born in Berlin and had degrees from the universities of Heidelberg, Vienna, and Oxford. All in history-related subjects.

'Maybe they were students together, at Oxford,' said Hannah. It was an obvious and not very helpful point to make, but she didn't know what he expected her to say. Or do. 'Had he never mentioned her to you before?'

'Not that I recall. What does she mean about him being on the right track—at last? And having something to show him—why couldn't she just send it?'

He looked at Hannah as if she would know. She looked at the screen again—as if that would tell her.

'How would you feel about following up on this?' he said.

'Me?' She really must stop saying that, but she was taken by surprise. 'What do you mean, following up?'

'Picking up where you left off.'

'Where *I* left off?'

'Where Michael left off, then.'

She almost laughed, but it would have been inappropriate. 'I wouldn't know where to start,' she said. This was probably not what she should have said, as a professional researcher, but she was not at her best.

'Well, you could start with this,' he inclined his head towards the screen.

'You want me to email her?'

'I think it would be better if you saw her in person.'

'You want me to go to *Berlin*?'

'You were going to go with my brother.'

Had she told him that? She didn't think so. This was Emily, again.

'But—*why*?' she said. 'What good would it do?'

'I'd just like to know what Mike was working on,' he said patiently. 'And what is this "right track" she's on about.'

'Why don't you give her a call and ask her?'

He was shaking his head. 'I can't do stuff like this. I don't know the first thing about it. Besides, it would be better coming from you. You were working for Mike, you speak German . . .'

'But she seems to speak English. I mean   ,'

She stopped. He had taken out his wallet. He pulled out a bundle of banknotes and stacked them on the table. She wasn't counting, but there seemed to be a lot of them. Maybe a thousand dollars or more. What kind of people carried that much money around with them in cash these days? She looked around the bar but it was still empty.

'Take this as an advance,' he said. 'It's all I have on me. If you give me details of your bank account, I'll transfer another three thousand tomorrow.'

'I'm sorry,' she said. 'I know you're upset but this is crazy.'

'Why? Have you got anything better to do?'

He had a point. But he must have decided this was the wrong approach.

'I'm just asking you to carry on whatever work you were going to do for my brother. This should cover the trip to Berlin. If you don't want to carry on after that, then, fine. At least we'll have tried.'

Did she owe it to Michael Blake? She had hardly known him but . . . She closed her eyes and massaged her brow. She saw him sitting at his desk during the job interview and then morphed onto the floor of that terrible room. She had an uncomfortable feeling that she did, but probably could have argued her way out of it, given time.

She looked at the man sitting opposite her now. 'She might not want to see me,' she said.

'I'll take a chance on that, but I think from the tone of that email . . .'

'But honestly—where is this going to get us? You really think this has something do with—with what happened on Long Island?'

'I'll never know if I don't ask.'

'You should do this yourself,' she said again.

'I can't. I've got to stick around for the inquest,' he said. 'Then I have to take him home.'

'Home?' She didn't get it for a moment.

'To bury him.'

Chapter Eight

The Funeral

Home was never an easy place to be.

They were born in Belfast during what people called the Troubles. Aiden in 1983, at the height of the IRA bombing campaign; Michael a couple of years later, during a quiet month. Their father always said this was what made them so different. Aiden was 'explosive' and 'bloody-minded'; Michael a quiet, calm, gentle little boy, inclined to be a bit of a wuss.

Aiden thought this was bollocks, even as a kid. Wisely, he didn't say so. His dad would have flattened him.

In fact, most people considered Aiden to be the calmer of the two, almost frighteningly so at times, and Michael, though quiet, had a temper on him—especially when he felt people were taking advantage of him, or in pursuit of justice, for himself and others, even others who were long dead.

In any case, the lull did not last long and the Blakes found themselves in the thick of it. There were particular reasons for this. It was a mixed marriage—their father, Derek, was a Protestant; their mother, Imelda, a Catholic. This did not go down well in Northern Ireland. To make matters worse, both of Imelda's brothers had connections with Sinn Fein and the Provos. This made the family a target for Protestant extremists and the security forces, while there were those within the IRA who had marked Degsy Blake down as someone to be watched, or seen to.

So the family moved to England, taking the route favoured by so many over the years—the night ferry to Liverpool—and home became a three-bedroom semi on a social housing estate in Garston, not far from the docks. Aiden's dad found work in a timber yard, his mum as a teaching assistant in a local primary.

Garston had begun life as a fishing village on the Mersey but by the nineteenth century it was part of Liverpool's sprawling docklands, specialising in the import of coal. To the young Aiden, coal dust seemed to have seeped into its every pore, but by the time he moved there the docks were in terminal decline, the former dockers mostly on benefits, and Garston as rough and tough a place to grow up as anywhere in England. At least people weren't trying to kill you for being a Catholic or a Protestant—or a bit of both—but they did their best to knock the bejasus out of you, simply for being different. And the Blake kids were different.

When Aiden was eight and Michael six, their mother sent them to a private school a bus-ride away in the relatively affluent suburb of Woolton. Every day they walked to the bus stop on Allerton Road, wearing their school uniforms: blue blazer, cap and badge with the school motto, *Ad Vitam Paramus*—We Prepare for Life. And every day they came back just after four and the local scallies gave them a practical lesson in what it meant. It wasn't just the uniforms they objected to; even worse were the accents. No one on that estate spoke like Aiden and Michael. It would have been bad enough if they'd had a Belfast accent, but every Thursday evening after school and on Saturday mornings after catechism, the two brothers were taken by their mother to Mrs Madison's Academy of Drama and Public Speaking in Woolton Village—to have elocution lessons.

It was one of Aiden's major grievances with his mum that she'd had the ambition to give them a good education but lacked the basic common sense to realise how their private school uniforms and their elocution-lesson accents would go down on a council housing estate in one of the most deprived areas of Liverpool. Day after day when they came home from school, there'd be a gang of scallies waiting for them near the bus stop. Their caps would be the first to go. They'd usually find them later in someone's front garden or thrown up a tree. Once or twice they'd been peed on or used to wipe up dog shit. Or some kind of shit. Michael would cry. Aiden would go into his shell. They soon learned to take their caps off before they got off the bus and stuff them in their school satchels, but the satchels themselves were an incitement to violence.

Their mother tried to stop it of course. She found out who the boys were and complained to their parents. This only made things worse. Their

48

father, characteristically, taught them to fight. Degsy, as his mates called him, was a boxing fan and a great admirer of Muhammad Ali, though it was then a good ten years since his last fight. But Degsy had grown up when he was the greatest, so he taught Aiden to fight like Muhammad Ali—to float like a butterfly and sting like a bee.

It took Aiden a while to get the hang of this and, as his dad admitted, he was a long way from reaching the standards of his idol, but it made an immediate impact at street level. Whenever the occasion arose, Aiden would calmly offer to fight the whole gang, one by one. Then he would take off his blazer and his cap, give them to his little brother to hold for him, and enter the ring of jeering boys. Amazingly, it was almost always a fair fight—or at least 'fair' by the standards of Garston. The gangs had their code. You had to watch out for the head butts—but no one else joined in, even when Aiden began to win.

To the astonishment of the onlookers, he would move around the improvised ring with his hands hanging loosely at the sides, just like his dad's hero, skipping and dancing and ducking and weaving, while his opponent unleashed a torrent of blows into thin air. Then he would start hitting back. He usually aimed for the nose, for he had found that a bloody nose would stop a fight faster than anything else and leave no lasting damage. Usually. If that failed, he would deliver a succession of rapid body blows with both fists, ripping up into his opponent's midriff—the tusked boar, his father called it—and then flattening him with a right cross as he reeled back. By the time he was eleven he was rarely beaten, even by boys two or three years older. The Louisville Lip would have loved it.

Unfortunately his mother didn't. When he came back with blood on his shirt and cheerfully announced it was all right 'cos it was some-one else's, she was not amused. And his father wasn't there to defend him—'cos if he wasn't at work in the timber yard he had other things to do. Imelda decided her firstborn was turning into a thug.

'Do you not have the wit to talk yourself out of trouble, like your little brother?' she would ask.

It was useless for Aiden to point out that his little brother's wit only worked because the other kids knew his big brother would beat the shit out of them if they as much as laid a finger on him.

But Aiden had enough wit of his own to work out that fists weren't the only answer. He learned to use his brain, too, and not only to avoid trouble. By the time he was sixteen he was the brains behind some very hard cases indeed. By then, he had fallen out with both parents and a great many other adults, too. Michael was the only witness of Aiden's misspent youth that he hadn't fallen out with, and Michael was the only reason he ever came home.

And it was because of Michael that he had come home now.

He sat next to his parents in the front row of the little chapel in Allerton Cemetery while Father Francis did his best with some fairly unpromising material.

It had been a surprise to Aiden than any kind of religious ceremony was permitted to a man who was suspected of being a suicide and a killer. But there had been no official verdict on that as yet, and apparently the Church no longer had a rigid policy as to who could and could not be buried on holy ground—it was left to the individual priests to decide for themselves. Even so, Father Francis had elected to conduct the funeral service in the cemetery chapel rather than the parish church and had clearly gone to some trouble to find prayers that might be considered suitable for the occasion.

'God of Hope, we come to you in shock and grief and confusion of heart. Help us to find peace in the knowledge of your loving mercy to all your children and give us light to guide us out of our darkness into the assurance of your love, in Jesus Christ our Lord, Amen.'

Aiden's mother made the sign of the cross. She sat, grim-faced and dry-eyed, almost within touching distance of her son's coffin. It was impossible to know what she was thinking—whether she thought Michael innocent or guilty, at peace with his Redeemer, or suffering the torments of the damned; whether this had tested her faith beyond endurance or whether she regarded it as yet another burden that God had placed upon her thin but stalwart shoulders. The sign of the cross indicated the latter.

It was Aiden's father who wept. Michael had always been his favourite as a child, even though he could never teach him to use his fists or to take the slightest notice of his homely words of advice. There had been issues between them but never the implacable, prolonged hostility he displayed to Aiden as a teenager. If he knew Michael was homosexual he never acknowledged it. Michael's academic achievements, his books, his television appearances, his increasing fame, they were the important thing. The Professor, he called him. "Ask the Professor here, he'll tell you." Whereas with Aiden—he was always wary, on his guard, as if one day his older boy might turn on him and beat him to a pulp.

Derek Blake was a small, ginger-haired man of fiery temperament, whereas Aiden took after his maternal grandfather, a big, calm, dark-haired man from County Tyrone who had been a blacksmith when there were still horses to be shoed. Aiden had outgrown his father by the time he was thirteen and this did not help an already abrasive relationship. There had been one occasion, about this time, when his father had leaned over the dinner table and whacked him across the head for some perceived disrespect—not in itself an unusual occurrence—and Aiden had stood up, already several inches taller, and looked at him in such a way that his father picked up his plate and took himself off to eat alone in front of the television. It was the last time he tried to hit either of his sons but there was no emotional contact either, not with Aiden. And despite the tears, there was none now.

When the service came to an end, Aiden stepped up to the altar with the men from the undertakers and took the front end of the coffin on his shoulder for the last part of it. They walked into a chill wind whipped across the Mersey, bringing a bitter, thin rain, and they lowered the coffin into the grave while Father Francis said the final words of consolation. There were a good few mourners, though Aiden knew none of them personally. Friends from Oxford, possibly, or people he had met during his career in television. No one from their schooldays that he recognised. He glanced briefly into the grave. No words came to mind, of sorrow or of parting, but he was determined that it would not end here, like this, in a cold, lonely graveyard in Garston.

He looked away across the bleak expanse of the cemetery. A few flowers, well past their prime, bowed their heads in the drizzle, and autumn leaves dripped onto the gravestones. Fuck this, he thought, get me out of here. He might have been speaking for his brother. And then he saw the van.

A large white van, parked in one of the lanes that crisscrossed the graveyard, not far from the little chapel they had just left. No one would have thought twice about it and nor would Aiden if he was not in the business he was in. It had a logo on the side and the name of an electrical contractor, 24-Hour Service. Aiden noted the single darkened window in the back and the studded panel that could be for ventilation or a directional mike.

He was still thinking about this and its implications, when he became aware that the mourners were moving away from the grave. Reluctantly he followed his parents back to the waiting cars. His mother had decided there would not be a wake, either back at the house or in some local hostelry. It was 'inappropriate,' she had declared. Aiden was thankful enough for this, but he did not look forward to going back home alone with his parents. He wondered how long before he could decently make his excuses and leave. Or perhaps he could leave now. It was not far to the airport. He doubted they would miss him. They'd probably be relieved to see the back of him.

But it was impossible, of course. Inappropriate.

Two men had appeared at the back of the white van. Aiden watched them as they took out a toolbox, crossed to one of the old lampposts lining the roads through the graveyard, and removed a metal plate from the base.

Paranoia was an occupational hazard. But it kept you alive.

He was about to join his parents in the funeral car when he felt a hand on his arm and turned to see the priest, Father Francis, squinting up at him through the drizzle. His eyes, surprisingly blue in so grizzled a countenance, were vaguely questioning.

He and Aiden had only a passing acquaintance. Aiden had stopped going to Mass about a year after Father Francis joined the parish. He remembered arguing with him once, but not what it was about. The priest had been closer to Michael, who had been one of the altar boys and sang in the choir. He was probably in his late sixties now, Aiden thought, with the look of a badly stuffed teddy bear. Aiden braced himself for the pious words of solace and consolation.

'Fancy a jar?'

Somewhat to his surprise, Aiden found himself nodding.

There was a pub near the cemetery, a big old Victorian building, much in use by funeral parties. It wore a suitable air of mourning, but there were no other mourners, as far as he could tell. Aiden got the drinks in. A pint of Caines for himself and a Guinness for the priest.

'Bloody awful weather,' said the barman. Aiden nodded. 'You've managed to find some sun though.' He was looking at Aiden's face.

'Just got back from Dubai,' said Aiden, who saw no reason for reticence when you could as easily lie. It was not far off, anyway.

'All right for some folk.'

Aiden picked up the two pints and carried them over to the priest. He was sitting at a table by the window, where there was a bit more light.

'Cheers.' They clinked glasses. 'To Michael,' said the priest.

They drank in silence for a moment.

'They always thought it'd be you they'd have to bury,' the priest said, by way of an ice-breaker. 'Especially when you were in Iraq.'

'I've always been a disappointment to them,' Aiden acknowledged.

The priest smiled.

From where he sat, he could see into the car park and down the drive to the road. There was no sign of the white van.

'You see much of him recently,' he asked the priest, 'Michael?'

'Oh aye. I usually saw him when he came back to the Pool. We'd have the occasional jar at the Mariners. Talk about football and that.'

This was a surprise. He couldn't see Michael having a jar at the Mariners, or any other pub in Liverpool, with or without a priest.

'So when was he last home, then?'

'Must have been last Christmas, before he went for the job in New York.'

'Say much about that, did he?'

'Can't say he did, really. Seemed to be looking forward to it, but . . . you know Michael. Didn't talk that much about his work.'

'Nothing about his new book?'

'Didn't know he was writing one. What was it about?'

'The usual, I think. World War Two. The Nazis. Hitler.'

'Well, I suppose it still gets people going. In this country anyway. It's all they've got some of them, and they weren't even born.'

'So you just talked about football?'

'Football, history, religion . . . He was always interested in the Church, Michael, though more from a historian's point of view. Not what you might call a believer.'

'There was a time, when he was a kid, I thought he might become a priest.'

'Michael? No. I don't think so. Not that I was around then.' He looked at Aiden speculatively. 'Your mother thought you'd be the one who went down that route, if either of you did.'

'Me?' Aiden blinked. 'What made her think that?'

'You went to a convent, didn't you, on Saturday mornings—for catechism?'

'Only because she sent us.'

'She said you'd come back like there was a halo round your head, like you'd seen a vision.'

'Bollocks,' he said. 'Sorry but . . .'

The priest waved it away. He'd heard worse.

But Aiden was thinking about it. 'Unless it was Sister Sarah,' he said.

'Oh aye?'

'She was the nun who taught us. American. Irish American from Boston. Young. Early twenties, I guess. Bit different from the usual line in nuns. Round here, anyway.'

'And you were?'

'Eleven, twelve? Old enough to think about it. If you're tempted in the night, say three Hail Marys, she'd say, and think of something else. If only she knew.'

The priest shook his head in mock censure. 'Be more than three Hail Marys, my son, for lusting after a nun. Father MacDermot it would have been in those days. He'd have had you doing the stations of the cross—on your knees.' He pointed at Aiden glass. 'Another pint?'

But Aiden's phone went. 'Sorry, I'll have to take this,' he said.

It was Hannah from Berlin.

'How'd it go?' she said.

She knew it was the funeral that morning.

'As you'd expect,' he said. 'How about you?'

'Well, she was not exactly forthcoming but—I think there is something. Only, she's not going to tell me about it.' There was a pause. 'I think it might be worth you coming over here yourself.'

54

CHAPTER NINE

The Schutzstaffel Museum

HANNAH HAD MET DOCTOR ULBRECHT IN HER OFFICE AT THE Schutzstaffel Museum.

It was probably fair to say it had not gone well.

Doctor Irma Ulbrecht was not at all the strait-laced academic Hannah had expected. She was much younger, for a start—probably in her mid-thirties, a little older than Hannah, maybe—part-Asian and very good-looking, even beautiful, though in a somewhat in-your-face way that Hannah did not normally favour, though she did not think it was aimed at her. But it was the way she dressed that Hannah found most surprising, at least in someone who was not only a respected historian, but a custodian of the horrors of the Third Reich. She wore a tight black sweater with a short black skirt and Lurex tights and cute little ankle boots with heels that must have brought her height up to six feet. She could have been a model.

It was clear from the start that they did not like each other much. But maybe Doctor Ulbrecht just did not like Americans. They had started the conversation in English, which she spoke perfectly, with only a slight German accent. Hannah thought it would be rude now to switch to German and almost certainly unnecessary so far as understanding was concerned, but she wondered if it put a barrier between them.

But there was also a sense of something territorial, which Hannah did not quite understand.

'You knew Michael well?' she asked. She used his first name to imply a degree of intimacy, but this too made her feel uncomfortable, a fraud.

'We met at Oxford maybe ten years ago. I was a Rhodes scholar and he was doing his doctorate, with some teaching. We have stayed in contact over the years. We have many interests in common—academically at least.' She had been staring at her phone, lying flat on her desk, as if expecting an urgent message, but now she looked up and gazed at Hannah directly. 'And you?'

Hannah confessed that they had only been working together for a short while before his death. She did not say how short. She and Aiden had talked over how much information was necessary. They had agreed it was impossible to say nothing at all—to maintain so gross a deception as to pretend Michael was still alive—but in her email, Hannah had said very little about the circumstances of his death. She had not disclosed that it was she who had found the bodies.

'And yet you are to continue with his work?'

'Well, that is what the family wanted. As a kind of legacy.'

This, too, had been Aiden's suggestion.

That direct stare again. 'You are an academic yourself?'

'No, but I've researched a number of television documentaries and ...'

'Really? Documentaries? For television?' The tone of polite interest did nothing to lessen the sting. 'So, what do Michael's publishers think of this?'

Hannah could feel the flush in her face and neck, a tincture of embarrassment and anger.

'The family has yet to discuss it with his publishers,' Hannah said. 'They wanted to get a clearer picture of where Michael was going with it—which is where I come in.'

'He did not discuss this with you, his assistant? Where he is *going with it.*'

'Well, of course—but he was at that stage when it could have gone a number of different ways.' Hannah floundered. 'As I said, the trip to Berlin was a sudden decision on his part, and we didn't have a chance to talk much about it before he was ... his death.'

She waited. Doctor Ulbrecht was also waiting, but it was she who broke the silence, with a hint of irritation.

'Well, he was writing about the bludgeoning to death of Nazism and here is where it happened. Mainly.'

Hannah took a chance. 'I had the impression that you shared an interest in certain people who were here at the time.'

'You mean the *Bunkervolk?*'

The expression was unfamiliar to Hannah. She assumed it meant the people of Berlin in Year Zero, hiding in their cellars while the bombs and the shells rained down and the Red Army advanced street by street. But it didn't. It meant the people who had been in *The* Bunker, the *Fuhrerbunker*, with Hitler, in the final days.

'There is some, what is the English word—*crossover*—I guess, but . . .' Doctor Ulbrecht gazed into space as if she was thinking about it or what she was prepared to reveal to Hannah. The office was in the basement of the museum, but Hannah did not think this was an indication of inferior status. The building was vast, but it was built mainly on one floor. Light flooded the spacious office from a large plate glass window set high in one wall, almost a skylight. The furniture was modern, minimalist. There were bookshelves on three walls, packed tight with books. None of them left lying about. No photographs that Hannah could see. Not even a notice board.

'As you probably know, I am preparing an exhibition on this subject.' Hannah had not known this. 'The topography of the bunker complex. Who was where and what they were doing in those last few weeks and days. Michael's interest was in what happened to them next, those that survived. Did they pass on their ideas, their fanaticism, to the next generation? Did they have a plan?'

'And did they?'

She shrugged. 'I would not call it a plan. There is no evidence that they wanted to save National Socialism from the ruins or prepare for a Second Coming, as Michael seems to have thought. Maybe they had had enough of it by then. But did he not talk to you about this?'

'Not really,' Hannah admitted. 'I think he was still trying to work out where he was going with this.'

'Yes.' A sad smile. 'This is Michael. He has a lead and he worries it like a dog with a bone. In many ways he was more of a journalist than a historian. It was his strength and his weakness. He would have some—what is the word?—half-baked idea that he would work at until it was almost convincing. This is why his books are so successful, I think. It gives the reviewers an opportunity to express their own opinion, which they like, of course. But some people have said that he bends the facts to fit the theory.'

This was by far the longest speech she had made in the short time Hannah had been with her, and it suggested that despite their apparent friendship, she was not uncritical of his methods, and perhaps envious of his success. There was certainly an element of competition between them.

'And what was the theory this time?' Hannah asked, chancing her luck.

'Oh, Michael has this idea that National Socialism is a virus that never goes away. It just mutates or finds another host. I think he is right about that but sometimes . . . Well, he is not here to defend himself, is he?' The cool eyes focused on Hannah with a glint in them that had nothing to do with tears. 'But I am surprised he did not discuss this with you, his research assistant.'

'He discussed most things with me,' Hannah said. Lied. They had not had enough time together for that. 'But not this, for some reason. But I think this is why he was planning the trip to Berlin.'

'Well, if you do not know, I am sure I do not.'

There was quite a bit of what Hannah's mother would have called 'the madam' about Irma Ulbrecht. And she obviously knew a lot more than she was prepared to admit.

'He did mention someone called Hanna that you wanted to talk to him about,' she proposed cautiously.

It was hardly a change of expression, but there was something in her face, a sudden tension that had not been there before.

'Hanna?' She frowned. 'But this is your name.'

'He didn't mean me. Perhaps one of the *Bunkervolk*?'

She shook her head again, still frowning. 'It means nothing to me, I am afraid.'

She's lying, Hannah thought, but she could think of no way of pursuing the subject, not without admitting she had read Michael Blake's emails after his death, and she was not ready to do that.

For the rest of the interview Doctor Ulbrecht ducked and dived or questioned Hannah about Blake's death and what Hannah knew about the police investigation. It was clear that this was the only reason she had agreed to see her in the first place. The meeting was almost certainly as unsatisfactory for her as it was for Hannah.

Surprisingly she escorted her to the stairs at the end of the corridor. Perhaps to make sure she left the premises.

'You must visit our current exhibition while you are here,' she said. 'You will see it on your way out. I was going to show Michael when he came here. You will find it instructive, I think.'

Hannah wondered if this was a clue or a diversion. She felt quite sure that this was not what Doctor Ulbrecht had meant in the email. But she took a look at it, all the same.

It was a photographic exhibition featuring members of the SS, the paramilitary guard that had propelled Hitler to power and maintained it through the years of repression and murder that followed. Hannah anticipated the usual images of jackbooted fanatics, strutting their stuff at mass rallies, beating up Jews and Communists in the streets and imposing their merciless regime throughout Europe, but the theme of the exhibition appeared to be the SS in their leisure hours, enjoying group outings in striped blazers and Panama hats, hiking in the coun- tryside in their lederhosen, playing football, drinking from large steins in beer gardens or picnicking beside a lake against a stunning back- ground of mountain and forest. The message appeared to be that these monsters of legend were not that different—at least in their appearance and their leisure pursuits—from other men in any other country in the world. That they were, in fact, quite ordinary. It was this that was so disturbing about the exhibition to Hannah. You could imagine the same kind of men anywhere, and in any era, dressed slightly differently perhaps, but of the same basic build and disposition—big and overweight for the most part, but not unduly threatening, quite amiably bovine, in fact, until you remembered what they had done as they went about the brutal business of making the world a better place for people like themselves.

It did not instil a new sense of purpose in Hannah, exactly—she was still far from convinced that there was any link between Michael Blake's death and his work—but she was less inclined to give up at the first hurdle. Irma Ulbrecht might come over as a condescending cow, but basically they were on the same side, if only she could be persuaded to see it.

'I think we should tell her the truth,' she told Aiden when she called him to report back. 'I think she knows more than she's prepared to say. But there's no way she's going to tell *me* about it.'

'Why not?'

'Because . . .' *What could she say? Because she feels I'm a threat? She just doesn't like me?* She settled for; 'I don't think she trusts me. She thinks I'm just trying to pick her brains.'

'Well, you are, aren't you?'

Hannah said nothing.

'So what do you think we should tell her that would make her any more trusting?'

He was being sardonic, but she was hardened to that. 'Be more open with her,' she proposed. 'Tell her what you really think about Michael's death. And I think it would be better coming from you than me.'

'Why would it make any difference coming from me?'

'It just would. You're his brother and—I think she was genuinely fond of him.' Was she? 'You can get a direct flight from Liverpool,' she said. 'It only takes a couple of hours.'

A moment's silence. 'Well, I *could* come to Berlin,' he said. 'There's no point in hanging around over here. Let me check the times.'

She already had, but she let him do it himself and spent the next few minutes wondering if this was a mistake. She couldn't even be sure Irma would agree to meet him.

'I can be there this afternoon,' he said when he called back. 'Lands just after three. Can you book me a room?'

Hannah stopped at Reception on her way out. Then she set off for her second rendezvous in the German capital, one that she hoped would be rather more rewarding than the first.

CHAPTER TEN

The War Hero

'I COULD NOT FIND MUCH ABOUT YOUR GRANDMOTHER I AM AFRAID, but there are some things I can show you.'

David Gradowski was a researcher at the Jewish Museum in Kreuzberg. Very intense with dark, probing eyes that peered at her through round-framed spectacles, and a mass of wiry black hair, he put Hannah in mind of the young Lev Bronstein before he became Trotsky. He seemed like a man on a mission, and he was. He was filling in the spaces where people's lives had once been.

'This is the one photograph we did find. Gabriele with two of her schoolfriends when she was eight years old. She is the one on the right.'

Hannah looked at the faded picture on the computer screen. A long, thinnish face framed by plaits and looking very serious, with no attempt to smile for the camera. She wore a plain, striped dress and white ankle socks. The caption read 'Ruth Adler, Lily Geissel, Gabriele Fabel, Juedische Freischule, June 1934.'

Gradowski explained that one of the first things the Nazis did after they came to power in 1933 was to forbid Jewish children to attend German state schools. They had to go to their own Jewish schools.

'But this was a very good school,' he said. 'It has its origin in the eighteenth century. In fact, one of the founders was the composer Mendelssohn. The building is still there, on Grosse Hamburger Strasse, and it is still a school, the Jewish High School it is called now, though you no longer have to be Jewish to attend. That is how I found the photograph—in the school archive. It was in a box with some others.

Unfortunately, they were in a very poor state. This is one of the better ones, and I have done my best to enhance it. The names were on the back.'

Hannah looked again at the girl who had been her grandmother. What was she thinking as she stared so seriously at the camera? Did she know how bad things were? Did she think it would get any better—or a lot worse? How bad *was* it, for a young Jewish schoolgirl in Nazi Germany in 1934? There were trees in the background and one of the girls was holding what could have been a napkin in her hands or a small towel. Was it a picnic? A school outing?

'Thank you. It is the only picture of her I have ever seen,' she said.

They were speaking German and it sounded very stilted to her ears, too formal to express her true feelings, though she might have struggled with English, too, in this instance. Gradowski made a small, self-deprecating gesture with his hands. 'It is little enough. I will make a copy for you if you wish. But you said that you were interested in the family background also? Well, here we have quite a lot of information. Gabriele's father was a prominent figure in prewar Berlin. A journalist and a filmmaker.'

'A filmmaker?' Her interest immediately stirred.

'Of documentaries, not movies, but you are interested in films?'

'Very much.'

'Then perhaps it is in the genes. This is him during the war. The first war. What we call the Kaiser's War.'

He clicked the mouse and the photograph of a young man appeared. A handsome young man, very upright in military uniform. His hair was cropped very short and he wore a small moustache on his upper lip, like a smudge on the print.

'Josef Fabel,' Gradowski said. 'Gabriele's father. Your great-grandfather.'

'He was a soldier?'

'An airman. At least to begin with. He joined the Luftwaffe in August 1914, a few days after the outbreak of the war. In his first week of training, there was an accident. Well, it was not an accident at all, in fact. When he was coming in to land, one of the other pilots, a fellow cadet, deliberately put his machine in the way of Josef's plane—as a protest against the employment of Jews in the German Air Force. He died instantly. Josef survived but spent several months in hospital.'

He noted the look on Hannah's face and shrugged.

'I suppose he thought it his patriotic duty—"taking a hit for the team." Or in this case for the Fatherland and the corps. Josef Fabel went on to fly over a hundred sorties on the Western Front. According to the logbooks, he shot down twelve Allied planes. *Ein Experten.* I think, in English, you would say *a fighter ace, a top gun.* Then a new commandant took over who refused to have a Jew in the corps. So Josef was transferred to ground crew—on aircraft maintenance behind the lines. It probably saved his life—the life expectation of the pilots was a few weeks at most, more often days. But still he wanted to fight. He was a true servant of the Fatherland, you see. So he volunteered for the Wehrmacht. He was a *Feldwebel-Leutnant* in the Twelfth Infantry Brigade, Sixth Division, Third Army Corps. He fought on the Eastern Front against the Russians. He was wounded at Tanenburg, which was one of the great battles of the war. A decisive victory for Germany.'

His sharp eyes took in her expression. It was probably not too difficult to read. 'You did not know any of this?'

'I had no idea. Not a thing. But he survived the war?'

'Oh yes. That war, at least.'

'So what happened to him then?

'After the war? Well, to begin with, he went to the University of Berlin. That is when he first began to practice journalism—for the university newspaper. Later he wrote for the mainstream press, and Jewish journals like the *Berliner Tageblatt.* Then he started making films. Documentaries.'

Why did my mother not tell me any of this? Hannah thought. It was something to be proud of, not to keep hidden in case it rattled the skeletons in the family cupboard. But perhaps she had no knowledge of it.

Hannah was almost afraid to ask, but what was the point of coming here if she didn't? 'What happened to him—and the rest of the family?'

He nodded. It would not be an unfamiliar question for him. 'I am afraid Josef Fabel was arrested shortly after Hitler came to power. We do not know what happened to him after that. He was one of those who simply disappeared. We suspect he was murdered in prison. His wife tried to find answers, for two years she tried, and then she left Germany with her daughter—Gabriele—for Italy. I have no record of what happened to them there.'

Hannah was silent for a moment, reflecting on the brutal reality behind those dispassionate words.

'And the films he made—the documentaries—do any of them survive?'

'If they do, I am afraid we have not been able to find them. But we have some of the articles he wrote, and a kind of journal—a fragment only, but covering the first three months of 1933 when Hitler first came to power. More memoir, really, than a diary—observations, notes for an article, maybe. Things he had thought worth jotting down, but well written for the most part, as if he meant them for publication someday, once he had edited them. He gave it to a friend of his for safekeeping a few days before he disappeared. He must have known, or at least feared the worst. I will print it out for you if you like and you can read it at your leisure.'

Hannah found a café overlooking a small park off Freidrichstrasse—everything organic and plant based—ordered a flat white with almond milk, and began reading the journal of her great-grandfather Josef Fabel, or the fragment that had survived. It looked like it had been written in a school exercise book, the pages individually scanned onto computer. Handwritten, and in German, of course, with some of the words in shorthand—so they were difficult and sometimes impossible for her to read, but there was no way she would not try. It was the first piece of family history she had ever found, the first positive evidence that she had even had family in Germany, in the time of the Nazis.

'It will give you some idea of what it was like for them,' Gradowski had said, 'in those early days when Hitler first came to power.'

The first entry was dated Sunday, January 8th, 1933:

Went with Marcus to a meeting of the Nazis at the Sportpalast. Goebbels was speaking. Marcus said it would be 'instructive.' . . .

Chapter Eleven

The Journalist and the Jesuit

The Journal of Josef Fabel

. . . The meeting started with a torchlit procession through the streets to the Sportpalast. *Torches and banners and thousands of men in the Nazi uniform, women too, though nothing like so many. Most of the men are unemployed, Marcus says, but they are paid a small sum out of Party funds. It usually guarantees a good turnout, he said, even on a night like this. But Goebbels* was speaking and he was second only to Hitler in the Nazi hierarchy so maybe they would have come anyway.*

It was raining, a thin drizzle but icy cold. I was wishing I had worn my leather flying jacket with its sheepskin lining, but Marcus said it would make me look like a Soviet commissar and we did not want that, we had to look shabby, he said. Rough, working men. Easier for him than me. As usual he looked like a stevedore. Possibly an out-of-work stevedore. He certainly did not look like a priest, but then he rarely does if he is not saying Mass. He had his coat buttoned up to the neck so you could not see his collar. I was surprised he was wearing it, but he said it might save us from a beating if I said something they did not like. He does not trust me to keep my mouth shut.

We joined a long queue outside the Sportpalast. There were better places to be on a Sunday evening in January and better things to do. I might have mentioned this to Marcus. Stop whingeing and take notes, he said. Mental notes, he added

---

*Joseph Goebbels was the Nazi *Gauleiter*, or district organiser, for Berlin and probably the man closest to the party leader Adolf Hitler.

hastily, in case I got my notebook out. You are supposed to know thine enemy, he said. And you are supposed to love them, I said. Not that I have seen much sign of it. He gave me a look. The first time we met he was being set on by three men in an alley in Kreuzberg. Red Front, as it turned out. I tried to give him a hand, but I am not sure he needed it—he had laid one of them out before I got there. As a Catholic priest there are certain doctrines he is obliged to express, at least in public, but as a Jesuit I am never quite sure what he really believes. Certainly it is not the innate goodness of human nature, unless he hides it well.

It is odd that Marcus and I have become such good friends. It astonishes everyone who think they know me. On the surface we would appear to have little in common besides a love of football and a quirky sense of humour, or perhaps I should say, a kind of professional interest, and at times delight, in the absurdity of human behaviour. But on some things we are agreed. Whatever he might say, he loathes Hitler. He thinks he is the Devil Incarnate—Jesuit for very bad indeed, as bad as it gets.

By the time we got there the Sportpalast was almost full and we had to go up on the balcony, a long way from the stage. But it gave us a view of the whole auditorium and personally I was not too bothered if we could hear the speeches or not. In fact, I preferred not. I had heard Hitler speak once and it was enough. They say Goebbels is better. More impassioned—if that is better. Hitler favours mockery. He has a gift for mimicry, they say. He makes people laugh. Some people, anyway. I have never been able to see the joke personally, but then I'm a Jew.

There was a more sombre atmosphere tonight. The Nazis had called the meeting to honour one of their young brownshirts who had been stabbed to death on New Year's Eve. In a drunken brawl, the police said, at least according to some newspapers, but the Nazis had their own view which Goebbels was about to express.

The meeting started with a roll of drums and the band struck up the Dead March. In came the standard bearers and the guard of honour. They formed ranks several deep in front of the stage and then Goebbels appeared. Roars of Seig Heil! and the Nazi salute which Goebbels returned. We were too far away for me to see his features, but I had seen plenty of photographs. I think one might say without risk of bias that he looks reptilian. His most notable feature is his mouth which is very wide but with very thin lips. I had thought of it before as a mouth like a trap. Now I realised it is designed for shouting. It opens very wide and the words come screaming out, like winged demons of hate. He may have had a microphone but I doubt he needed it. His voice, once released from that rattrap of a mouth, would have carried to the thousands outside who could not get in.

He started by reminding them of the meaning of National Socialism, which was about making Germany great again, he said, and eliminating all who place 'internationalism' and the interests of other countries and ideologies above their loyalty to the Fatherland. He moved on to a denunciation of Schleicher* who was neither Catholic nor Protestant, socialist or capitalist, he said, but had no purpose beyond his own ambition. When Hitler took over he would govern Germany according to his unshakeable Nazi principles, he said. He would never cooperate or compromise with those failed politicians and generals who had failed the Fatherland. Pause for cheers which surprisingly never came.

In fact apart from the beginning, when he had stepped onto the stage, the whole speech up to now had been greeted in near-silence. Where was the passion, where was the fury? The only applause came when he reminded them that Germany was a Christian country and that Christ was a kind of prototype Hitler who had whipped the moneylenders out of the temple, all of them being Jewish of course. But most of the audience were looking a bit puzzled. Maybe they had come to the wrong rally. Then he started to talk about the murdered brownshirt.

We know the names of the murderers, he said. Shouts of 'Name them! Name them!' 'But the murderer of this poor boy is not to blame'— they looked a bit puzzled again—then, his voice rising: 'The real murderers are the bloody Jews who publish their newspapers on Lindenstrasse.'

Uproar. The audience transformed into a howling mob. His own voice rose to a shriek. From where I was situated his face seemed all mouth. 'Their hands are red with the blood of our beloved young comrade. The Jews have stolen our national life, our economy, our elections. . . . We no longer have a German people, we have a nation of slaves dominated by a handful of Jews and their friends in the press and political life.'

The audience cheering and shaking their fists, shrieking curses, Goebbels screaming at the top of his voice, his whole body charged with emotion. 'It is to rescue Germany from the hands of the Jews that the National Socialist Party

---

*Kurt von Schleicher was the Chancellor of Germany at the time and a former general.

was formed and until we do that we are all slaves. We must take back control, make Germany great again! Heil Hitler!' He throws his arm up in the Nazi salute and they are all saluting back, straining at the leash like savage dogs, longing to be unchained and tear someone's throat out, preferably a Jew's.

—Well, that was interesting, says Marcus as we make our way back to Mitte.

—What particular part of it, I said.

—Well, you must have noticed they were ready to go to sleep until he mentioned the Jews, he says.

—Yes, I did notice that, I said. So what is your point?

—Well, if that is all they have to offer, he says . . . No policies, no platform, no ideology even—only a denunciation of the Jews.

I asked him if I was supposed to be reassured by this. He patted me on the shoulder. Do not worry, he says. They have reached the limit of their power and influence. They reached it a year ago. They will never win over the rest of Germany with this kind of stuff. You heard what the man said, 'Germany is a Christian nation.'

Went home feeling depressed. But then that is nothing new these days.

Monday, January 16th

Spent some time at the Old Academy. I sometimes go there to write. The atmosphere is conducive to writing. I sit there with my notebook staring at a painting but not really seeing it while I think of what it is I am trying to say. But today there was a power cut. I was surprised they let me in but they still had a couple of galleries open, lit by candles, and I found myself looking at the paintings properly, probably for the first time. Then I thought, this is how people would have seen them for hundreds of years. It was the first time I had thought about this. Before electric lighting, or gaslight even, people would have seen them mostly by candlelight, certainly at this time of the year when the sun never really breaks through the cloud layer and it is dark by three o'clock.

I spent most of my time looking at one painting. It was by Caspar David Friedrich. Called the Monk by the Sea. It shows the tiny figure of a monk, shrouded in black, against this immense panorama of sea and sky. Dark sea, black, threatening clouds, rolling in from the horizon, like some monstrous beast. It was so dark you could not see much of the foreground, you could hardly see the figure of the monk at all, and yet I sat there staring at it for a long time. I cannot explain what it was. Maybe the insignificance of the individual against the immensity of sea and sky, the elemental forces stacked up against him. Perhaps you would say it was an obvious analogy for the times we are living through. Too obvious. Friedrich painted it in 1808. I looked it up in the handbook and was told that it contrasts the meagre figure of the monk with the vastness of nature and the presence of God. I guess God had to be in it somewhere; it was Caspar David Friedrich and it was 1808. The monk has no individuality; he is like a piece of driftwood on the shore, at the mercy of the tide, or in this case, God and the Heavens. His sole purpose is the glory of God, and you might say, if you were well-disposed towards him and his religion, the greater good of humanity.

I cannot say I felt much cheered by this. I suppose it is not bad to be reminded of your own insignificance in the scheme of things, that there are limits to what you can achieve as an individual in this world, but I think I knew that already. Certainly, there are people who would benefit from it a lot more than me, but they are not the kind of people you would find in an art gallery during a power cut, staring at a picture of a monk by Caspar David Friedrich, by candlelight.

Thursday, January 19th
Picked up Gabriele from school today and as we are walking home she says to me, Papa, why is it people say Jews are dirty? I thought this was something they must have been talking about at school, but no, it was while she was out shopping with her mother at the weekend, and it was not spoken to her, or her mother, but someone else. It helps that they are both blonde I suppose. 'Dirty Jew, filthy Jew, I don't speak to Jews.' I've heard worse, of course, seen it, suffered it, but still—that Gabriele should be aware of it, at the age of eight. Ruth says I am naïve, where have I been? Do I not realise how much they hate us? I thought this was a bit rich. I am probably the only Jew she knows who was nearly killed for being a Jew. I still have the scars.

But Ruth is right in a way. (Ruth? Hannah thought. But it was not her mother. As she read on, she realised this was Josef's wife. They had the same name.) *I am always being surprised by the extent of it. I think perhaps because I am more German than Ruth, or at least more patriotic. There*

69

has always been anti-Semitism in Germany of course but I do not think it was so evident, certainly not in Berlin. It was never so widespread or acceptable. People might say things to family or friends, but not in public, not in the street, to perfect strangers. It has become respectable. Dirty Jew. I think it is because our political leaders, the Nazis especially, but not only them, have made them think it is all right to say stuff like this. As if it is their patriotic duty as Germans. Hate Jews, hate foreigners. Incredible to think that four years ago, we had never heard of Hitler or Goebbels—or even the Nazi Party. They were a tiny minority, NASDAP, a sect, like some crazy religious fanatics. Now they are the biggest party in the Reichstag. I know all the reasons, of course. I have written about them often enough. Losing the war, economic collapse, poverty, mass unemployment, national humiliation, people looking for someone to blame, but there had to be something there already, something that was much larger and deeper, more entrenched in the national psyche than I ever thought it was. Something visceral. All right, I might have said, maybe twenty, twenty-five per cent of people think this way, in the small towns, the rural areas where Jews have always been thought of as outsiders, but now—now I think it is more like fifty per cent, maybe more.

We talked about it again last night, after we put Gaby to bed. Ruth started on about emigrating again. She worries about me, she thinks my name will be on a list because I write for Tageblatt.* *But she worries about Gabriele even more. I worry about Gabriele, too. Of course I do. But we are German. Where are we going to go? We could stay with her sister in Rome for a while, she says, until things settle down. But the Fascists are already in power in Italy, at least in Germany they have still some way to go. England, then, she says, or America. But what would I do, how would I write? The only language I speak is German, and a bit of Yiddish. Besides, I think we have to stay and fight this, not run away from it. I want to fight for the Germany I believe in. And what is that, Josef? she said. Where will I find it?*

The Berliner Tageblatt *was published from 1872 to 1939 and was one of the leading liberal newspapers in Germany and the most hostile and critical towards the Nazis, before Hitler came to power. It was known to the Nazis as* das Judenblatt.

Saturday, January 28th

Schleicher has resigned. Everyone saw it coming but it was still a shock when it actually came. They say Hindenburg will ask Hitler to form a government. The Nazis are the biggest party in the Reichstag but they don't have a majority, nowhere near. Out of 608 seats the Nazis have 196, the Social Democrats 121 and the Communists 100. The smaller parties would probably vote with the Nazis, but not all the time, not without Hitler having to dump most of his policies. He says in public that he will never compromise. But Marcus says the wolves have had a hard winter. The Nazis lost nearly a million votes in the November election. The days after the Great Crash when it seemed like they would carry all before them are over, he says, and they are short of money. There have been signs that the bankers and industrialists are getting cold feet. They have been scared off by Hitler's ranting and raving, and the violence. He could be right. The brownshirts have stopped beating people up and are trying to raise money. They were out collecting when I walked over to Mitte this morning. Some of them even smiled at me as they thrust their tin boxes at me.

Tuesday, January 31st

So, it has finally happened. What we've been dreading for months—and yet it seemed like an anti-climax when it came. Hitler has been appointed Reich Chancellor. We now have a Nazi government—though the right-wing press does not call it that. They call it a government of national unity. Hindenburg insisted on making von Papen vice-Chancellor and the word is that he is the one pulling the strings. The Nazis get only three out of ten members of the Cabinet—and they have to rely on the Nationalists to support them in the Reichstag. Not much consolation there—the Nationalists are almost as bad as the Nazis, but the Zentrum is a different matter and they hold the balance of power. They think they can use Hitler as a front while they run the show. Hitler has insisted that Hindenburg call a new election—the third in a year—and the hope is that he'll lose even more seats than he did in the last one. The German people have their faults but they are just too conservative, too pragmatic, to elect someone as clearly insane as Hitler. Ruth thinks I'm being wilfully optimistic and it will be the death of us all.

We try to hide our differences for Gabriele's sake but it is difficult some-times, and she can sense the tension in the air. As usual we talk about her day at school, her progress at swimming and gymnastics, the school trip to Potsdam, more cheerfully and determinedly than we usually do perhaps, poor girl. All the time I feel the rat gnawing at my insides. It was there during the war, of course, especially in the trenches but I don't remember it being as bad as this. My fear then was just for myself. But it was nothing like the fear I have for Gabriele. She let me read to her before she went to sleep—a rare indulgence on her part; she has been reading to herself since she was seven. I looked back on her from the bedroom door as she snuggled down in her Federbedett and I thought my heart would break. I still think we should stay and fight, but do I have a right to even contemplate this when I have a wife and an eight-year-old daughter? And do I have the guts for it, when I am so scared for them?

Friday, February 24th

I have been commissioned to write a piece on how Berlin nightlife is adjusting to the new regime—Hitler has a reputation for being a puritan, unlike many of his followers—and I decided to take Marcel with me. A Jesuit priest might not seem the obvious companion for a tour of Berlin nightlife, but he has a surprising knowledge of every bar, brothel, and lowlife dive in the city. He says that if your job is saving sinners, you have to go to the places where there is sin—what is the point of confining your pastoral care to those who attend Mass every Sunday? Fair enough, I suppose, but I do not think he is meant to enjoy it so much. I was paying of course.

We started off in one of the small unlicensed bars in the streets at the back of the Alexanderplatz. Kneipe, they are called, and they are usually in the living room of a private house with an entrance directly off the street. They serve beer and schnapps, and 'bar snacks' like sausages and pickled eggs. More and more of them have sprung up in the past year or two, but they are more about avoiding taxes than Nazis. As well as the usual fare it served up a rough red wine 'from our own estates in the Spessart.' I think this was irony but maybe not. Marcus said he had tasted better Communion wine. Personally, I think that is what it was. He probably sold it to them.

We moved on to der Platz which used to specialise in political burlesque, but they seem to have dropped the political stuff. Now it is all overtly sexual and frankly rather boring—to me at least though Marcus seemed to enjoy it.

The only spark of originality was when seven naked women combined to form a kind of tableau in the shape of a skull. Quite artistic. I will not attempt to describe it. Marcus laughed so loudly he drew more attention to us than I would have wished. Sex and death, he said, is what the Nazis like best.

Out on the streets again. I wanted to do something on the rise of the illicit street market in drink and drugs. I am not sure this has anything to do with the rise of the Nazis but with a bit of journalistic licence I am sure I can make a link. We met our first dealer on Erichstrasse selling what he calls schnapps for one mark a shot. It smelled more like aviation fuel to me. I took a cautious sip and was unable to speak for several minutes. Marcus downed it in one of course. The dealer told us he used to work in a bar but it was smashed up by the brownshirts along with the proprietor because he threw out one of their collectors, so there is my link. Further along the street was a man selling cocaine, at five marks a capsule. While we were talking to him two street girls turned up. Marcus introduced them as Rose and Mauzi—obviously parishioners of his or nuns in disguise. I asked them if drug use had increased since Hitler became Chancellor. It had. The Nazis are very good for business, the dealer said.

By now I needed something to eat and we made our way to another little kneipe where we had sausage with sauerkraut and bread, washed down with a strong Bavarian beer. All very good. The bar-owner was called Adolf. Not a fan of the other Adolf. Thought he was mad. A mad clown, he called him. But he didn't like the Communists, either, and he thought the Social Democrats were useless. Things were better in the Kaiser's day, he said. This was something I heard a lot in the course of the evening. Marcus repeated his mantra about the Catholics saving us. Hitler needed the support of the Zentrum he said, and this would force him to be more moderate: 'to steer the ship of state on a less turbulent course' as he put it. Marcus has a weakness for maritime analogies which I often find annoying. He comes from the Sudtirol, which is about as far from the sea as anywhere in Europe.

Searching for an analogy myself, I reminded him of Dr. Faust.

I could see the Jesuit mind ticking over.

'I think you forget,' he said, 'that the message Goethe wished to convey is that man must learn to come to terms with the world in which he lives, and that after all his trials and accommodations, Faust goes to Heaven. The final

message of the second play, delivered by the angels sent to escort him there, is that "he who strives on and lives to strive, can earn redemption still."'

But by this time he had lost me—and the bar owner. This is the problem with Jesuits, too clever by half. Even so, I was impressed he could string two words together after all the aviation fuel and Communion wine. I am not sure I could. I cannot even remember how I got home. I think Marcus took me. Ruth not amused.

Tuesday, February 28th

Four o'clock in the morning. I am sitting in the kitchen drinking schnapps, exhausted but almost too tired to sleep. My clothes stink of smoke and I expect my hair does too.

I was out on the town again, alone this time, trying to get more stuff for my piece on Berlin nightlife when someone said the Reichstag was on fire. By the time I got there the whole place was ablaze and the flames were shooting through the roof. It was already clear that it was beyond saving. The home of German democracy. The police had thrown up a cordon, and they would not let me through even with my press pass. The name Fabel of course does not help. But I got close enough to take pictures on my little Leica. There were dozens of fire engines and even more police vehicles. The ground was covered with fire hoses and they were pumping water from the Spree but there was obviously nothing they could do. Then I saw Hitler. He was on the other side of the cordon with Goebbels, surrounded by half a dozen of their SA thugs, talking to some high-ranking police and fire officers. He was throwing his arms about and looking at the building as if it was his own home going up in flames, which I thought was a bit rich given he has never had a good word to say for it. Then he turned towards me and his eyes made direct contact with mine. I swear there was a look in them that was—the word that came to mind was exultant. I might even say demonic. But of course people would say it was in my imagination. I raised my Leica to take a picture but a policeman stood in my way.

Too tired to write more, it will be in the papers anyway, in the morning. I will write a more reflective piece for the weeklies, or one of the foreign newspapers that do not mind translating.

Wednesday, March 1st

Different accounts of what happened, depending on what paper you read. The official account is that it was the Communists. The police have already arrested one of them—a Dutchman called van der Lebe or Lubbe—who was caught as he rushed out of the building. But Hitler is saying it is a conspiracy of the KDP* and the first step in a Communist putsch. He has pressured Hindenburg to sign an emergency decree which suspends all civil liberties including free speech and the freedom of the press. Thousands of SA and SS have been called up as police auxiliaries and there have been mass arrests of Communists and other 'subversives' including all the KDP delegates in the Reichstag and even some Social Democrats. Of course, this will give the Nazis and their allies a permanent majority in the Reichstag—if it ever meets again.

The other account is that the fire was planned and executed by an SA einsatzgruppe† under the supervision of Goring and Goebbels and that van der Lubbe was 'planted' on the scene by the Nazis. According to this version, he is a mental defective with a record of arson who was picked up from an asylum and taken to the Reichstag by the brownshirts. But when they got there they found the building was already ablaze. Another einsatzgruppe had jumped the gun and set fire to it already—before the arsonist arrived! The story goes that the first group—the ones with van der Lubbe—have complained to their superiors about this and there is an unholy row going on behind the scenes. It sounds too good to be true, but the head of the Berlin fire department, Walter Gempp, was reported in the foreign press as saying that some of his men saw a car arrive at a back entrance to the building and three men entered, after *the fire had started. Two of them came out almost immediately. Then ten minutes later a third man came running out, stripped to the waist, and was picked up by the police. There is a picture of him at the time being marched away. He is recognisable as the arsonist van der Lubbe.*

I have just had a message from Marcus. He says one of the firemen is a parishioner of his and that he is willing to talk to me about what he saw, so long as I do not use his name.

---

*The German Communist Party.
†A special SS task force or death squad.

Thursday, March 2nd

Went into Tageblatt *for a meeting with Theo.* I told him about Marcus and his fireman friend, but he says it does not matter who set fire to the Reichstag and we would not be able to publish it in any case. I have never seen him so low. He wants to leave the country, if he can get out. He says I should leave, too. I tried to persuade him to wait until after the election—I am sure the Nazis are going to lose. Even if the KDP is banned, most of their followers will vote for the SD or the Zentrum just to keep the Nazis out. He said I was out of my mind. The SD was finished, he said, and the Zentrum had agreed to support the Nazis. The Vatican were sending one of their top men to Berlin to make a deal, and my friend Marcus was one of the people setting it up for them. He has been having talks with Goebbels and his people since Hitler became Chancellor, Theo said.*

I said it must be a mistake. Marcus and Goebbels! It was unthinkable. But Theo showed me the report—Father Marcus Senner, of Saint Michael's in Kreuzberg, appointed special adviser to Cardinal Pacelli, Foreign Secretary to the Vatican.

I still cannot believe it. Apart from anything else, I cannot believe that Marcus moves in such elevated circles.

He is still trying to arrange this meeting with the fireman for me.

---

*Theodor Wolff, the editor of the *Berliner Tageblatt.*

Chapter Twelve

Shadowlands

It was almost four in the afternoon when Hannah finished reading. The journal ended abruptly with the entry on March 2nd. According to Gradowski, Josef Fabel had been arrested the following day by members of the SA who had been drafted into the police as 'auxiliaries.' He was never seen again. Gradowski said he was believed to have been taken to one of the temporary prisons set up in Berlin immediately after the fire and was almost certainly murdered there, though his body was never found and his fate remained a mystery. The official account was that he had been released from prison on March 6th and fled the country to avoid being prosecuted for sedition.

His wife Ruth had spent the next two years trying to find out what had happened to him, then left Germany for good, taking Gabriele with her. They stayed for a while with her sister and her family in Rome and then Ruth rented her own apartment, finding work as a dressmaker. She died in 1940, of breast cancer, just before Italy entered the war on the side of Nazi Germany.

So far as Gradowski was aware, Gabriele stayed on in Rome, living with her aunt's family and attending the Jewish High School. He had no idea of how she had died until Hannah told him.

The waitress came to the table, not for the first time, and asked if there was anything else she could bring her. Hannah told her no—she was just going. She had lingered over her coffee for more than an hour. Aiden would have landed ten minutes ago, but there was nothing from him on voicemail, no texts. She knew she should be back at the hotel to greet him, but there was something else she wanted to do first.

Friedrich's painting was still in the same building where Josef Fabel had seen it during a power cut in the winter of 1933—the Old National Gallery, on Museum Island. The gallery had been badly damaged by air raids during the war but the painting had been stashed away in a safe location and brought back after the postwar restoration. It was not hard for Hannah to imagine that she was sitting more or less where her great-grandfather had been sitting eighty-six years ago, just before his arrest.

The guidebook informed her that the solitary figure of the monk represented the insignificance of man 'against the immensity of God and Nature . . . floating between hope and despair at a time of great change and uncertainty.' 'The monk' was thought to be the artist himself, identified by his reddish beard, but naturally Hannah wondered if Josef had seen himself in the image. She thought it very likely that he would.

Even after reading the entries in his journal, or perhaps because of them, she had no clear image of the man who had been Gabriele's father, and her own great-grandfather. The voice had been distinct and yet the man himself remained in darkness; perhaps because of the mystery of how his life had ended, perhaps because the voice seemed a trifle 'forced,' or too self-conscious, the jottings of a journalist with an eye to publication—after they had been polished up in several rewrites. The strongest image in her mind was not the fire at the Reichstag, but that of the eight-year-old Gabriele snuggling down into her *Federbedett* after her father had read her a bedtime story.

But she also had a very strong image of Josef as a fighter. A man who would not give up, no matter how great the odds. And she remembered that line in the journal: *I think we have to stay and fight this, not run away from it. I want to fight for the Germany I believe in.*

She suddenly remembered Aiden and dug in her bag for her phone. It was five past five. If the plane had landed on time, he would be back at the hotel by now. Guiltily she hurried through the rooms of the gallery and down the steps to the street. Rush hour was in full swing. There were no taxis, but it was only a ten-minute walk to the hotel, less if she ran. She began to run.

But he had been and gone.

The woman on reception told her that he had arrived a half ago or more, checked into his room, and gone straight out again. There was no message for her.

Hannah wondered if he had gone to see Irma Ulbrecht. Well, best of luck to him. There was nothing she could do to help him there. Feeling a little lost and not a little useless, she went up to her room to shower and change. Then she came down again to sit in the lobby and wait for his return. It felt less lonely than in her room. Besides, she wouldn't put it past Aiden to come in and go out again without telling her.

It was almost dark, the rain streaming down the windows of the hotel lobby and the passersby hurrying past with their heads down, or under black umbrellas. At least they seemed black to Hannah. She sat at a table in one of the windows and opened up her laptop to look at the photograph Gradowski had scanned in for her of Gabriele with her two friends. It would have been over a year since Josef had disappeared by then. Did Gabriele know he was dead, or did she think he might still be alive somewhere, maybe in prison, maybe in exile? Either way, she would be grieving for him. She would cling to the hope that he was still alive, that she would see him again.

Hannah sat there for a long time looking at the photograph of Gabriele and her friends, trying to figure out what bothered her most about it. Perhaps it was a sense of impending doom, the idea of clinging to what remains of ordinary life, hoping it will get better, or at least not worse, and all the time the shadows are lengthening.

The door opened and a man came in from the street, bringing a flurry of rain with him. He wore blue Levi's and a black leather hoodie, a rucksack slung over one shoulder. She did not know it was Aiden until he pushed back the hood. He looked younger than she remembered him and better looking. Possibly there was less tension in his face, or it might just have been that the hoodie suited him better than a jacket and tie. It seemed more in character, though what did she know about his character? He saw her at once and came over to where she was sitting, flopping down in the chair opposite without any formal greeting. She started to say she was sorry she had not been here to greet him but he cut her short.

'I've been to see Irma,' he said. Irma already.

'Any good?'

He shook his head, looked away towards the empty reception desk. 'Can you get a drink around here?'

'You told her what you thought about—what happened to Michael?'

'Yeah.'

'And?'

'She wanted to know if that's what the police thought.' He was still looking restlessly around the reception area. 'There's a bar next door, do you fancy a drink?'

They were the only customers in the little bar. Hannah had a glass of wine, Aiden a litre of beer.

'I'm sorry,' she said. 'Looks like I dragged you over here for nothing.'

He shrugged. 'Beer's all right.' He had already drunk half of it.

'So what now?' She was embarrassed. He had spent a lot of money for a litre of German beer.

'I might just get rat-arsed,' he said. 'What about you?'

The expression was unfamiliar to her but she guessed what it meant. Most women she knew would not object to getting 'rat-arsed' in Berlin with a man who looked like Aiden Blake. But not Hannah. There was something about him that did not exactly repulse her but that made her wary, even if she was not sure why.

'I honestly don't think there's much more I can do,' she said. 'I was sure she knew more than she's prepared to say, but . . .'

'Is that a yes,' he said, 'or a no?'

Before she could reply, his phone went. She knew from his manner who it was. The conversation was brief.

'She wants to meet up,' he told her. 'In half an hour.'

'Both of us?'

He looked a bit embarrassed, but perhaps that was in her imagination. 'She didn't say anything about you. She says she has something she wants to show me.'

CHAPTER THIRTEEN

The Fallen Angels

AIDEN WAITED JUST INSIDE THE BERLIN MALL AT THE EXIT ONTO Volkstrasse. The shops were still open and there were plenty of people about. He had no idea why she had suggested meeting here but he doubted it was to go shopping. He could see the rain pouring down in the light of the street lamps.

The last time he had been here was about twenty years ago on a school trip. It was organised by the history department because they were doing World War Two and the Cold War. This whole area—the heart of old Berlin—had been flattened by Allied bombing or Russian shells and then left as a wasteland. For nearly thirty years the Berlin Wall had run straight through the middle of it, dividing the city into capitalist West and communist East, but by the time of their visit most of the wall had gone and it had been turned into a building site—the biggest in Europe they were told—destined to be the centre of the new Berlin, the new unified Germany. They had trooped around all the historical sites, taken pictures, some of them even made notes, but mostly they were here for the beer.

One night a few of the older boys sneaked out of their hotel and went to a nightclub, not far from where he was standing now. The club was in an old cellar, which the Germans called a Bunker, and it was decorated with memoribilia of the Cold War, so you could say it was part of their education. Aiden would, anyway, if they'd been found out. The women serving at the tables wore Red Army uniform, though not like the Red Army wore it.

'Hi. Sorry to keep you waiting.' Aiden felt a hand on his arm and Irma was there, wearing a blue belted raincoat and carrying an umbrella. Smiling, too. A lot more cheeful than she had been in her office.

'We have to go out into the rain, I am afraid,' she told him, 'but you can share my umbrella.'

She did not say where they were going and he didn't ask. If she wanted to make a mystery of it, it was all right with him, provided they didn't have to walk too far. He was walking awkwardly with his head bent, trying to stay under the umbrella and not get his eye poked out. After a few minutes he gave up and moved away a little, pulling up his hood. They had crossed Volkstrasse heading north and now they were walking through a residential area of modern apartment blocks. He was about to ask how much further it was when she stopped beside what he took to be a parking lot behind a wire mesh fence. Then he noticed a sign on the fence that said *Fahrradvermeitung* with a picture of a bicycle and the words in English: Bikes for hire. This, surely, was not what she had in mind.

She was speaking into an entry phone by the side of a double gate, and after a moment it opened to reveal a compound about the size of a basketball or five-a-side football pitch. As soon as they entered, floodlights came on and he noted at least two CCTV cameras mounted on towers above the fence. There were no bicycles that he could see, but presumably they would be kept out of the rain.

There were a couple of portacabins to the left of the entrance, and a security guard who had just emerged from the one nearest to them. Irma went over to speak to him and he looked across at Aiden, who put his hand up to push his hood back, but it was not necessary; the guard was already turning away and heading back to his lair. With a jerk of her head Irma indicated that Aiden should follow her to the other cabin, which was far more substantial and had wire mesh over the windows and an alarm above the door. Irma keyed in numbers and pushed the door open.

Strip lighting came on as soon as they entered and Aiden saw they were in what appeared to be an office, with a couple of desks, a table and chairs, all very basic, apart from the coffee machine in one corner.

'This is my other office,' Irma said, 'where I come to write.'

He nodded, as if this made sense, but he was wondering what the hell they were doing here.

'Come,' she said, 'and all will be clear.'

She led the way to another door at the far end of the room, tapped in another code, and opened it onto a smaller area with a washroom off to one side and a spiral staircase on the other, going down. Aiden shot her a look.

'No need to be frightened,' she said. 'Keep close to me and you will be quite safe. Here there are only the ghosts.'

She led the way down the spiral stair, holding on to the metal rail with both hands and taking care in her high heels. After the first two or three steps she triggered another sensor and a light snapped on to reveal concrete walls and a few pipes, with felt lagging hanging down like thick cobwebs. The steps were quite steep and they descended for about five or six metres to an area, not much wider than the stair shaft, with a heavy door, like the door to a vault or a nuclear bunker, but pushed back against the wall beyond. As they stepped through, another sensor light came on, revealing a long corridor with doors on either side, all closed. There was a smell of damp and possibly disinfectant, something sharp anyway.

Aiden followed his guide down the corridor until she paused at one of the doors, pushed it open, and switched on a light to reveal what might have been a medium-sized dining or conference room containing a long metal table and a dozen or so straight metal chairs. His eye was drawn immediately to the murals that entirely covered the walls. They were not unlike the primitive daubings made by cave-dwellers, except that they were not of running horses and deer and bison. They were of soldiers, wearing the familiar coal-scuttle helmets and field-grey uniforms of the German Army in World War Two, but carrying kite-shaped shields from a more distant past. Some were holding them high above their heads, like umbrellas or wings, and beneath the shields there were other figures, less martial—men in lederhosen drinking from foaming beer steins, women in dirndls serving them; men in overalls operating lathes and other machinery, women holding children by the hand or carrying babes in arms. And from the sky above, bombs rained down from crudely drawn aircraft with the silver star of the USA or the red-white-and-blue roundels of the Royal Air Force.

'What do you think?' Irma enquired, head to one side, her expression faintly mocking.

'Very nice,' he said. 'What is it, a nightclub?' He was thinking of the one he had visited as a school sixth-former.

This amused her. 'A nightclub. Very good. I guess it would make a good nightclub. Perhaps we should discuss it. We could use it to raise money. But no, can you not guess? It is part of the old bunker complex where Hitler and his staff spent the last months of World War Two, when the Red Army was fighting its way into Berlin and the British and Americans were bombing night and day.'

Aiden wondered if this was her idea of a joke. 'I thought it was all sealed up and filled with rubble.' He had heard about this on the school trip. 'I thought the Russians sealed it up at the end of the war.'

'That was the *Fuhrerbunker*. This is the one next to it. We call it the *Chaufferbunker*—for the SS drivers and bodyguards.'

Aiden gazed about him, trying to take it in. He supposed it was possible. They had places like this in London, but London had not been occupied by the Russians for forty-odd years. 'So what is it used for now?' he said.

'Nothing. We are thinking what to do with it. Very few people know about it. And now you are one of them.'

She took a small flask out of her bag. 'Schnapps?' she said.

He blinked a little. 'You brought schnapps?'

'Why not? We will make our own nightclub.'

They sat in the metal chairs at the metal table and she poured into two small metal cups. '*Prost!*'

She clinked her cup against his. He looked around the walls again. 'So it has been like this since the war?'

'I guess so, but hidden. Forgotten. Deep underground. It was in the middle of the Death Strip—on the eastern side of the Berlin Wall. Then, when the wall came down, in 1990 I think, there was a rock concert on the Potsdamerplatz to celebrate. Pink Floyd came. They called it the Wall Concert, Live in Berlin.'

She began to sing softly, her eyes still mocking. *'We don't need no education, we don't need no thought control . . . All in all you're just another—brick in the wall.'*

'I remember,' he said. The older kids used to sing it in Belfast when he was still at primary school.

'The whole area was wasteland, left derelict since the war, and they fear there are unexploded bombs dropped by the Allies, or a few land mines from the Cold War planted by the Russians or the East German border guards, to stop people escaping to the West. And so they send in security guards to make it safe. And as they search, they find a metal door in the ground, what do you say for this in English? *Die Schachtdeckel.*'

'A manhole cover?' he offered.

'Is it?' She considered this with a frown. 'Why *man*-hole?'

'I have no idea,' he said honestly. He spread his arms apologetically. Not his fault.

'Well, below the *man*hole was this. As if the people had left the day before. The authorities had pictures taken, then it was filled with sand and the entrance sealed. They were afraid it would become a shrine for the neo-Nazis. And so it stayed like that for twenty years, on a piece of wasteland with a fence around it.'

'And a bike hire?'

A short laugh. 'Ah yes, I do not know how the bike hire came to be here. Maybe it was a cover. I have never seen any sign of any bikes.'

'And now what?'

'Ah, that is a good question. At first there is an idea they will make it a kind of exhibition, a warning museum, like the concentration camps. The authorities have appointed a committee to do this and I am the *Vorsitzende*—what is it you say?—the chairperson. We move in the earth machines, we take out the sand, and then—they begin to worry. What is it you say in English, to get cold feet? There is the rise of the neo-Nazis—the new Right. Maybe is not so good, they say, to open this to the public. Maybe is not the right time, when the Far Right takes so much of the vote. But I'm fighting this. I think the people should see it, to show the great delusion of the SS who think they are the guardians of western civilisation. So—' she shrugged, 'that is how it is at the moment. We wait for them to make a decision. And while we wait, there is just me and whoever I wish to bring down here.'

'And this is where you planned to bring Michael—when he came to Berlin?'

'Yes. Because of his great interest in the Knights of the Black Cross.' She spoke lightly but she was watching him carefully, as if it might mean something to him.

It didn't.

'Another name for them is the Teutonic Knights,' she said after a moment. 'Warrior monks. Crusaders. You do not know of them?'

'I've heard of the Teutonic Knights, but not from Michael. So what have they got to do with anything?'

'Look at the pictures on the walls. Can you not see? They are not ordinary soldiers. They are the Waffen-SS. See the sign on the shields and the collars? The double flash of lightning? These are the men of the First SS Division, *Leibstandarte Adolf Hitler*. They provided the personal bodyguard of the Fuhrer, and the elite of his stormtroopers. But what is important is how they see themselves. The guardian angels of the German people. This is the idea of Heinrich Himmler—you know of Himmler, the head of the SS?—the architect of the Holocaust. Raised as a devout Roman Catholic. So, he makes them like the Teutonic Knights, one of the great Catholic military orders at the time of the Crusades. The Knights of the Black Cross. So they guard not only the German people but all of Christendom—against the Jews and the Bolsheviks. And against the stupid Anglo-Saxons who do not know who is their real enemy.' She threw out her arm. 'You see that man there?'

She was pointing to one of the soldiers in the mural. He was standing with both arms held out from his sides—with a kite-shaped shield strapped to each of them, like the statue of a dark angel about to take flight.

'His name is Bechmann. *SS-Sturmbannfuhrer* Heinrich Bechmann.'

'You know his name?'

'I do. I have done the research. He was one of Hitler's bodyguards. There are many, but this one, he is very close to the Fuhrer. And the people under the shields, these are Hitler and his mistress, Eva Braun. See?'

Aiden noted the two smaller figures under the steel wings: one a woman, blonde and curvaceous, the other a man stripped to the waist, lifting weights. The muscles stood out in his chest and arms and he had great abs. Only the moustache gave him away.

'That's Hitler?' It was not the image of Hitler that he knew, or most of the world.

'Oh, but this is the point, it is all delusion. The real Hitler, he is a sick old man by now, mad with disease and defeat, a rat in a trap, shaking with the tremors he cannot control, and the Red Army is closing in on him. But delusion, this is all they have left and soon they will all be dead. The Knights of the Black Cross. The brave champions of Christendom, ready to die for the Fatherland. And Bechmann, he believes in this. More than anyone. You are sure Michael never speaks of this man?'

'No. Never. Not to me.' It felt like an interrogation. And of course it was, and she had chosen the right place for it.

'Strange. Michael was very interested in this man. Even, I would say, it is an obsession with him. Of course, he is very handsome. Tall, dark, and handsome, like you. Not the classic blond Aryan, but not many were.' She returned to her contemplation of Bechmann. 'Maybe he is like, to Hitler, a son. His ideal of the perfect German soldier. But you could say he was Italian, from the Italian side of the Tyrol.'

Aiden stood up to inspect the mural more closely. The square-jawed Nazi archangel with the bombs raining down on his metallic wings. The pictures had faded somewhat and though you could still see details of the uniforms and even the features, Aiden did not think she would be able to recognise a particular individual, unless she had other information she had not yet disclosed.

'How much do you know of what happens here?' she asked him. 'In the bunkers in the last days of the war?'

'Not a lot,' he said. 'But I saw the movie. Hitler dies.'

'But not soon enough for all those who die because of him. Imagine what it is like. In April 1945. Above us, the bombs and the shells are falling like rain, thousands of tons of explosives, every hour of every day and night. And the Red Army is coming closer and closer to the centre of the city. The war is over, Germany has lost. Everyone knows this except

Hitler. And maybe even Hitler knows it by now, somewhere in that diseased, demented brain of his. But still he will not surrender. He talks to his generals, his party bosses, even to Mussolini in Italy. Still he is making his plans. Officers of the Wehrmacht and the Waffen-SS and the Nazi Party send in their reports, news of another defeat, another army that is surrounded, on the point of surrender. Without hope. And Hitler says, fight on. The rat in the hole, he believes only what he wants to believe. He came to this room many times.'

She reached across the table and topped up Aiden's metal cup with schnapps, then her own, but not so much, he noted. 'He liked to eat with his men, the drivers and the bodyguards. He was more comfortable with them than with the generals and the diplomats, or his own party officials. Especially near the end. The women, too, his secretaries. Traudl Junge, you may have heard of her? She was here. Hitler—he might even sit where you are sitting now.'

He wondered where all this was heading, and where Michael came into it, but she was slowly getting there.

'In the first week of April, just before the final assault by the Russians, Hitler sends for Bechmann. He has a special mission for him. He is to go to the Reich Archives in Potsdam on the edge of Berlin. This is where all the government papers were moved for safe keeping during the bombing. A complete record of all the Nazis had done since Hitler came to power in 1933. But now the Russians were very close to Potsdam, and Bechmann was sent to bring them back, some of them, to the *Fuhrerbunker*. Berlin is on fire and Hitler, he is sending for more paper. And what do you think is the most important for him, that he wants it with him in the bunker, in the spring of 1945, in the final days?'

She gave him a moment. It would have needed longer than that.

'Go on,' he said.

But she shivered. 'It is very cold here. If you have seen enough, we will go and find somewhere a little more comfortable and I will tell you.'

Aiden took a final look around the room. The SS men looked not so much like angels as aliens. Something from *Star Wars*. The Teutonic Knights from Mustofar.

'Delusions,' said Irma Ulbrecht again. 'This is what history is about, the story of delusions. And the people who die because of them.'

It was still raining outside. They walked towards Ebertstrasse, where Irma thought they might pick up a cab, and she kept up a running commentary on the way.

'This was called Herman-Goering-Strasse in the time of the Nazis, after Reich Marshal Goering, you have heard of him?' He had. When they were doing World War Two. The fat man who liked dressing up in uniforms, and women's frilly frocks. 'This was the heart of the old Berlin but in the last days of the war there was not much of it left. The British and the Americans had seen to that. The bombing went on day and night until the Russians arrived. The only building still standing, or still intact, was the Brandenburger Tor, with the quadriga—the four-horse chariot— and the goddess of victory.'

They could see it now, the floodlit monolith at the end of the road.

'I wonder if they saw the irony in that. Probably not. Besides, they were not here to see it, they were down in the bunkers, those that were still alive.'

Aiden's hoodie was dripping with rain, he could feel it running down his nose and his neck at the front into his T-shirt. He was looking for a taxi but the only ones he saw were taken. She drew him into the shelter of a doorway and pointed across the road to the darker mass of the Tiergarten, though there were lights along the pathways and many of the trees were floodlit. He could see the rain in the lights.

'Imagine it, the way it was,' she said, 'in that last month of the war.'

Michael used to do this to him, before he gave him up as a bad job. *Imagine what it was like, back then.* As if everyone lived in the past as much as he did, or if not, they should, and he would help them get there.

'Every second another shell is falling, and the Katyusha rockets they call Stalin's Organ because of the noise they made, the scream, like an organ played by the Devil. And the Red Army is coming on street by street, running from building to building, with flame throwers that they fire into the cellars. It is like the air itself is on fire, and it is full of flying shards of metal. Hot metal rain. No one can live in that rain. The shells are landing in the cemeteries even and blowing open the graves, blowing the bodies in the air, so that they hang in the trees, the bodies of the dead. The Berliners who are still alive, they crouch in the cellars and the air-raid shelters, waiting for the Russians to come. And Hitler, he is in his *Fuhrerbunker*, waiting for someone to save him.'

She looked across the road that had once been called after the fat man, towards the Tiergarten, with the rain glinting in the lights, and the lights in her eyes.

'They had made a small airstrip in the Tiergarten, and one night, late in April, with the Red Army only a few blocks away, a plane flies in, coming in very low over the city, over the Russian lines. Flown by a woman.'

Chapter Fourteen

The Aviatrix

Berlin, April 1945

She came in at street level, so low she could see the surprise on their faces, her appearance so swift and sudden she was a block away before they began firing at her, though not always. The Storch's wings were so full of holes it was a wonder she was still flying—and flying blind, for the instrument panel was shot to bits and the landmarks that had once been so familiar were long gone. There was a larger hole under her feet caused by a shell fragment that had torn through the cockpit when they began their descent over Berlin. Ritter had been in the pilot's seat then and it had taken off most of his left foot. Somehow she had pulled him out and taken over the controls, but she had little hope of finding anywhere to land. You only had to look down through the hole in the cockpit floor to see that.

She headed for where the smoke was thickest, and the shells were still landing, on the basis that if the Russians were still firing, there had to be someone left to fire back. Then directly ahead of her she saw the best guide she could have hoped for: the Goddess of Victory and her four horses, still miraculously intact and facing the enemy to the East, except that now the enemy was all around them. She banked sharply and suddenly the air was clear, and ahead of her she could see the Tiergarten, the trees bright with the fresh green growth of spring, even the ones that had been brought down by the bombs and the shells, and an open stretch of grass not much bigger than the lawn of her home in Hirschberg. But you could land a Storch on a postage stamp and there was nowhere else to go.

She had made gentler landings. She heard an anguished cry of 'Scheisse!' from the man lying on the floor of the fuselage behind her, but at least it told her he was still alive, still able to curse, and the soldiers running towards them were their own and not Russians. She climbed out of the cockpit and hands reached out to help her down.

'Welcome to Berlin,' said one, giving her an oddly formal bow. She was a celebrity, perhaps he felt it was expected. In the past there would have been flowers and flashing lights.

'Have you got a stretcher?' she said. 'There's a man in there with his foot blown off.'

They pulled him out and carried him away, crouching and running, as if crouching and running could save them from the mayhem that was exploding all around them, and she ran beside them, across what must once have been the garden of the Reich-Chancellery, until they reached the entrance to the bunker.

She bent down to Ritter and asked him how he was.

'I'll live,' he said. She took this as ironic.

The guards took them down into the bunker and here was Magda Goebbels with a face like a ghoul, slashed with lipstick. They hugged, brushing cheeks, like it was the old days.

'The Fuhrer will be pleased to see you,' she said. 'It will cheer him up.'

But when she saw him she was shocked. He shuffled along like an old man, stooped and broken, and his voice was a croak, a ghost of the voice that had moved millions, a voice from the grave. He seized her hand and held it in both of his and she felt the tremor in them. It was as if he was clutching her for support.

'Why have you come here, my dear?' he said.

She thought of telling him the truth, that she had come to die with him, but she wasn't sure if it struck the right tone. He still thinks we can win, Magda had told her. He thinks they will fall out before the end, the Reds and the Amis.

'I thought there might be something I can do,' she said, hoping it didn't sound as ludicrous to him as it did to her, when what he needed was an army— five armies—not one crazy woman and her crippled lover, and a plane full of holes that would never fly again. But it was the right answer. There was something she could do. Even if it was not what she had expected—even if it confirmed her worst fears about his state of mind.

'Ich möchte dass du nimmst für mich eine Nachricht zum Papst,' he said.

'I want you to take a message for me—to the Pope.'

CHAPTER FIFTEEN

The Vatican Papers

'Her name was Hanna Reitsch,' said Irma, 'and she was the most famous aviatrix in Germany. She could fly anything. She even flew a V2 rocket once, to see if it could be done. The world's first guided missile.'

The name seemed familiar to Aiden but he did not know why. He wondered if Michael had ever told him about her. It could only have been Michael.

'The plane she flew into Berlin was a Fieseler Storch, short take-off and landing. It can land in thirty metres. To begin there was a man in control, as there usually was. Ritter von Greim, her lover, one of the top men in the Luftwaffe, but he was wounded in the foot and Hanna had to take over. She flew through the streets, only a few feet above the ground, with hundreds of Russian soldiers firing at her, and landed close to where we are standing now. On the night of April 26th, 1945, four days before Hitler took his own life. It is thought they came to die with him, but he had other plans for them. Some I have spoken with, they say that Hanna gave him hope. That all was not lost. He saw a way out of the trap he was in. So, he sent her away again. And with her went Heinrich Bechmann.'

'The soldier with the wings?'

'The soldier with the wings.' She nodded with satisfaction. He had been paying attention. Good boy. Gold star.

'And the papers?'

'I am coming to them. Ah, at last!'

She had seen a cab and this time it was not taken. She stepped out into the road and flagged it down.

'You want to eat?' she asked Aiden. He did. She gave the driver the name of a restaurant and they drove north towards the Brandenburg Gate. She leaned forward, peering through the window.

'Here is where they kept the plane,' she said. 'In a garage right under the Tor.'

'The Storch?'

'No. The Storch was finished. It was hit by a shell, minutes after they landed. This was another plane, kept for the Fuhrer in case he wished to escape. Arado AR96, advanced trainer, two-seater, range over six hundred miles.'

She saw that he was smiling. 'Did I say something funny?'

'I'm sorry. Do you know the names of all the military hardware?'

'You are surprised? Because I am a woman?'

'No.' He probably did mean that, but not just because she was a woman. 'Because it is so long ago.'

'Ah, but I know the modern ones, too. Planes, guns, tanks. My father is a general in the *Bundeswehr*. He wants a boy so I give him a boy. Better than a boy. When I was twelve years old I knew how to strip and fire a G36. You know what is a G36?'

He did. It was an automatic rifle on general issue to the German Army. He had even fired one. But he did not mention it.

'I drove my first AVF when I was fourteen—a *Luchs*. A Lynx I think you say in English. Armoured car. You have been a soldier, I think?'

'Of sorts. How can you tell?'

'I can tell. The British Army?'

'Royal Marines.'

'What rank?'

He had played this game before, with less gentle companions. Name, rank, and number.

'I was a sergeant,' he said.

'On active service?'

'Sometimes. Do you know many soldiers?'

She made a moue with her lips. 'I used to. I even married one. A captain in the French Foreign Legion.' She looked at him to make sure he was impressed. 'It did not last very long. And what do you do now?'

'A bit of this, a bit of that.'

She considered him with a curious half-smile. 'You do not like questions about yourself?'

He shrugged as if he didn't care one way or another. He could always lie. 'Have you always lived in Berlin?' he asked.

She looked away, out of the window of the cab. They had turned right at the Tor and they were heading east, into darker streets.

'No. I came to Berlin when I was eight. I was born in Japan. My father was military attaché in the German Embassy in Tokyo. My mother is Japanese.' She turned to him again. 'So why do you not want to tell me what it is you do now?'

He appeared to consider. 'I'm a security guard. Kind of.'

A dry laugh. 'And what is it you guard?'

'People, mostly.'

'I see. A bodyguard. Like Heinrich Bechmann. And what do they do while you are in Berlin?'

'I have no idea. I expect they don't get out much.'

The cab came to a halt outside a building that looked like an old Gothic church. In fact, it had been a brewery, Irma told him, but now it was one of the best restaurants in Berlin. It was clearly a place she knew well. She was welcomed with enthusiasm and relieved of her umbrella and her coat. She did not wear a great deal beneath it. A black sweater, a short skirt in yellow tartan, black leggings, and those ankle-length boots with the heels. It could have been worn by a schoolgirl, but she carried it well. Aiden hung his leather hoodie on the back of his chair and let it drip. It was quite warm in the restaurant, a lot warmer than it had been in the bunker.

They had been given a table at the window overlooking a large flood-lit courtyard, empty now in the rain. He ordered the wild boar, with gravy, cabbage, and chips. She went for a salad. 'I am not a big eater,' she said. She also ordered a bottle of wine—a Saxon Weissburgunder. 'But you will have to drink most of it,' she said.

When the wine arrived, and their glasses were filled, she sat back in her chair with that tease of a smile but her eyes appraising.

'So —tell me what you know about Michael's work. His recent work.'

Aiden looked at her. Was this what it was all about? A deal, like they had with the girls in Garston? I'll show you mine if you show me yours. But he had nothing to show.

'I haven't the slightest idea what Michael was working on,' he said. 'I probably wouldn't understand it if I did.'

She frowned. 'This woman who was working for him, she has not told you?'

'I don't think she knew that much.'

'No, I don't think she did. Well, I will tell you what he told me. But he was still scratching in the dirt, turning over stones. I do not know what he might have found—without me.'

'So, what did you find for him?'

'I will come to that in a minute. But first, what is he looking for, what kind of book is he writing? It is a history, yes, so it is set in the past. He is looking at the lives of people who were alive in the spring and summer of 1945, Year Zero, the year of destiny. What was it like for the people who lived through this and what message do they have for those of us who live now? But he wants more than that. He is looking for an angle. Something that will catch people's attention. Make it relevant to today. Make headlines. That was always Michael's way. Something that makes people think this did not just matter then, it matters now.'

He shrugged. 'Big ask.'

'Maybe but—look at the people he wrote about in *The Murder Factory*. He showed how quite ordinary people—local builders, traders, manufacturers, upstanding members of the community—were drawn into something that was beyond evil. And he named them, he named their children, he named the companies they ran and still run. And he named the big companies that were involved in this and those who run them still, and what they are doing now. He makes it personal. You have read Michael's books?'

'Of course. They're not my kind of reading, but he was my brother. Of course I've read them.'

'Well then, Michael is always trying to make history relevant to what is happening today. Even if it means bending the facts a little.

Even if it means drawing parallels, pointing fingers. Look—see what happened then and see what happens now, and my God, it is the same people. Or the same kind of people. Not everyone is happy about this. And I am not just talking about historians.'

They were bringing the food. Aiden looked at his piled plate and at hers. Well, he probably did more exercise. He started sawing at his pig.

She took a sip of wine, watching him over the rim of the glass. Then she set it down carefully on the table.

'Very well. So, now I will tell you about Bechmann,' she said. 'And these papers that he brings out of Berlin.'

He inclined his head attentively but carried on eating. Despite what she had said about Michael's passion for making history relevant, it was hard to see any connection between his death and this story of the last days of the war.

'When the Russians see this plane taking off from the centre of Berlin, they think it is carrying the Fuhrer. Out of the ruins he has made of Germany and to a place of greater safety. But no. It is not the Fuhrer. He is still in his bunker making plans for the next war. In the plane is his insurance policy. His "get-out-of-jail" card. But now I must give you a history lesson. Have something more to eat.'

Her tone was ironic and he wondered if Michael had ever told her that if he insisted on giving him one of his history lessons, Aiden would insist on grabbing something to eat or drink, preferably both.

'History is the story of delusions,' she said. 'You have seen the paintings on the wall. The Nazis think they are fighting to save what we used to call Christendom. Now we call it western civilisation. And when Hitler comes to power in 1933, one of the first things he does is to make a deal with the Church of Rome. Hitler thinks they are in this fight together, like the Pope and Emperor in the days of the Holy Roman Empire.' She saw that this was perhaps a step too far for her present audience. 'Another delusion, but it is what Hitler thinks, so he sends for all the documents, all the correspondence between them, puts them in a folder and sends it off with Bechmann to Rome. To the man who made the deal, Cardinal Pacelli, who is now Pope Pius the Twelfth.'

'And this is his get-out-of-jail card?'

'This is what I am telling you. Hitler spoke about it before he died. He had a plan to save them all, and what was left of Germany. He told his mistress Eva Braun, and she told it to Traudl Junge, the secretary who was closest to him—and years later she told me.' He looked up at this, if only to see if she was serious. She appeared to be.

'When was this?'

'Never mind. She lived a long time after the bunker. What is important is Hitler's plan. He will ask the Pope to intercede with the Allies to save his skin. Make peace with Nazi Germany and unite against Stalin's Russia—to defend the Christian West against the godless Bolsheviks.' She noted his disbelief. 'You think this is insane and of course it is. He is a mad old man, older than his years, trapped in a hole in the ground. It is his last throw of the dice. But he was always a gambler. And if the Pope will not help them—then all his dealings with Hitler and the Nazis, they will be made known to the world.'

'Does this all come from this, what's her name, Trudie?'

A flicker of the brow. This is what came of mixing with the other ranks. 'Traudl. Not just her. I spoke to three of the survivors before they died. I have read all the memoirs, all the eyewitness accounts. I know better than anyone in Germany, better than anyone in the world maybe, what happens in the *Fuhrerbunker* in the last days of the war. And I have seen the paper Bechmann signed for the release of these documents from the archives. This is the German way, even in the last days of the Third Reich, if you want something you must sign for it. I found it in the Russian state archives in Moscow. A list of all the documents that Bechmann took from Potsdam on Hitler's orders, and his signature in receipt. But the list does not tell us a great deal. Not without the papers themselves. Only that they related to the Vatican. So where are they, what happened to them—and what is in them?'

Again, he waited for her to tell him. But she seemed to be waiting for him. She started chasing a piece of lettuce around her plate, watching it keenly as if it really mattered that it did not get away.

'Did Michael know about these papers?' he asked her.

She speared the lettuce and folded it into in her mouth before replying. 'I do not think so. I was going to tell him when he came to Berlin.'

I think I know what Hanna took with her, when she left Berlin. He thought he would keep that to himself for the time being.

'Maybe someone did not want him to come to Berlin,' Aiden said.

Now she was after a slice of beetroot. 'Seems unlikely,' she said. 'Either that they knew or would go to such extreme lengths to stop him. They would have to care very much about what I was going to tell him. And they would have to think it would mean more to him than to me, or I would be the one who is dead.'

'But you have no idea what was in them, these papers?'

'No. As I have said, only a list—and the titles do not tell us much. Mostly dates and numbers. We cannot know for sure without seeing them.' The beetroot went between the parted lips, leaving them a brighter shade of red. 'But there is speculation that Pope Pius knew about the Final Solution, Hitler's plan for the Jews, long before he said he did.'

'And why does that matter? Now?'

'It matters to a lot of Jews. And Catholics. And people who do not want it all stirred up again, all this shit from the past. It sounds crazy, I know, but there are a lot of crazy people in America these days.'

'But not in Germany?'

'In Germany you could say that we learned the lessons of history. Not to listen to crazy people, not to choose them as our leaders.'

'Okay. But where are we going with this?'

'We?'

'Figure of speech,' he said.

She drank some more wine. Set the glass down again in that deliberate, thoughtful way.

'Okay. Well, as I say, I am not sure where Michael was going with this. I would have to see his notes. But I think he needed this story— Hanna Reitsch and her flight out of Berlin with Hitler's henchman and the Vatican papers. I think this would have given him his angle. Made it relevant.'

'Why would it be relevant?'

'Because the Pope—the one we have now—is going to open up the Secret Archives. In the Vatican. This is what he says. To let people know the truth about his predecessor Pope Pius and his relations with the Nazis. To settle things once and for all. What he did or did not know about the Final Solution. If these papers are there, then it will be known—if they are not and they stay hidden . . . Well, here is Michael's book with his own take on the subject.'

'Pity he didn't finish it.'

'It is not too late. Is this not what you want? His final book. The last flight out of Berlin.'

'Shouldn't that be your book?'

'We could have both names on the cover.' She gazed at him speculatively. 'For me it would be an honour. And a tribute to Michael.'

'Well, it's not a bad thought,' he said.

She smiled and held his gaze. The moment was broken by one of the waiters who came to take away their plates. Aiden hadn't quite finished but he let it go. There was a brief exchange in German.

'Do you want coffee?' she said to Aiden. 'Or shall we have it back at my place?'

CHAPTER SIXTEEN

The File on Heinrich Bechmann

THERE WAS NO SIGN OF AIDEN AT BREAKFAST AND HIS KEY WAS STILL on the hook. Hannah was about to try his phone when he walked in through the front door. He was unshaven and she could have sworn he was wearing the same clothes he had gone out in to meet Irma Ulbrecht. She looked at him thoughtfully, saying nothing. He grinned at her a little sheepishly, though in fact it was not the image of a sheep that came to mind.

'Sorry about last night,' he said. 'I was given a bit of a run around.'

'You might have called me,' she said. 'I was worried.'

'I tried but I couldn't get a signal. I was underground.'

'What? On the subway?'

'No, not on the subway. But let me grab something to eat.'

Over breakfast he told her about his visit to the *Chaufferbunker* and what Irma had told him about Hanna Reitsch and Heinrich Bechmann.

'So that's where you spent the night,' she said, 'in the *Chaufferbunker*.'

He just gave her a look and it was Hannah who blushed.

'Well, I mean, it's all very interesting,' she said to cover her confusion, 'but it happened seventy-five years ago. I don't see how it could bother anyone today. Not enough to kill someone.'

'No?'

'Do *you*?'

He didn't answer directly. 'I've been thinking, you know when you were in the bath and the guy held you under the water?'

It was not something she was ever likely to forget. 'What about it?'

'When he let you up you said he said something that sounded like "Hannah, right?"'

'Yes? So?'

'Could you have misheard him? Could he have said Hanna *Reitsch*?'

'Well, I wasn't exactly at my best so far as hearing is concerned, or anything else for that matter. But why would he say that?'

'To see if it meant anything to you.'

'Well, I guess it could have been. But that would mean . . .' What did it mean?

'We're on the right track,' he said. 'Like Michael.'

She thought 'the right track' was something of an exaggeration, but she kept it to herself. 'So what do you want me to do now?' she asked him.

'I've made an appointment for you,' he said. 'At the Schutzstaffel Museum.'

The librarian was expecting her. He led her to a work station.

'Most of the files are now online,' he explained, 'but in a number of cases we have had to restrict the access. The file on Heinrich Bechmann is one of them.'

He was less forthcoming, certainly less than convincing, about the reason for this. 'Some of the people referenced may still be alive or have family whose feelings we have to respect. There could be legal complications. Anyway, you must clear it with us first, if there is anything you wish to use.' But he tapped in a password and left Hannah alone with the file on Heinrich Bechmann.

It began with a brief history of the SS—the Schutz-Staffel, or Shield Squadron, formed in 1925 as a bodyguard for Hitler and the other party leaders. To begin with there were just eight of them, all ex-servicemen, and their chief role was to police their public meetings and beat up hecklers. By the time Bechmann joined them, it had grown into a monster, a state within a state. Its commander-in-chief was Heinrich Himmler, who had become Hitler's right-hand man, and its chief function was state security, but it ran its own industries and banks; it had its own law courts, a scientific and education division, and a medical corps which supervised the euthanasia programme; it ran the concentration camps; and it had its own army—the Waffen-SS—a million fanatical party cadres who fought alongside the regular troops of the Wehrmacht. Bechmann was one of these. Indisputably Aryan and a fanatical Nazi, he was ideal material for the storm troopers of the master race.

In fact, he had been born in Italy—in a small mountain village in the South Tyrol—but he grew up among a resentful German-speaking population, agitating to be part of the new Fatherland which Hitler was building to the north. In 1936 the family moved to Munich, and a year later Bechmann was enrolled in the *Leibstandarte SS Adolf Hitler*, the Fuhrer's Praetorian Guard, the elite of the elite. In 1938 he was among the troops who marched into Vienna to impose the *Anschluss*—the union of Germany and Austria—and in 1939 he took part in the invasions of Czechoslovakia and Poland. The following year he was among the frontline troops who stormed through Holland and France.

It was in France, in May 1940, that he became involved in his first recorded atrocity—the massacre of eighty British prisoners-of-war during the retreat to Dunkirk. Most of them blown up with grenades tossed into a crowded barn; the rest shot as they tried to escape.

In January 1942, he joined a unit sent into the Ukraine on a mission code-named Operation Werewolf. Their job was to clear Jews from the site chosen as Hitler's field headquarters on the Eastern Front. According to depositions taken by the Red Army, he was one of two SS officers who supervised the mass execution of 272 Jews at Strizhavka, on the construction site itself, and over 300 in the surrounding area. They were lined up on the side of a mass grave and mown down by machine guns mounted in the back of a truck.

Shortly afterwards, he asked to be transferred to active service and was present at several of the major engagements in North Africa and Italy, winning the Iron Cross Second Class, the Knights Cross, and the Silver Wound Badge. Badly wounded in Italy, he was flown back to Germany and spent several months recuperating before serving again in France during the Allied invasion of Normandy. Then, in December 1944, he took part in the Battle of the Bulge, the German bid to repulse the Allied forces marching into the Fatherland—and it was at this point he played a key role in what, from the American perspective, was one of the worst atrocities of the war.

According to the file, *Sturmbannfuhrer* Bechmann had been attached to a special unit of shock troops known as *Kampfgruppe Peiper*, charged with spearheading the German advance.

The story that followed was compiled from eyewitness accounts and interrogations of Bechmann's captured comrades.

Between noon and 1 p.m. on December 17th, 1944, Kampfgruppe Peiper approached the crossroads at Baugnez, where they encountered un American convoy of about thirty vehicles. The advance guard of Peiper's group, led by Sturmbannfuhrer Bechmann, opened fire on the first and last vehicles of the convoy, forcing it to stop. With only small arms to defend themselves, the Americans surrendered.

While the main German column continued on the road towards Ligneuville, the unit under Bechmann led the American prisoners into a field, where they were joined by others captured by the SS earlier in the day. Most of the testimonies from survivors state that about 120 men were gathered in the field when the Germans fired on them with machine guns. As soon as the Germans opened fire, many of the prisoners tried to flee and a few sought shelter in a café at the crossroads. The SS then set fire to the building and shot any who tried to escape the flames. Some of those in the field had dropped to the ground and feigned death, but the SS troops walked among the bodies and shot any who were found to be alive. Most of the bodies recovered showed bullet wounds to the head.

Former members of Kampfgruppe Peiper, interviewed at Schwabisch prison in the immediate postwar period, variously reported that the American prisoners had tried to flee or had recovered their discarded weapons and opened fire upon their captors. Many of those interviewed claimed that the order to return fire was given by SS-Sturmbannfuhrer Bechmann and several reported that Bechmann had also given the order to execute the wounded with a shot to the head.

There was a footnote to say that in 1946 over seventy members of the SS unit were tried by a US military tribunal in the former concentration camp of Dachau. Forty-three were sentenced to death by hanging and twenty-two to life imprisonment. But for whatever reason Bechmann was not among them.

Hannah looked at the photographs that accompanied this report. The huddled bodies of the victims in the snow-covered field by the crossroads. The SS defendants in the trial at Dachau. Pictures of bodies being recovered from a mass grave near the site of Hitler's Werewolf headquarters in the Ukraine. And two pictures of the man thought to be Heinrich Bechmann. The first showed a group of Waffen-SS at a pavement café in Paris in 1940, shortly after the German victory over France. According to the caption, Bechmann was second from the right, a clean-cut German officer, strikingly handsome, smiling. The other picture showed two old men with long beards on their hands and knees, scrubbing the pavement with what looked like toothbrushes. The caption read 'Vienna 1936: Pro-Nazis celebrate the union of Germany and Austria by making Jewish citizens clean the streets.' Bechmann was at the front of the crowd, a tall young man in a black uniform with a swastika armband. He seemed to be laughing.

Bechmann's SS career had ended in Berlin, where he had served as one of Hitler's personal bodyguards in the *Fuhrerbunker*. He was presumed to have been there on the night of May 28th, 1945, when Hitler took his own life. He was still only in his mid-twenties.

'As the news of Hitler's death spread through the bunker,' Hannah read,

> *many of his remaining staff planned to escape from Berlin and give themselves up to the Allies on the western side of the River Elbe. One group led by SS-Brigadefuhrer Wilhelm Mohnke left the Fuhrerbunker on the night of May 1st, 1945. It included Hitler's personal pilot Hans Baur, the chief of his bodyguard Hans Rattenhuber, his secretaries Traudl Junge, Gerda Christian, and Else Kruger, his dietician Constanze Manziarly, Doctor Ernst-Gunter Schenck, and*

various others. The group headed along the subway but their route was blocked, so they went aboveground and joined hundreds of other German civilians and military personnel who had sought refuge at the Schultheiss-Patzenhofer Brewery. On May 2nd, upon learning of General Weidling's order for the complete surrender of all German forces in Berlin, Mohnke decided to surrender the group to the Soviet Army but a number of SS men chose to commit suicide and others fought on in pockets of resistance until May 8th, 1945.

Bechmann was not listed among those taken prisoner. It was assumed that he had been among those who committed suicide in the bunkers or were killed in action on the streets of Berlin.

That was it. There was nothing about being sent to collect documents from the Reich Archives in Potsdam and nothing about Bechmann leaving the bunker with Hanna Reitsch.

So how had Irma Ulbrecht learned of this—and why had it not been added to the information in the file, even as speculation? Even more surprisingly, Hannah was not allowed to make a copy of the file. She had to be content with making notes. And why could you not access it online? Because they didn't want him to become a hero of the Far Right? It was chilling to even think of it as a remote possibility.

It was just after one o'clock when she left the building. The sky was overcast but at least it wasn't raining. Aiden still wasn't answering his phone so she left a terse voicemail and a text message and headed back in the direction of the hotel.

The streets were crowded with office workers on their way to lunch. Looking around her she could have been back in New York. Perhaps not quite, but it was not at all like the Berlin of her dreams, which were informed as much by fiction as by the factual history: Isherwood's dissolute city of the early thirties, or Le Carré's shabbier, Cold War version, or even the whimsical wasteland portrayed by Wim Wenders in *Wings of Desire*, a continuing burlesque in which suspendered trollops strutted their stuff for fat Weimar businessmen, and Nazi brownshirts sang in beer gardens, and sequined acrobats danced with angels in the Death Strip beside what was left of the Berlin Wall.

She suddenly realised she had no idea where she was going, and not just in the abstract sense. She looked for a street sign, but there was nothing obviously helpful. Like everywhere in Berlin, the sidewalk had a cycle lane with cyclists speeding past in both directions, and the pedestrians seemed to be in almost as much of a hurry. Rather than stop one of them to ask the way, she looked up Google Maps on her phone and she was waiting for a signal when she felt a violent tug on the strap of her shoulder bag. The next moment she was sprawling on the sidewalk and the bag was gone. From her prone position she caught a glimpse of the cyclist who had mugged her speeding away from her with his prize.

A number of people came running to help, though there was little to do beyond express their concern. In fact, she was more shocked than hurt. Then the enormity of what she had lost hit her. Her wallet with all her credit cards, almost two hundred Euros in cash, her address book and diary, her iPad—and her passport . . . And, of course, her notes on Heinrich Bechmann.

CHAPTER SEVENTEEN

Cycling in Berlin

HANNAH WAS SURROUNDED BY A SYMPATHETIC CROWD. ONE YOUNG woman offered her a disinfectant wipe, an older woman stood by with a first-aid kit. Hannah was impressed. Was this standard equipment for pedestrians in Berlin? A man offered her his phone. He had the police on, he said, they wanted to talk to her. Then the crowd suddenly parted and there was the cyclist again—with her bag slung round his neck.

He presented it to her with a small bow.

Hannah was confused. Had he been stricken by remorse? Was this a joke? But no. It was a different cyclist. Although she had caught only a fleeting glimpse of her assailant, she'd had a distinct impression of someone thin and wiry—a young man, or even a woman—wearing tight cycling gear and a black helmet. This man wore cycling gear but he was taller and much more solid. And he had a silver and blue helmet.

All this was by the way. The important thing was that he had brought back her bag.

'He threw it away when I was about to catch him,' he said in German as he handed it to her. 'You had better check that everything is there.'

Hannah did. Nothing seemed to be missing.

'*Danke schön! Vielen Dank!*' she gushed. People in the crowd began to applaud. They slapped the cyclist on the shoulders. He looked embarrassed.

Someone rather diffidently explained that the police were still on the line. Hannah spoke to them. She explained what had happened and that her bag had been restored to her. No, she had not been hurt. No, she did not wish to make a formal complaint. All she wanted to do was to return to her hotel. She wondered if she should offer the cyclist a reward and if so, how much? She looked at him, her knight in shining armour. He was older than she had first thought, possibly in his forties, but very fit with strong, almost chiselled features. The offer of a reward might offend him, she thought.

'I really don't know how to thank you,' she said.

'There is really no need, Fraulein.' Another small bow. There was something quaintly old-fashioned about him, but also a hint of parody. 'I am glad to have been of assistance. But you must permit me to see you safely back to your hotel.'

She demurred. He insisted. It would have been ungracious for Hannah to refuse. And so they walked on together, Hannah clutching her bag rather more tightly than before, the cyclist pushing his bike.

His name was Emil, he told her, Emil Brandt, and he worked as a press officer for the Auswärtiges Amt, the German Foreign Office. He had worked in several Middle Eastern countries and in Washington. Now he was based at the embassy in Rome and he was visiting Berlin for a conference. He spoke English but not as good as her German, he assured her.

Hannah was a little more reticent when she told him about herself. But it was better to tell him something approaching the truth, if only to explain what she was doing in Berlin. So she settled for the line that she was a television researcher, working on a story about the *Bunkervolk*, the people who had been with Hitler in the final days.

He shook his head in apparent bemusement. He had taken his cycle helmet off and hung it over the handlebars. His hair was closely cropped, but not quite shaved, a touch of grey at the temple. His features were almost gaunt but not unattractive. 'This is something I do not understand,' he told her. 'This fascination in your country with a war that ended three-quarters of a century ago. Why is this do you think? Are there not enough wars in the present day to worry about?'

'You sound like my mother,' she said.

He laughed. 'This is not something one wishes to hear from a beautiful young woman. But really, I do not say this to flatter you—' he had noted the expression on her face—'but you are a modern, intelligent young woman, your future is before you, so why do you concern yourself with the past—and such a dark period of the past?'

'It's my job,' she shrugged. 'I don't get to choose the subjects I work on. Next week it could be killer dogs.'

'Killer dogs?'

'That was a joke,' she said. This was not entirely true, television being what it was. 'People *like* the dark,' she said. 'Inhumanity, cruelty, man's infinite capacity for inflicting pain.' She frowned at the pomposity of this, even if it was probably true. She would never have said this in English, but the German language inclined one to seriousness. Her German tutor at Uni—a German himself—had once told her that when he wanted to talk of frivolous things, or to gossip, he spoke in English, but when he wanted to be serious he spoke German. A little later he had asked her out. In English.

'Anyway, do you think it should be forgotten?' she demanded primly.

'But how could we forget? Here in Berlin, especially, with so many things to remind us. Down every street we turn.' They had just turned down Kurfürstendamm, in fact, which was entirely devoted to the serious business of shopping. 'We do not need to make feature films and documentaries. Instead we have museums and memorials. You could say that Berlin is a prisoner of its own past. Every district must have its museum, its shrine to the crimes that were committed here. You have heard probably about the one for the homosexuals who were persecuted by the Nazis?'

Hannah shook her head. She braced herself for the joke and hoped it would not be too offensive.

'It is a concrete block with a hole in the middle. Or a window. Through which you may, if you wish, watch a video of two men kissing. At least this was the idea when they built it. But then there was a complaint from the lesbians. They said, "Why is it only the men who are kissing?" So the authorities decided to make a change. Instead of the men, we would see a film of two women kissing. So then the men complained. They said the Nazis did not kill lesbians, only the male homosexuals.'

'So what happened?'

'Oh, I do not know. I expect they are still arguing about it. They will be arguing until the next war. This is what happens in Berlin.'

'You are not a Berliner?'

He laughed. 'No, I am not a Berliner. I am actually from Switzerland.'

'And you're based in Rome?'

'I am. Have you ever been to Rome?'

'No. But my grandmother lived there once, in the 1940s.'

And then, rather to her surprise, she told him about Gabriele. She was by no means sure why she did this, or that it was such a good idea. She thought it was partly because she was a little ashamed of her remark about killer dogs, as if she did not care what subject she worked on. For some reason, she did not want him to think badly of her.

'So you would like to know what happened to her, during the war?'

'Yes, I think so. Wouldn't you? I mean if she was *your* grandmother.'

'Possibly. Then again, I might prefer not to know. However, perhaps I can be of some assistance to you. I have many contacts in Rome.'

He asked her to write down her grandmother's name. 'If she was a German there might be a record in the archives at the embassy,' he said. 'And there are people I know in Rome who might be able to help—officials in the Italian Foreign Office. Perhaps if you would permit me to make enquiries on your behalf?'

Hannah did not see how she could refuse. Nor to give him her phone number—so he could contact her if he came up with anything.

They had reached the hotel. She thanked him yet again, for coming to her rescue. They shook hands and he cycled off, back the way they had come.

If Aiden had been back at the hotel Hannah would have told him about the incident but he wasn't, nor was there any message from him. Somewhat put out, she retired to her room to clean up. She looked a wreck and she had a small graze on her chin. This was what happened when you left Brooklyn.

She took a shower and put on some clean clothes. Still no word from Aiden, but she found a pleasant little café-bar a short walk from the hotel and ordered lunch. This helped put her in a better frame of mind. The food was good, the staff attentive and friendly. She ate sparingly—a mushroom omelette and salad—but indulged herself with a carafe of white wine. It made her slightly maudlin, but it was not a disagreeable mood to be in, alone in a foreign city. She googled Bechmann and found a Wikipedia reference, not quite as much as in the Schutzstaffel Museum but enough to make her wonder why they had been so officious about her not downloading it. She even found the picture of him in Vienna. But it did not mention the last flight out of Berlin, and he had died, it said, in May 1945.

When she left the café she went for a walk in the Tiergarten, keeping a firm grip on her shoulder bag. She walked along the Landwehrkanal as far as the bridge where the killers of Rosa Luxemburg dumped her body after the failed Revolution of 1919. She sat on a bench nearby, thinking about the cyclist Emil Brandt and what he had said to her about Berlin being a prisoner of its own past. She did not think this was true. The past was all around them, but the Berliners were moving on, quite confidently into the future. But he was right about all the reminders. There were even little brass plaques in the sidewalk, *Stolperstein*, they called them—stumbling stones—marking the places where victims of the Nazi terror had been murdered, or taken away to be murdered. There might even be one of her great-grandfather Josef Fabel. She should try and find out. And then there were the memories of the Cold War when Berlin had been the divided city. Everyone who had been shot trying to escape from East to West was commemorated with a cross, a whole new crop of memorials for a whole new generation of victims. Victims of history, her mother would probably have said.

Hannah had always understood the saying 'the past is a foreign country' to mean a distant place, difficult to reach, even more difficult to understand, but in Berlin the past was a close neighbour to the present, a parallel universe with porous borders. Maybe it was the same in all historic capitals, but in Berlin the dark parts seemed that much darker, or perhaps they were just more recent.

Her phone alerted her to a text message. She did not recognise the number but the message was from Irma and it had been sent to both Aiden and herself. 'Can you meet me at 6pm at the bike hire on Gertrud-Kolmar-Strasse. It is important. Please be there.'

The peremptory nature of the message annoyed her—and why a bike hire? She surely couldn't mean them to go cycling. After what had just happened to her it was like someone was playing a joke. She thought of speaking to Aiden first but decided against it and just included him in her reply to say she would be there. She looked up the address. It was only a few minutes' walk from where she was now and it was not yet five o'clock. She found another café where she could pass the time reading a novel she had brought with her—a detective story set in Berlin in the 1930s. It was almost dark when she set off and it had started to rain again, a soft but persistent drizzle. She put her hood up and joined the rush-hour crowds making their way home from work.

She walked down Gertrud-Kolmar-Strasse looking for the bike hire. It was a long road and she was annoyed that Irma hadn't given a number. Also, the more she thought about it, the odder it seemed. A bike hire? She had to be kidding. Unless she lived above the shop. Or perhaps it *was* a joke. Perhaps they were both in on it, Irma and Aiden. There would be a message waiting in the shop instructing her to hire a bike and cycle out into the Grunewald or somewhere equally remote to meet them, like a kind of treasure hunt, in the rain. They were probably testing her to see how far she would go.

She thought again about calling Aiden but then she saw the sign on the opposite side of the road. It wasn't a shop, it was a compound inside a wire fence. It looked like a building site. She crossed the road and found the entrance. It had been wedged open with a concrete bike stand and the gates kept trying to close but then stopped just before one of them hit it, flapping backwards and forwards like a bird with a broken wing. Hannah found this faintly sinister. Inside the compound she could see a couple of portacabins and a parked car—a Porsche. No sign of any bikes or people, but one of the cabins had lights in the windows, and the car was parked right outside.

Hannah entered the compound and a pair of floodlights came on. She walked over to the cabin and knocked on the door. Nothing. She knocked again. Still no reply. She looked at the Porsche to see if either or both of them was waiting there for her, but they weren't, unless they were hiding under the seats. There wasn't a lot of room to hide in a Porsche. It was a convertible, a classic, probably from the 1960s. She thought it might be Irma's car. It was her style. This annoyed Hannah even more.

In her irritation she tried the door of the portacabin, and rather to her surprise it opened. Inwardly. It seemed to be a site office. Maybe she was meant to wait here for them. It had only just turned six-thirty.

'*Hallo!*' she said. '*Hallo, ist jemand da?* Is anyone there?'

Then she went in.

Irma was sitting at a desk on the far side of the room. Her body was slumped as if she was asleep, but her eyes were open, her face was the colour of a bruise, and her tongue was hanging out. Before Hannah could take anything else in, or make a move or scream, or do one of half a dozen things that might have occurred to her, given time, she heard the door close behind her and a hand was clamped across her mouth.

Chapter Eighteen

'Breathe deeply'

WHEN SHE HAD FIRST MOVED TO NEW YORK, JUST TO KEEP HER FATHER happy, Hannah had attended a series of self-defence classes called 'Survive the Streets.' Her father had paid for the course and Hannah had learned a number of techniques for defending herself which she had never, in all her time in New York, had to employ, but she still had a rough idea of what to do if the circumstances appeared to require it. When grabbed from behind you were supposed to ground your heel in your assailant's instep and drive your elbow violently into his stomach. Then, when he obligingly relaxed his hold and doubled up at the waist, you swivelled round and delivered a rabbit punch to the back of his neck. And then you ran like hell.

All of which posed something of a challenge.

She did manage to stamp on her assailant's foot, but when she drove her elbow into his midriff, it did not sink in to anything like the extent required; nor did she hear the anticipated sound of expelled air. Instead the grip tightened on her arm and a voice in her ear said, 'Hannah! It's me—Aiden.'

Hannah broke away, but only because he let her. She turned to confront him and he stepped back, arms raised in a gesture of surrender or supplication.

'Take it easy,' he said.

She turned again and looked at Irma. The first look would have been enough.

'Oh my God!' This time she clamped her own hand over her mouth. She did not seem to be able to tear her eyes away. She could feel a moan starting in her throat.

'Steady.' Aiden was holding both of her arms. She was probably swaying. Or if she wasn't, the room was. She tried to push past him and out of the door. But he just held her a little more tightly.

'I think you'd better sit down,' he said. He led her across the room, gripping her arms very firmly, and sat her down on a chair at the end of a table.

'Put your head down on your knees.' She felt his hand on her shoulder, bending her over. 'Breathe deeply.'

When she thought she was no longer going to faint she sat up, shaking off his hand.

'What the fuck?' she said.

Aiden took this as a serious question, which in its way, it was.

'She was strangled,' he said. She saw that he was wearing gloves. Disposable, plastic gloves.

'Why are you wearing those?'

Several possible explanations had already occurred to her.

'Because I don't want to leave any prints,' he said. 'And nor should you. Don't touch anything.' He picked up her hands and placed them firmly in her lap, like she was a little girl. She wanted to look at Irma again but didn't. She was very conscious of her, though, sitting just a few yards away at the far end of the room.

'She was like this when you . . .'

'Yeah.'

'Have you called the police?'

'Not yet.'

'Why not? How long have you been here?'

'I don't know. Fifteen minutes? I got here early.'

'Fifteen minutes!' This was a long time to be here with a dead body. What had he been doing?

'And you haven't called the police?'

'I needed time to think.'

'What about?'

He didn't answer but she saw his eyes move further down the table, and she followed his gaze and saw a shoulder bag and something else next to it. It looked like a parcel bound up with tape. Not very neatly. And there were wires sticking out.

'What's that?' she said. She felt a rising alarm. 'Aiden?'

'IED,' he said.

'What?'

'Improvised. Explosive. Device.'

He pushed her gently back into the chair.

'Don't worry, I've disabled it.'

She looked at it. She had never seen a bomb before, not outside a museum. It looked like there were several canisters bound together with gaffer tape, what appeared to be a mobile phone, and a circuit board with lots of wiring.

'Why did you bring it here?'

'I didn't bring it here, Hannah. I found it here. It was in one of the drawers. Of her desk.' He spoke in the same tone of weary patience that had, now she thought about it, characterised his manner since she got here. He crossed to the window.

'You searched her desk?' She spoke to the back of his head. 'Why?'

'I was looking for clues.' He was peering into the compound. 'Whoever planted it was probably waiting for both of us to get here before they detonated it. And that means they must be keeping an eye on the place.' He seemed to be talking more to himself than her, but she felt compelled to make a response.

'What are we going to do?'

He turned and looked at her thoughtfully.

'We've got to phone the police,' she insisted.

She pulled her phone out of her bag. What was the number for the emergency services in Berlin? She should know. He took it off her, not violently but firmly, and put it in his pocket.

'Just bear with me,' he said. 'I'm trying to get us out of this.'

He walked over to the desk where Irma was sitting. Hannah thought of making a dash for the door but she wasn't sure she could make it, and in any case, if what he said was true . . . She looked at the bomb again, if that was what it was. It looked like it was. She didn't know what to believe. Had he disabled it? How did you disable a bomb?

He came back and put something in the shoulder bag. Then he picked up the bomb in both hands and put that in, too. Quite carefully.

'What are you doing?' she asked him.

'I'm taking it with us,' he said.

'What?'

'It's quite safe,' he said, 'and I don't want them activating it again.'

Before she could pursue this any further he took her arm and led her to the door. He opened it cautiously and looked out.

'Okay,' he said. 'We're going to take Irma's car. Don't touch anything. And pull your hood right up over your face. I think they've disabled the CCTV, but just in case.'

The moan began again but he didn't let it distract him. He kept hold of her arm until they reached the car, then he opened the door for her and strapped her into the passenger seat as if she were a child. He still had the gloves on. She couldn't understand why he was so worried about fingerprints if he had nothing to hide.

'You *are* going to tell the police,' she said. It was part question, part instruction, but he just shut the door on her and went round the other side of the car and got into the driver's seat, handing her the shoulder bag. She stared at it in horror.

'Sorry,' he said. 'But I don't know where else to put it. It's quite safe, just hold on to it.'

He started the engine. She found her voice at last.

'Where are we going?'

'Let's worry about that if we're still alive when we get out of here,' he said. 'If that's all right with you.'

Then he put his foot down.

CHAPTER NINETEEN

The Houseboat on the Spree

HE DROVE ACROSS THE COMPOUND LIKE A BOY RACER. THERE WAS A LOT of surface water about and she could see it flying past the windows. She felt like she was in a powerboat. They shot through the gates and out onto the road. After a couple of blocks he slowed down a bit.

'You don't have to hug it,' he said.

'What if there's a jolt?' she said.

'It's not nitroglycerin,' he said. This was not quite the reassurance she might have been looking for. There was nowhere else to put it except at her feet. She kept it on her lap.

Aiden made a left turn and then a right and she could see the Brandenburger Tor ahead of them.

'Where are we going?'

'Irma's,' he said.

This was a shock, though in her current state the best she could do was a faint 'Uh?'

'There are some things I have to do there,' he said.

She stared at his hands on the wheel, in the disposable plastic gloves. Even if he hadn't killed Irma himself, and her personal jury was still out on that, what kind of man carried disposable plastic gloves around with him, just in case he might need them? She watched the hands sliding competently up and down the leather wheel.

'Why won't you call the police?' she said.

He did not answer right away. But then he said: 'I don't trust them.'

She stared at him. 'Why not?' No answer. 'The German police or any police?' Still no answer. 'Have you had much to do with the police?'

'Hannah—let's just say I'm paranoid and leave it at that.'

'No,' she said. 'I want to know why you won't call the police. Or why you won't let me call them, or why you've still got my phone.'

He sighed. 'Okay. Let's say my experience of the police, in most countries, is that they are inclined to take the easy option and in this case the easy option is us. Or me, at any rate.'

Hannah thought about this. It didn't get her very far. Surprisingly he spoke again.

'I need time to figure this out,' he said. 'I don't want to spend the next few days banged up in a police cell being asked stupid questions while every scrap of evidence disappears.'

This did not make a lot of sense to Hannah. Wouldn't the police be gathering evidence?

'Is that why we're going to Irma's?' she said.

'One of the reasons.'

'So you can see if there's any evidence—and get rid of it?' This was provocative but she didn't care. She had a bomb in her lap.

'If you like.' He glanced swiftly at her and then back at the road. 'What possible reason do you think I might have for killing Irma Ulbrecht?'

She had been thinking about this. 'You may have thought she had something to do with killing your brother.'

'Well, I certainly think she had something to do with the *reason* he was killed. And it probably got her killed, too.' She was going to ask another question but then he spoke again. 'She'd been tortured.'

'What?' She stared at him but he was looking straight ahead through the windscreen wipers and the rain. Swish, swish. 'Why would . . .'

'They'd tied her to the chair and they burned her face,' he said. 'Probably with a lighter.'

'Oh no, oh God.' She put her hands to her own face, then quickly grabbed the bag as he turned another corner. She thought about the body in the beach house. 'Why would they do that?'

'Possibly because they wanted to know how much *she* knew.'

'About what?'

'If I knew that, we wouldn't be where we are now, would we?'

Hannah was not sure exactly where they were now or how they had got here. She closed her eyes, but when she opened them she would still be in the same place, clutching a bag that may or may not contain a bomb that may or may not go off at any moment, in the vehicle of a woman who had just been murdered with the man who may or may not have murdered her.

'Why did she want to meet us?' she said. 'And why there?'

'It's her other office,' he said. Then after a moment: 'I'm not sure she did.'

'Did what?'

'Meet us there. It probably wasn't her who sent the text.'

'But it was from her phone?'

'Yeah.'

'But if it was—whoever killed her—they must know about us.'

He took his eyes off the road for a moment and looked at her instead. His lips compressed and widened, but you would never call it a smile.

Eyes back on the road. He turned another corner and stopped the car. They were in a dead end, a cul-de-sac. Ahead of them she saw lights glinting on water.

He looked at her. 'Before you get out of the car,' he said, 'put your hood up. And don't say anything.'

'Why? Are we being recorded?'

'No, I don't think so. Not at the moment. But it will irritate me less.'

He took the bag off her and put it over his shoulder. Then they walked to the end of the street where she had seen the water. It was a river. The Havel or the Spree, she thought. It seemed important to know where she was, and where she was going, though she would have been pushed to say why. They walked for a minute or so along the side of the river. Then Aiden led her down a flight of steps that ended in a metal gate. Beyond the gate were some moorings. He tapped in a code that opened the gate and they went through.

She followed him along a wooden walkway between the moorings until he came to the boat at the very end. Quite large, as boats go. There were potted plants on the deck, even small trees, and what looked like a garden shed. He had clearly been here before. He marched straight up the gangplank to the wheelhouse and produced a bunch of keys. Had he taken them from Irma? She had seen him take something. There appeared to be two locks on the door. The keys opened both of them.

Hannah followed him in and he switched on some lights. Then he led her down a few steps to what in any other kind of boat she might have called the saloon. She had grown up with boats in Black Rock, but she had never seen one like this outside a fashion magazine. There was soft lighting, woven silk rugs, expensive throws over chairs and sofas, bookshelves, and hangings on the walls—or bulkheads as Hannah had been taught to call them, though perhaps not in this case.

Aiden had gone straight over to a large desk that occupied one end of the room and was tapping instructions into the keyboard of a laptop which was connected to a large monitor above the desk. It came up with a screen display—a mountain landscape in snow, possibly the Alps—and a request for the password. Which judging from the single expletive he uttered, Aiden did not have. He tried something but whatever it was, it didn't work.

'It will be in German, won't it?' Hannah said, standing behind him.

He looked at her.

'How is that supposed to help?'

'Well, maybe you've got the spelling wrong.'

'I don't know the password,' he said in his default tone of weary patience. 'So whether it's in German or Middle English or fucking Swahili it doesn't make a hell of a lot of difference, does it?'

'You knew the pass for the marina,' she pointed out.

'Only because she gave it me when I went to buy a toothbrush and some croissants. And how is that relevant, anyway?'

He went to buy a toothbrush and some croissants. This small intimacy brought home to Hannah what had happened between them, and what had happened to Irma since, and what it must have done to Aiden to find her like that.

If he didn't kill her himself.

'I thought maybe she'd used the same number with the name of her first pet—or something.' She floundered.

'I spent the night with her, Hannah. We didn't get around to discussing the names of our first pet.'

He was searching through the papers on the desk. 'What are you looking for anyway?' she said.

'I don't know. But she made a couple of calls this morning. They were in German so I didn't pick up much but I thought I heard the words *Fuhrerbunker* and *Bunkervolk* and Heinrich Bechmann. Then she started looking stuff up on the laptop.'

He had found something. She looked over his shoulder. It was a scribbled list of names.

Meran. Schlossraben. Einsatzgruppe. Bozen. Bolzano Dolomiti. Stahlberg von. And what looked like a couple of long telephone numbers starting with the international code 0039.

'Make anything of this?' he asked her.

'*Meran* could be the German for Merano,' she said, 'in the South Tyrol. *Schlossraben* sounds like a castle—the castle of the ravens. *Einsatzgruppe* means—deployment group, literally. Special group or task force. In the SS it was the name for a death squad. *Dolomiti* is the Dolomites. Stahlberg, I don't know. I think Bozen is another place. If I had my phone I could check.'

He took it out of his pocket and gave it to her.

'Yes,' she said. 'Bozen. The German name for Bolzano in the South Tyrol. Bolzano Dolomiti is the name of the airport. It's a ski resort.'

'Phone the numbers,' he said, 'but don't say anything if anyone answers.'

The first one was the Merano Tourist Office, the second was the Merano Municipal Police. Both were voicemails. In both Italian and German. Hannah didn't leave a message.

'Why was she interested in Merano?' Aiden said, but she didn't think he was asking her.

He checked it on his own phone and read aloud: '*Merano. Once a Germanic stronghold in the South Tyrol, Merano acquired the chic hotels and elegant promenades of a belle époque spa when the beautiful but batty Empress Sisi of Austria made it a fashionable haunt of the nineteenth-century European aristocracy.* Blah-di-blah di blah.'

'Maybe she was planning a holiday,' said Hannah. 'Or a research trip.'

'To research what?' He had got *Schlossraben* up on his phone. There was a picture of a Gothic castle against a mountain background. But the text was in German. He handed it to Hannah.

'You want me to translate?'

'That would be a good idea,' he said. 'Then I'd be able to understand it.'

'*Schlossraben was built in the thirteenth century by Crusaders returning from the Holy Land,*' she read. '*In the eighteenth century, it was destroyed by Napoleon but restored in the nineteenth century and has been in private ownership ever since.*'

'Fascinating,' he murmured. She took this as sardonic.

'Do you want me to go on?'

'Please.'

'*In 1943 it became the headquarters of an SS Einsatzgruppen who used it as a clearinghouse for Nazi war loot. Gold, jewellery, paintings, and antiques were channelled through the Schloss to secret destinations outside Europe to provide for Nazi exiles in the event of a German defeat. Also forged documents. Then, when defeat became a certainty, it became a staging post for Nazis escaping from Germany across the Brenner Pass.*'

She looked at him again, waiting for a reaction.

'And after the war?'

'*In 1945 it was occupied by Allied forces until its restoration to the Stahlberg family in 1947.*'

'That's all?'

'That's all.'

'What the hell was she doing?' Aiden started searching among the papers again.

'It could be anything,' Hannah said. 'It's what she did.' No comment. 'Bechmann was born near Merano,' Hannah recalled.

'What?'

'You sent me to the Schutzstaffel Museum to research him, remember? Irma arranged it.'

He was looking at her now with a different expression, an improvement on the usual. She gathered she had said something useful for once.

He picked his shoulder bag up from the floor and took out the taped-up parcel.

'You'd better leave,' he said. 'In case I fuck this up. Wait for me outside. Some distance away.'

Fuck this up?

After a couple of false starts she managed to form a complete sentence.

'What are you going to do?'

'Put the fuse back in.'

Words, once again, failed her, but her expression was enough.

'I spent the night here,' he said. 'I probably shouldn't have, but I did. They'll find my DNA all over it. It will be a bit harder for them if it's at the bottom of the Spree. Now will you get the fuck out of here? I need to concentrate.'

Hannah stopped a little way down the quayside and looked back. He could not possibly be serious, she thought. He was just teasing her. Even Aiden wasn't that mad.

She saw him emerge from the wheelhouse and come striding briskly towards her. When he saw her standing there watching, he frowned fiercely and waved his arms at her like he was shooing her away. She took a few steps back but his gestures became more determined, so she turned and began to walk properly, but in no particular hurry. He caught her up and took her roughly by the arm, almost dragging her along with him at a half-run. Then the bomb went off.

She tried to look back but he was going too fast. They got into Irma's car and he drove off at normal speed.

'I can't believe you just did that,' she said.

No comment.

'Where are we going now?' she said. She was starting to adopt the same weary tone as he did.

'Merano,' he said.

Chapter Twenty

Night Train to Munich

They left Irma's car in a street near the Zoogarten and took a cab back to the hotel to pick up the tab and their luggage before going on to the station, where they took the night train to Munich. In different couchettes. In another life Hannah might have felt thrilled to be making such a journey. In fact, something like it had figured in her adolescent fantasies. An intercity express rushing through the night filled with murderous psychos and mysterious women, one of whom was her. She would have been sipping champagne at a white-clothed table and dining on quails' eggs and stuffed carp (which had seemed quintessentially *European* to the teenage Hannah) while the train sped through a landscape of mountain and forest, and small country stations with unreadable names flashed by in a blur of lights and a clatter of crossrails. At other times the windows would have reflected an entirely satisfactory image of a young woman with cool eyes and dark red lipstick, wearing a waist-hugging suit in the style of the late 1940s, poised, elegant, ravishingly beautiful, sometimes in a wide-brimmed hat, sometimes not. Always alone.

In fact it was a nightmare. The train left five minutes before midnight and she was shown straight into her economy sleeper. She had not eaten, nor was there an opportunity to do so. The events of the evening had not, in any case, been conducive to eating. The sleeper felt like a prison cell in motion, the bed was a rack on which she writhed in torment for most of the night. She was torn by doubt and indecision. There was some amount of self-recrimination in there too, as she reviewed the events of the past twenty-four hours and compiled a long mental list of all the things she should have done differently. But perhaps she would have to go back further than that.

As the train sped through the night, her imagination began to paint new and ever more alarming scenarios. She even began to doubt that Aiden was Michael's brother. She had checked him out on the internet of course, but with little success. There were a number of Aiden Blakes—some with extensive profiles—but none even remotely resembling what she knew of this one. There was no Facebook page, no Twitter account, no Instagram or any other obvious social media reference. He could be a professional killer, a hit man who had murdered her previous employer and his partner and was now tying up the loose ends, one of whom had been Irma. Another was herself. It was surprising he hadn't dealt with her already. Possibly he was using her to find out how much Michael knew, and to lead him to others in the know—like Irma. When he had eliminated them all, one by one, it would be Hannah's turn.

Sleep was impossible. She squirmed about on the narrow bed, twisting her brain into something resembling the sheets. She felt like her late grandmother Gabriele Fabel, making the same journey as a schoolgirl, the victim of events beyond her control or understanding. But at least Gabriele knew who her enemy was.

Hannah had always known that the key to power was knowledge. You had to know what was happening and why. This was why she was drawn to history. Not just because she loved the mystery but from a compulsion to solve it, and to at least have an informed opinion on why people had acted as they did.

Why, why, why, mummy's going to cry, her mother would wail in desperation when Hannah was a child, always pestering her with questions, forever searching for answers. And all along she had feared this very situation. This sense of being trapped, of being swept along by a series of events she was helpless to change or influence, ceaselessly wailing *Why?* Locked in her moving cell, rushing through the night, with Aiden the demonic switchman pulling the levers. There were other times when she recognised the contradictions in her narrative and knew that she had become paranoid and that Aiden was caught up in these events as much as she was, though he seemed a lot better at handling them. He had seemed genuinely upset about Irma, upset and angry. But it didn't mean he hadn't killed her.

And so it went on, round and around in her head.

The first chance she had to talk to him was at the central station in Munich over breakfast—or coffee in her case because her stomach felt too tense to digest solids, and especially not one of the cheese and ham paninis Aiden bought for them. Whatever personal stress he might be enduring, it didn't seem to affect his appetite. They had almost an hour before the next stage of their journey—a five-hour trek via Innsbruck to Merano.

'I'm not sure I can go through with this,' Hannah told him after sitting in silence for a couple of minutes trying not to watch him eat.

He looked at her in that thoughtful way of his. 'So what do you want to do?'

'I want to go home.'

'Well, there's probably an airport in Munich,' he said. 'But I wouldn't advise it. Not just yet.'

'You think I might miss something?'

Sarcasm was the only weapon at her disposal and this time it brought a rare response.

'Okay. Go home. But don't forget they tried to kill us. And don't think they won't try again.'

'What do you mean, *they*?'

'I don't know yet—but it's probably not a gang of homophobic psychos from Long Island.'

She closed her eyes. When she was a very little girl, she used to think if you closed your eyes and hid behind your hands people couldn't see you. It hadn't worked then and it didn't now.

'And what about the police?' she said.

'What about them?'

'You don't think there'll be a problem when they find the body?'

'I don't know. It depends what they've got to go on.' He took another bite of his panini. The cheese was stringy and she had to turn her head away again.

'I'm pretty sure the CCTV had been disabled,' he said. 'Just like the security locks. And anyway, we both had our hoods up. And it was raining.'

She wondered if he was trying to reassure himself as much as her.

'And what about the houseboat?'

He frowned like he didn't see the connection. She made it for him.

'The houseboat you blew up. In the middle of Berlin. Which just happens to belong to a woman who has just been murdered. Or don't you think an exploding houseboat makes the news these days?'

'It could have been a gas leak.'

'A what?'

'From the cooker. It happens a lot on boats.'

She sat back a little and regarded him carefully. She wondered if he was insane. Not just given to the odd insane remark, but properly certifiable. 'How do you know about all this stuff?' she said.

'What stuff?'

'Well—like, bombs for a start?'

'I did a course once.'

'Oh. So you know what you're doing when you disable bombs?'

'I wouldn't say that. It wasn't really my thing. Didn't have the patience for it.'

She let her jaw drop but he didn't even notice.

'So when they find Irma's body and they realise the houseboat was actually blown up by a bomb and not someone leaving the gas on, what do you think they'll do next?'

'Well—there'll be an autopsy to find out how she died, and then they'll make a connection with the boat, and then I guess they'll start looking for whoever it was who killed her.'

'Do you think we might be high up on the list?'

He seemed to be thinking about this seriously. 'Well, they'll look at her recent activities. They'll question her work colleagues. They'll check her appointments diary and her desktop at the Schutzstaffel Museum. They'll have a record of our names in reception . . . So sooner or later—yeah, I guess they'll want to check us out.'

'You're just trying to cheer me up.'

'You did ask.'

'And then what?'

'We'll tell them the truth.'

'What—about finding the body?'

He looked at her in that thoughtful way again. It occurred to her that he probably thought she was as mad as she thought he was. But probably for different reasons. 'No, we don't tell them about finding the body. But everything up to that point. Almost everything, anyway.'

'You're not going to tell them about spending the night with her?'

'Probably not.'

'And when are we going to do this?'

'When they catch up with us.'

'Won't they want to know why we didn't call them when we heard about Irma?'

'We haven't heard about Irma, yet. We left Berlin before they found the body. I haven't seen anything on the news, have you?'

'Is that the line we're going to take?'

'It's the line I'm going to take.'

'And what are we going to do in Merano?'

It struck her as odd that she had waited until they were in Munich before asking this. She put it down to shock and the fact that she had a lot of other things on her mind.

'We're going to find out what it was that made Irma want to go there.'

'We don't know for sure that she did—want to go there.'

This clearly struck home, or near enough to wherever home was to be an irritant.

'Pick, pick. Hannah, I'm just trying to work through this. To find out who killed her and who killed my brother. But to do that we need to know *why* they killed him. And why they killed Irma. And why they're trying to kill us.'

'You think they're trying to kill us now?'

'Well, all things considered, I'm moving towards that conclusion. What do *you* think?'

'And you think we'll find the answers in Merano?'

'I'm following a lead. Leads don't always lead anywhere, but sometimes they do. I live in hope.'

Hannah was quiet for a moment, mulling this over. Then she said: 'There's something I should tell you.'

'Go on.'

'When we were in Berlin I got mugged.'

She told him about the incident with the shoulder bag and the cyclist.

He took it badly.

'Why didn't you tell me this at the time?'

'Because you weren't around. And then we got the text from Irma—or whoever sent it. And then—well, you know what happened then. Besides, I didn't think it was important. I got it back, didn't I?'

'That's the oldest trick in the game, Hannah. Someone steals your bag. Gets your card numbers, date of birth, address, everything. Then his accomplice brings it back, wins your confidence, and picks up the reward. And anything else you're prepared to give him. Then they clean you out.'

'No one's cleaned me out,' she said. 'My bank would have let me know.'

He put his hand to his forehead and massaged it for a moment. When he spoke again he was calmer.

'What else was in the bag?'

'Do you think I should cancel my credit cards?'

'What else was in the bag?' he repeated in the same flat tone, if possibly flatter.

'Well, my passport, my phone—and the stuff I'd copied from the library at the Schutzstaffel Museum. From the file on Heinrich Bechmann.'

He closed his eyes and made a kind of strangled noise deep in his throat.

'I'm sure you're making too big a deal of this,' she said. 'He wasn't that kind of guy. He was a cyclist.'

This opened his eyes.

'A cyclist. Oh well. So. That's a relief. Sorry, I'm being paranoid.'

'He walked me back to the hotel. His name's Emil Brandt and he works for the German Foreign Office.'

'He told you that?'

'How else would I know?'

'Did he give you his phone number?'

'No but . . .'

'Did you give him yours? You did, didn't you? Great. Well, tell me if he calls you, won't you? I mean, before you decide to go on a date with him. Or tell him where we are now.'

She could have wept. Thrown years of training out the window and wept tears of anguish and self-pity onto her uneaten panini. 'I'm sorry,' she said. 'I'm not cut out for this kind of thing.'

'You still want to go home?'

'What was it you said that might have changed my mind?' she asked him. 'I must have missed it.'

'They are not going to go away, Hannah. We're a threat to them. We have to stay one step ahead of the game.'

'Is that what we're doing?'

'Okay. That's very funny. I appreciate your sardonic sense of humour. Very New York. Or, where is it, Brooklyn? However—if we can find out why this is happening we'll go some way to knowing who's doing it, and if we know that, we stand some chance of staying alive.'

She knew she wasn't going home any time soon.

'Anyway,' he said with a shrug, 'believe it or not, you're better off with me than without me.'

'Shit,' she said. 'I'm really fucked, aren't I?'

'That's very good,' he nodded as if in appreciation. 'Probably.' He indicated her panini. 'If you're not going to eat that, can I have it?'

CHAPTER TWENTY-ONE

The Castle of the Ravens

ON THE WAY INTO MERANO IT BEGAN TO SNOW. FROM THE TRAIN WINdow it was like looking at a fairytale city in a paperweight. Aiden was not impressed.

'Fucking snow,' he said.

They took a cab to the information office. There was eidelweiss in a vase on the counter and the woman behind it wore a dirndl and a professional smile. Hannah asked if she knew of a place called *Schlossraben*. She spoke in English for Aiden's benefit.

'I do,' said the woman. 'What is it you wish to know?'

'Well, how to get there would be a help,' said Hannah. For some reason the woman annoyed her. Perhaps it was the dirndl, but it could have been the smile.

The smile morphed into a concerned frown. 'You were not thinking of going there today?'

'Well, yes, we were as a matter of fact,' Hannah told her. 'Why? Is it far?'

'It is only a few kilometres out of town, but it is off the road, up a small track, and in this weather . . . You are expected?'

Hannah said no, but she had heard it was very picturesque.

The woman laughed. It was that all right. There was something about the laugh and her tone of voice to suggest that 'picturesque' was not the whole story.

'But it is private residence,' she said. 'You should speak to the owner before you pay them a visit.'

'And who would that be?' Aiden put in. 'So we can ask him.'

'Well, he is the Count von Stahlberg, but he is not always there. However, he has staff who look after the place while he is away and they will not take kindly to unexpected visitors.'

'Well, we just want to take a look at it,' he told her kindly. 'We weren't planning on going in for the guided tour and the cream tea.'

The professional smile again, taut with dislike. But if the snow continued, the road would be very bad. Impassable even. Did they have their own car?

'No, we were thinking of hiring one. Do you have any recommendations?'

She drew a couple of circles on a street map.

'Stahlberg was one of the names on Irma's list,' said Hannah when they were back in the street.

'I know,' said Aiden. 'Aren't you glad you came?'

'The forecast is for more snow,' said the man at the car hire. 'So I would advise you do not go out of town until the weather improves.'

'We won't,' said Aiden, taking the key.

'You're sure about this?' Hannah asked him as they followed the signs to Austria. Dense forest pressed in on either side and the road was climbing all the time.

'See if you can find the news on your phone,' he said. 'The Berlin news.'

'What—for the weather?'

'No, not for the weather. Why would the Berlin news carry the weather in Italy? Besides, we can see the weather. It's snowing. I want to know if there's anything on Irma, or the explosion.'

The explosion was there but a fair way down the headlines.

'They think it might have been a gas leak,' said Hannah.

Aiden said nothing, but he didn't have to.

There was nothing on Irma. But then she found a story about a security guard who had been found badly injured on a building site in the centre of Berlin. He had been struck on the head with a blunt instrument and was in intensive care.

'Does it say where?'

'No. Hang on. In the government quarter.'

'That'll be it. Nothing about a woman?'

'No.'

'They must have moved the body,' he said. 'Or else the police are keeping it to themselves for some reason.'

'Why would they move the body?'

'I don't know. DNA. Whatever. They thought the explosion would fix that. When it didn't happen they must have gone back in and cleaned up after themselves.'

She sat there thinking about this without coming to any helpful conclusions.

'We didn't see a security guard.'

'That's because he was unconscious. There was one the last time I went there. In the other cabin.'

They drove on in silence. The snow seemed to have eased off a little.

'What do we tell this Count person when we get there?' Hannah said after a few minutes. 'If he's there.'

'I've been thinking about that,' he said. She refrained from comment. They had to try to get on better, and as the more mature adult, it was up to her to make a start. 'We say we're working for a TV company—making a documentary about the *Bunkervolk* in the last days of the war.'

'Do you know anything about making a documentary?'

'No. But I assume you do.'

Fair enough. 'So how are we supposed to know about this place?'

'Irma Ulbrecht told us about it. She said it was a refuge for the SS after the war, and she thought Bechmann might have come here.'

'So we're going to tell him about Irma—and being in Berlin?'

'That's right. We met Irma at the Schutzstaffel Museum. She's helping us with the research. I think she's probably been in touch with this bloke already.'

'But what if they find the body? And he hears about it?'

'Then we look shocked. You say "you're shitting me" in your fluent German and we clear off as fast as we can. Does that look like a raven to you?'

He had slowed down and she looked up to see two stone pillars, or gateposts, at the right-hand side of the road, each topped by a stone bird with wings spread, beaks in an aggressive gape. They could have been ravens. There was no gate, but a narrow track led off through the forest covered with snow. They followed it for about five minutes through the forest, always climbing, and then they emerged from the trees and saw the *Schloss* ahead of them, on a steep rise.

'Bloody hell,' said Aiden. 'Did you bring the garlic?'

The nineteenth-century restorers had obviously tried to keep as much of the Gothic as possible. They may even have added to it. The high stone walls were flanked by turrets topped with conical roofs, the few windows narrow and mullioned, none lit. A few swirling snowflakes supplied what little atmosphere was lacking. From a distance it looked abandoned. They drove through a narrow archway into an enclosed courtyard. A flight of stone steps ascended to a door built to withstand a siege and looking as if it hadn't been opened since the last one. Someone must have seen them coming though, for after a few moments it did open and a figure stood gazing down at them. It could have been a bear.

Aiden cut the engine and stepped out of the car. Hannah opened the door on her side but stayed put for the time being. She heard Aiden call up the steps. 'Count von Stahlberg?'

'*Was wollen Sie?*' The bear spoke. In German. *Who's asking?*

'*Ich heisse Herr Blake*,' said Aiden. '*Ich komme aus England. Darf ich mit Graf von Stahlberg sprechen.*'

He looked back at Hannah and with a jerk of the head that indicated he would appreciate her assistance. With some reluctance she stepped out of the car.

'If the Count is at home, I wonder if you would be kind enough to ask him if he could spare us a few minutes of his time?' she requested politely. She had to raise her voice somewhat, but smiled to show she was friendly. The bear did not smile back but from a closer perspective was revealed to be human, or as near as damn it, wearing a fur coat, a fur hat with ear flaps, and a black beard. His nose was large, his eyes unusually small. Igor, she thought. The Count's manservant.

'And what is your business with the Count?'

Hannah looked at Aiden for support, but he gazed back at her blankly. Clearly, he had exceeded the limits of his German.

'We work for a television production company,' Hannah said. 'We are making a documentary about the history of Merano.' She thought she would leave the *Bunkervolk* until later.

Igor regarded them for a moment or two and then stepped back into the shadows. '*Kommen*,' he said.

She glanced questioningly at Aiden.

'You heard the man,' he said.

They went in and the door creaked shut behind them.

'You will wait here please,' said Igor.

'Here' was a large empty hallway. Stone floor, a massive stone fireplace but no fire, and no furniture worth speaking of. There were a couple of high windows but they let in very little light. Igor was heading up another flight of stairs into greater darkness. They heard his receding footsteps for a few moments, and then silence.

They waited. Hannah moved about a bit to keep warm. After a couple of minutes, they heard someone coming back. Not Igor. A younger man, also bearded but of more modest proportions and without fur. On the downside, he had a very large dog with him. It bounded down the stairs, showing its teeth and snarling until its owner called it to heel.

'Hugo von Stahlberg,' he said as he advanced towards them. 'What can I do for you?'

He appeared friendly—friendlier than the dog and the bear at any rate—and to Hannah's relief he spoke to them in English. This meant Aiden could do all the lying. He was wearing a thick woollen sweater with a knitted scarf wrapped at least once round his neck and trailing almost to the floor. Heating at *Schlossraben* was clearly an issue.

Aiden told him they were making a documentary for the Discovery Channel on the last days of Hitler's Reich.

'We met Doctor Ulbrecht in Berlin,' Aiden was saying. 'I gather you have spoken to her about some of the events that occurred in Merano around that time.'

Hannah braced herself, but the name clearly meant something to him, and not as the object of a murder enquiry.

'Ah yes,' he said. 'Doctor Ulbrecht. I am afraid I could not help her very much. I was not here myself at the time. I am not quite that old. But I told her what I had heard from my father who was here for most of the war as a young boy, and I said I would send her some notes and any photographs I can find, but I am afraid I have not done so, yet. She is still planning her exhibition for the spring?'

'So I believe.' Hannah wondered if Irma had told Aiden about this, or he was making it up as he went along.

'It is a very good idea,' said the Count seriously. 'The world needs to be reminded of such things, especially in these difficult times. She said she would invite me to the opening.'

'Yes—she mentioned that. She said you might be able to help us with one or two of the people we are interested in. In particular, a man called Heinrich Bechmann?'

'Ah yes. *Sturmbannfuhrer* Bechmann.' His tone did not change. 'But why are you interested in him in particular?'

'Well, he was one of the few *Bunkervolk* to have escaped the net and I wondered if he might have come here.'

'Oh, but he did not escape the net. At least, not for long. Did Doctor Ulbrecht not tell you?'

Hannah looked at Aiden to see if he wanted to answer this. Apparently he didn't.

'He was shot,' said the Count. 'By the *partigiani*. Excuse me, the partisans. I am not so used to speaking English these days. I think it is no longer snowing, or at least not very much, so if you will wait a moment I will put on my coat and show you his grave.'

CHAPTER TWENTY-TWO

Il Vescovo

THEY TRUDGED THROUGH THE CASTLE GROUNDS, THREE HOODED figures with the hound of the Baskervilles bounding ahead of them snapping at a few swirling snowflakes in lieu of anything more substantial. Rising before them were the ruins of what had once been a chapel perhaps, or part of a monastery, a single surviving wall with a rose window that framed the darkening sky. Hannah felt a strong sense of déjà vu, but after a few moments she tracked it down to the memory of a painting, used as the cover of a book by Herman Hesse—*Narziss und Goldmund*—showing a group of cowled monks emerging from an ancient abbey in the snow. It had been one of her favourite books as an adolescent. In fact, for some years she had been hopeful of finding a boyfriend who combined the intellect and spirituality of the monk Narziss and the physicality of the gorgeous carpenter Goldmund. She had not been fortunate in that respect, but she was probably over it now.

Beyond the chapel was a small cemetery, the gravestones leaning this way and that in their thin sprinkling of snow, as if they had been dumped there by an avalanche. The castellans and members of their immediate family, servants, soldiers, even their favourite hounds, had been buried here since the Middle Ages, the Count informed them, adding with a grim smile, 'and now they are joined by these *diavoli* of the SS.'

They were planted in a straight line, a little distanced from the rest and more upright: five stone slabs each engraved with the Maltese cross and the name of a German soldier, with his rank, number, and the date of his death, May 6, 1945.

Sturmbannfuhrer Bechmann was the second from the left.

'It was a week after Hitler's death,' their host informed them, 'a day before the German surrender. But here in the Sudtirol, the war continued for a little longer. The Allies were in Meran, but the *partigiano* were up in the mountains, and the SS they were here in the *Schloss*.'

They had been here for two years by then, he told them—an SS *Einsatzgruppen* with no obvious mission and no apparent duties, rarely seen outside the grounds of the *Schloss*, but visited once a month, regular as German clockwork, by the equally mysterious convoys from the North. He looked back at the grim outline of the *Schloss*, as if remembering, though these things must have happened thirty or forty years before he was born.

'But then the *partigiani* came down from the mountains and those they could find, who have not already fled, they lined them up in the courtyard where you leave your car, and shot them—by firing squad.'

Aiden asked him if he could take some pictures on his phone.

'As you wish. But please do not say where you find them. I do not want to make of this place a shrine, and all the neo-Nazis to come up here in their thousands to worship them.'

'I am surprised they were given a decent burial,' said Aiden, 'in the family plot.'

'Ah, but that is not the wish of my family—or the Communists. That is *il Vescovo*. The Bishop of Merano. Or one of his priests. But come, if you have taken your pictures, we will go back inside and I will tell you the whole story.'

As they walked back the heavens opened and the snow did what it had been threatening all day, obliterating every feature of the landscape except the dark mass of the *Schloss* rising before them. They began to walk faster, stumbling on the rough ground, until they reached its welcome shelter, though it was not noticeably warmer inside than out. After they had stamped the snow off their boots, their host led them up a spiral of stone steps into a room at the top of one of the turrets. It was comfortably furnished with a desk, rugs from dead animals which might once have been bear or wolf, and two leather armchairs on either side of an ornate iron stove. There were bookshelves on the walls, separated by small casement windows. On a clear day there would probably be a fine view of the mountains, Hannah thought, maybe even down into Merano, but all she could see now was the snow.

'Over there is Hohe Weisse and Hohe Wilde,' said the Count, who had seen her looking. 'I am sorry you cannot see them at present. We speak the German names still, for the mountains. As you may know, for centuries this was a province of the Hapsburg Empire. The Empress Sisi, she made Meran famous in the *grand epoque*, and the *haut monde,* they come here for the waters—and, I must say, for the sex and the scandal.'

He opened the stove door to throw more logs on the fire.

'Please—sit.' He indicated the two armchairs and they sat, with the dog on the floor between them, steam rising from its flanks. The Count produced a bottle of Apfelschnapps and three glasses, which he filled almost to the brim. Then he wheeled the swivel chair from behind his desk and joined them at the fire. All they needed was a story, Hannah thought, and that was on its way.

'So—now I will tell you the story as my father told it to me many times when I was a child,' the Count began, 'about when the Germans came here, in the spring of 1943, at the height of the war.'

Hannah stretched her feet out towards the stove and felt the schnapps burning a path to her stomach. For the first time in a long while she felt strangely safe. It was, of course, an illusion, but she held on to it while it lasted.

'My father lived here with his little sister, my Tante Mimi, and my Opa Matthias, my grandfather. Just the three of them. My grandmother was already in her grave, in the graveyard out there—' a nod to the window and the falling snow. 'She died in 1940 just after Italy entered the war on the side of Nazi Germany. Only thirty-six. My *Opa* always said she died of shame, but it was cancer I think. The servants had either gone away to fight for Italy and soon were either dead or in a prison camp, or they joined the *partigiani* in the mountains, the women and the men both.

'We are blamed, of course, that the SS came here, my *Opa* especially. He was an Austrian and an aristocrat, he had fought for the old emperor Joseph in the first war, here on the Italian front. But he was no friend to the Nazis. This is what I want to say to you, to set the record straight, that he was not a collaborator, as some people say of him. It is not with his permission that the SS come here, but they permit the family to stay in the *Bauernhaus*—the old farmhouse in the grounds—and maybe this was a mistake. But where else is he to go, my *Opa*, with his two children, and his wife in the graveyard here?'

'But *why* did the SS come here in the first place?' Aiden wanted to know.

'Yes. A good question. At the time, of course, no one knew this, no one who was not in the SS, but now we do. They were an *Einsatzgruppen* with a special mission and their mission was to make money. The leader, his name was Schultz. Erik Schultz. In civilian life he was a banker but now he was *Standartenführer*—a colonel in the SS. A man with a very high regard for himself. My father remembers him riding in the grounds on a big white horse. But he treats my *Opa* with respect. I think because he was old Austrian nobility and Schultz was—in German the word is *der Snob*.'

'The same in English,' said Hannah.

'So. The Snob. And of course he knows my *Opa* is a hero of the Kaiser's war—One of Us—so he invites him up to the *Schloss* many times. They have a strange—I do not know what you call it that is with them, my *Opa* and Herr Schultz. *Leichfertig*, they say in German. A kind of understanding. My grandfather laughs at him. And Schultz, he seems okay with this, but this is what my father said, who knows? And of course, my *Opa* wishes to know what is happening up here, up in his family home, what the SS are doing here.'

'And what were they doing?'

'Ah, this is what is so interesting. They make of it a *Laagerhaus*. A great storehouse for the things they steal, from all over Europe. Paintings, works of art, precious stones, even the books and ancient manuscripts, anything that is of value. They have *der Schätzer*—what is it, the people who put the price to these things?'

'Valuers?' Hannah proposed.

'Yes. That is it. Also, they are connoisseurs. They love the art, the good food, the good wine. It belongs to other people, of course, but—they are the conquerors, they have *Da Eroberungsrecht*—the right of conquest. We are familiar with this in Italy. It is wonderful that we have anything we keep for ourselves. To show to the tourists.

'So—they bring them here, these things, from all over Europe, and they put a price on them and move them out. How, or where, no one knows, only the SS, and the money they make, it goes into bank accounts in Switzerland. For the SS. To pay their *intelligenza*, their secret operations, things they do not want even Hitler to know. But, also, I think it is a way to make a *Pension* for them, for when the war is over.

'Even at the end, when Hitler is in his bunker in Berlin, here at the *Schloss* it is, what do you say, *normale Geschafte*—business as usual. My father remembers the trucks that come in the night, come and go, all night long. And in the *Schloss*, there were lights, all through the night, as they load them up. Everything is for sale. Bargain prices.

'And now, my *Opa* discovers they have a new purpose. More urgent. To make an escape route for themselves and their comrades in Germany and in Austria. A way out of Europe. To make a new identity with false papers. And the money to make a new life wherever they go. Enough to bribe the politicos and the government officials who are willing to give them a sanctuary, a refuge. They forge the documents, with the *provenenza* for all the jewellery and the paintings they steal. The proof of ownership. In the spring of 1945 I think it is the most creative place in Europe. All around there is death and destruction, but here they prepare only for the future.'

He reached over with the bottle and topped up their glasses. 'Now I come to the important part, the part that interests you, I think. On the second of May, 1945, the German Army in Italy surrenders. But here *normale Geschafte*, even when the Americans arrive. I have seen photographs of them here in the town, the SS, in the centre of Merano, sitting with the officers of the Allies in the bars and the cafés—also civilians in suits, like the American gangsters or the mafiosi. And an American military policeman—the MP with the white helmet and the band around his arm—to direct the traffic.'

'Why would the Allies allow this?' Hannah asked.

Hugo shrugged. 'Your guess is as good as mine. But always there is something in it for them. I do not know, I was not here, and my father was a young boy, what does he know? But there is speculation. I think that certain deals were made here. A Modigliani or a Monet for the safe passage to South America. A necklace of pearls they take from a Jewish heiress in Vienna, before they send her to Auschwitz. You know?'

'But why did they not just come up here and take them?'

'Yes. I ask my father this. He thinks the place is filled with explosive, ready to blow up with all that is in it. But maybe it is more complicated than that. They need the *provenenza*, and the bill of sale, the proof that it is not war loot, even if it is. And there are many secret places in the *Schloss*, many places to hide. There are people in Merano who believe the Nazis buried their treasure here. They still do, though no one can find it. My father searched for many years and found nothing, just a few trinkets, cap badges and medals. But there are things that are of value more than pearls or paintings, and these are papers. Certificates of ownership. Shares in some of the biggest companies in the western world. The SS, they were buying shares for years—and now at the end of the war they sell them to the highest bidder. And *Schlossraben*— it is the stock market.

'Then the Communists arrive and it is all over. No more partying, no more drinking at pavement cafés with the Americanos. No more secret deals. The SS go to their Black Castle and they "pull up the drawbridge." And then the *partigiani* come for them.'

He put another log on the fire. It may have needed it, but Hannah sensed that he knew how to tell a good story and he was coming to the climax. It was getting darker outside and the fire was throwing shadows on the walls.

'So. I tell it as my father tells it to me. The night of May fourteen and he is in the *Bauernhaus* with Tante Mimi when he hears the noise from the *Schloss* and he is very much afraid for my *Opa* because he knows he is up here. So when he hears the guns he escapes from Tante Mimi and runs up here to find him—and the *partigiani* are here, with five dead bodies in the courtyard, all in the black uniform of the SS— and one of them is *Sturmbannfuhrer* Heinrich Bechmann. So that is the end of his journey.'

And ours, thought Hannah. The dead end.

'But why would he come here in the first place?' Aiden wanted to know. 'All the way from Berlin?'

'Maybe because he is born near here. This is what my father told me. In a small village in the mountains near Bolzano, so at the end he comes back to his *Heimat*. Maybe he seeks a refuge, maybe it is a—what is the word?—halfway house on his way to some other place, outside Europe, I do not know, but he is one of them and now he is dead, shot by firing squad in *der Innenhof*, the courtyard where you first come—and buried in the family cemetery.'

'So the partisans shot them and then gave them a decent Christian burial? Was that normal for the SS?'

'Of course, it is not normal. Only a few miles from here, Mussolini and his mistress, Claretta Petacci, they were shot by *partigiani* and then they hang them upside down from the metal girder of a gas station and shoot at them again and again before they are thrown in a shallow grave. This is the usual way with Fascists. So I ask this question myself of my father—why the stone crosses in the family plot? What he told me is that there was a priest with them, a young priest from Merano, and it was he who said that even the SS must have a proper burial. So that is why they are here, in the cemetery, and that is why my *Opa* and even my Papa maybe, why they were not shot with them, because the priest speaks for them.'

'He seems to have had a lot of clout,' said Aiden, 'this priest.'

'*Clout*? What is this?'

'Authority.'

'Ah yes. True. But that is because he was the secretary to *il Vescovo*—the Bishop of Merano—and *il Vescovo* he has . . . "clout," you say? Very much. He talks with both the Communists and the *Fascisti*—with the German Army and with the Allies. I do not know why this is. It was a confusing time in Italy, in all of Europe. And now they are all dead—*il Vescovo*, his secretary, the partisans—and my father, who is also in the graveyard out there. So you will not interview any of them for your documentary, I am afraid.'

Hannah glanced towards the window. It was dark now, but she could still see the snowflakes flapping at the glass like a great army of moths fatally drawn to the light and the warmth.

'I think perhaps we should make a move,' she said, 'before we get snowed in.'

'Oh, you will not go anywhere tonight,' said the Count. 'Believe me, it is quite impossible. No, you are my guests for as long as the snow falls, and maybe longer if they do not clear the road in the morning.'

Despite their protests, he insisted it was no trouble and that he would welcome the company. With the help of the manservant, whose real name, it appeared, was Karl-Luca, they brought their luggage from the car and were shown to their rooms. Hannah had stayed in worse places, but few quite so cold. There was an ancient radiator, but she had to sit on top of it to feel any heat. She checked her phone but there was no signal, which was no surprise and actually gave her some small comfort. Hopefully the snow had cut them off from the internet too, and even television, but she could hardly count on it, and if their host was watching the right channel and learned of the murder of Irma Ulbrecht, he might not be quite so welcoming.

They had been invited to join him for dinner, so she changed into the one dress she had brought with her—which was fortunately made of wool. That and a shawl, thick black tights, and a pair of boots, and she was at least ready for the cold, if not what else might happen if their host had picked up the news from Berlin.

She had been given directions to *der Saal*, where they were to have drinks before dinner. This was the largest and most comfortable room she had seen thus far, with an open fireplace and a log fire, Oriental rugs on the stone floor, and a great many paintings and tapestries on the walls. There was no sign of the Count or Karl-Luca, so after warming herself at the fire she inspected the paintings and the family photographs on the sideboard. There was one that looked like it might be a photo of their host as a young man, on skis and wearing the white camouflage suit of the *Alpini*, the elite Italian mountain troops, a rifle slung over his shoulder. And another of him in civilian clothes with a woman and a boy of about six or seven. His wife and son? If so, where were they now?

'Ah, you are here before me.'

He had changed into a dark green jacket with a leather collar, trousers tucked into thick Alpine socks, quite the Austrian nobleman, in fact, with the hound—which answered to the name of Bruno—at his heels. His manner indicated that if he had any news of the outside world it had not included a reference to murders and bombings in Berlin. May I call you Hannah, he asked politely, adding that she should call him Hugo. This only made her feel worse, of course. She had always hated deceit, even if it did not always stop her from practising it.

He was fixing drinks for them when Aiden entered the room, looking more like when she first met him, in a jacket and tie. But he appeared unusually tense. The *Schloss* would appear far more of a trap to him than a refuge. But the snow that kept them here would surely keep others away. She focused on directing the conversation away from the documentary they were supposed to be making, partly to stop Aiden saying the wrong thing, but mostly because she felt uncomfortable telling even more lies to someone who had made them so welcome. Even so, she felt a total fraud chatting to him about the castle and its history, and when Aiden asked about the number of staff it took to keep the place going she felt he had an ulterior motive, and that he wanted to know how many people he might have to kill if they became a threat to him. Not many, it appeared. There were only two permanent servants, Hugo told them—Karl-Luca and his wife Francesca, who did most of the cooking—and they had a couple of women from the village who came in once a week to help clean the few rooms that were still habitable.

'To tell you the truth, I do not know what to do with the place,' he said. 'It was bought by my great-grandfather when the Sudtirol was still a part of Austria. The story is that he came here on holiday with his young wife and they saw it and fell in love with it—the romantic Gothic—so of course, he buys it. It is a dream for him, a plaything. But he has money, he can afford it. Then comes the war—the Kaiser's War—and after there is no money, only the *Schloss*. My father made a living from the farm and the vineyard—he had a plan even to hire the place out for fashion photography, or a film location, but it did not happen. But me, I have no talent for these things. First I was in the *Alpini*, then I became an anthropologist. That is my profession now.'

'So why do you stay here?' Hannah asked him.

That hopeless smile. 'I do not think I can explain this, even to myself. Perhaps because my family is here. Even if they are in the graveyard.'

He was silent for a moment, and when he spoke again it seemed like a change of subject. 'It is good you make this documentary. People say there are too many stories about the war, it was all so long ago, but it is good to remind people what they were like, these *Fascisti*, now we have them back again. Mussolini has become respectable in Italy, his heirs sit in the *Parliamento Italiano*—and in the parliament at Strasbourg. All these—*scorpioni*—that crawl out from behind the stone. And me, I hide in my castle, and wait for the SS to come back.'

He was interrupted by the appearance of Karl-Luca to announce that dinner was served, and Hugo led the way into the dining room. Another impressive relic of the castle's golden age, with an open fire and a long table that looked as if it might be made of oak and was big enough to seat about thirty people, with enough candlesticks and gleaming cutlery to suggest their host hadn't quite reached the end of the family resources.

The food, however, was something of a jolt. A vegetable and bean soup that was more wholesome than appetising, followed by meat and two veg. Clearly more Austrian than Italian. The meat was wild boar, Hannah thought, and the wine a robust, earthy red, which Hugo told them came from the castle vineyard. It was he who did most of the talking—he had a great store of anecdotes, mostly about Merano and the surrounding area, which were entertaining enough to see them through the first two courses. Then, while they were waiting for whatever came next, he said: 'I have been thinking—why is it that Bechmann comes here to Merano, in these last days of the war, all the way from Berlin?'

They waited for him to tell them. They had come a long way to see a grave.

'I know he was born near here, but to come back then—in the spring of 1945 when the Allies were victorious, and the partisans out for revenge. It makes no sense. Did he think they would leave him in peace after what he did during the war?'

Aiden exchanged a quick glance with Hannah. Then he told Hugo the story about the Vatican papers, as Irma had told it to him, and her theory that Hanna Reitsch had flown Bechmann out of Berlin with them, to make a deal with the Pope.

'She was arrested not far from here,' he said. 'Just over the border into Austria.'

Hannah had not known that. Irma must have told him. She wondered if there was anything else he had learned from Irma and neglected to tell her until now.

'But why would she bring Bechmann here?' she said. 'It is a long way from Rome.'

'Probably as close as they could get,' offered Aiden. 'By plane, anyway, and she probably ran out of fuel.'

'Unless it was to see *il Vescovo*,' said Hugo thoughtfully. 'The man who has clout.'

They looked at him.

'He was a big man in these parts. Still is, among Catholics. My father spoke much about him. Marcus Senner. He was a local man. Born in a village near Bolzano. He was bishop in Merano for most of the war. Afterwards he was made a cardinal and went to Rome.'

'Senner?' Hannah repeated the name, wondering why it rang a bell. 'You have heard of him?'

'Yes. I think so. But I don't know why.'

'Something Michael said?' Aiden offered hopefully, but she shook her head. But if it wasn't Michael, where else could she have got it from? A moment later she excused herself and said she needed something from her room.

It did not take her long to find it. It was in the notes her great-grandfather had made that David Gradowski had printed out for her. Josef's friend Marcus, the Jesuit priest from Kreuzberg. Father Marcus Senner, who had been special adviser to Cardinal Pacelli when he was sent to Berlin to make a deal with the Nazis.

'I think I heard something of this from my father,' Hugo said, when Hannah returned to the dining room with this new information. 'Yes, it was a big black mark against him, that he helped to make this deal with the Nazis. But it did good for him in the Vatican. He and Pacelli stayed close, even when Pacelli became Pope, and they probably would have known that in Berlin. But I am wondering now, why his secretary was here with the *partigiani*.'

'You think he might have sent word to them?' Aiden suggested.

'Maybe. It would have solved a big problem for him. But let us see what else we can find out about *il Vescovo*.'

The wifi was down, as they had hoped, but Hugo had kept most of his father's records from the war and attached to them was an obituary from the local newspaper.

Marcus Senner had been born to a German Roman Catholic family in the South Tyrol in 1898 when it was part of the Austrian Empire. His father was a schoolmaster and Marcus was educated at a Church school in Klausen and then a Catholic seminary in Salzburg. Shortly after becoming a priest he had been sent to Berlin, possibly because German was his native tongue, and took up a curacy in the working class district of Kreuzberg, which was then a stronghold of the Communist Party. It was 1929—the year of the Wall Street crash and the beginning of the Great Depression. By 1932 over six million Germans were out of work and Berlin had become a battleground between the Communists and the Fascists. Senner made a name for himself as a skilful negotiator, cutting deals with the local party bosses to protect Church property and interests, and it was this that first brought him to the attention of the papal nuncio—Archbishop Eugenio Pacelli—who had been sent to Berlin to make a deal with the new German chancellor, Adolf Hitler.

When Pacelli became Pope, Senner was made Bishop of Merano, but he spent a lot of time in Rome. In 1970 he became Vatican Foreign Minister and he was made a cardinal. He died in 1985.

'So he would have been in a good position to take these documents to the Pope?' Aiden proposed when Hannah translated this for him.

'Possibly—if they existed,' Hugo agreed. 'For sure he would know of their value—or their danger, so far as the Church was concerned.'

'You say, if they existed?'

'Only because it is strange that they were not found. The partisans were Communists. They would not have seen any reason to keep them secret. On the contrary. Not if they could be used against the Church.'

'Unless Senner got hold of them first,' Aiden persisted. 'You said his secretary was here when the SS were killed.'

'This is true,' Hugo agreed. 'Perhaps they are still here, hidden in the *Schloss*. With all the other treasures we have never found.' But he obviously thought not.

'I don't suppose any of these people are still alive?' Aiden asked him.

'No one that I know. If they are, they would be very old.'

'Would there be any records?' Hannah wondered aloud. 'The bishop's secretary must have reported back about what happened that night. Senner might have sent a despatch to Rome. Could there be anything in the Bishop's Palace in Merano?'

But Hugo was already shaking his head: 'There is no longer a Bishop's Palace in Merano, or a bishop. Not for many years. In fact, I think Marcus Senner might have been the last. Now we are in the diocese of Bolzano. But—maybe there is someone I can ask.' He checked the time. 'It is a little late, but if you will excuse me I will try. I will have to use the landline in this weather.'

They could hear the wind in the chimney and Bruno moaning in harmony in his sleep.

'How did you know about Senner?' Aiden wanted to know. 'If it wasn't Michael—or Irma?'

'It was just something I read,' she told him. 'And his name cropped up.'

He gave her a searching look but she was reluctant to tell him about her visit to the Holocaust Museum and what she had learned of her own family history, if only because it had been a diversion from the job she had been paid to do.

'So—that was very interesting.' Hugo came back looking pleased with himself. 'I have spoken to Monsignore Abruzzo, the chief man of the Church here in Merano. He knows of one person who was here the night the SS men were killed. A boy, a little older than my father. He was a messenger—what do you say?—a courier between the bishop's people and the *partigiani*. A boy is less suspicious maybe. His name was Johann Winkler, and later he became a priest. A Jesuit. Later he was on the staff of Cardinal Senner in Rome, so they were close I think.'

'And he is still alive?'

'Yes. Retired of course, but he lives in the South—in Sicily. The Monsignore says he will look for an address and let me know. You think to speak with him for your documentary?'

'If he will speak with us,' Aiden said. 'I guess it depends how much he cares to say. Or remembers. How old is he?'

'Well, he was fourteen then, so he must be in his late eighties? But they say the long-term memory improves with age. You may be lucky. Also the Monsignore says there *are* records for the time that Senner was bishop here. The bad news is that they are in the Secret Archives of the Pope. In the Vatican.'

'The secret archives?' Aiden flicked a glance at Hannah. Another dead end. 'Why are they secret?'

'It is from the Latin *secretum*, which means, I think, private. The private papers of the Popes—that go back to the eighth century at least.'

'But why would the records of Merano be in the Pope's private papers?' Hannah pressed him.

'Because they include many letters that *il Vescovo* writes to Pope Pius during the war.'

'And how secret are they? I mean, is there any access to them?'

'I think if you have the right credentials—for the academic research. I do not know if the television is good for this. But you cannot do it online. If you want to see them, you will have to go to Rome.'

CHAPTER TWENTY-THREE

Rome

HANNAH WOKE TO THE SOUND OF CHURCH BELLS. FOR A MOMENT SHE had no clear idea of where she was. Then she heard raised voices outside her window, and the more discordant noise of motor horns. Rome, in a small hotel in Trastevere, and . . .

The rest came in a rush and it was all bad.

She reached for her phone to check if there was anything on the German news. There was. The body of a woman had been found in the Landscanal, not far from where Rosa Luxemburg had been disposed of in 1919 after her murder by the right-wing thugs of the Freikorps. It had been identified as that of Doctor Irma Ulbrecht, a deputy curator at the Schutzstaffel Museum, and according to the Berlin police she had been strangled. Her Porsche sports car had been found abandoned not far from the Zoogarten and it was believed that the houseboat on the River Spree which had been destroyed by an explosion was registered in her name. The media made much of her work for the Schutzstaffel Museum and her known opposition to the neo-Nazis—her friends and colleagues claimed that she had been extensively and viciously trolled on social media. The police were appealing for witnesses but there was no mention of an American woman or a British ex-Marine. Yet.

Hannah was interrupted by a beeping noise in the square outside her window—and the hint of a flashing light. She crossed to the window, braced for police cars, SWAT teams, or their Italian equivalent, but it was only a little street-cleaning vehicle, chugging its way across the square. There were no more raised voices and it was as tranquil a scene as she could have wished. The early morning sun gilded the terracotta rooftops, spring flowers bloomed in the window boxes, and the ramparts of a medieval tower rose impressively in the background.

Rome. She had thought about it so much in the past, and now she was here—and a fugitive, like Gabriele. In her mind's eye she could see her crossing the square below, the little blonde girl in the clothes she wore for school, with her schoolbag full of books and her mind full of—what? Worries about her friends and family back in Berlin, or the dark shadows that were reaching out for her here in Rome? Or just the homework she had not done?

It was still there, the school. By the Porto Ottavia, just across the Garibaldi Bridge, a short walk from the hotel where they were staying. She could be there in a few minutes. If she did not have more immediate concerns.

And right on cue came the sound of her phone.

Aiden. 'I hope I didn't wake you.' She couldn't tell if he was being sarcastic or not, but she suspected he was.

'No,' she said. 'I was just getting up.'

'I'm in the breakfast room,' he said. 'I'll order coffee.'

The breakfast room was in the basement and he was at a table in the corner, studying his iPad.

'The Vatican Library is just inside the Porto Sant'Anna,' he said. 'The Archives aren't marked but apparently they're right next to it.' He looked up at her and frowned slightly. 'You okay?'

'Great,' she said. She meant it to sting but it would take more than that.

'Good. Got your passport—and your student pass?'

'Do you mind if I have something to eat first?'

'Sure. No hurry. It opens at 8:15.'

Twenty minutes. She poured herself a coffee.

They took a cab to the Vatican. The capital of the Holy Roman Church, the State within a State. Not that you'd know. Hannah had read that it was barely half a mile from one end to the other, but she thought there might have been some kind of a frontier, even if it was only a welcome sign in a few different languages and a Swiss Guard in medieval armour carrying a pike. Something to distinguish it from the rest of the city. But there was nothing. Perhaps they thought that when you saw St Peter's Basilica you would know. Certainly it was big enough, if not quite as impressive as Hannah had anticipated from what she had seen of it on the television news with the square filled with thousands of the faithful and the Pope up on his balcony giving the blessing. At this time of morning it was almost empty.

They cut through a broad colonnade into the street beyond. The Vatican on one side of the road, Italy on the other. Halfway down was the Porto Sant'Anna, gateway to the papal offices and the Secret Archives.

Aiden hung back. 'I'll wait for you here,' he said.

She was surprised. 'You're not coming in?'

'Best not,' he said. 'There's no point in going in mob-handed. I'll just hang round here for a while, in case you come straight out. If they let you in, I'll meet you back at the hotel.'

She had to suppress an angry retort. If he wasn't going to come in with her, why bother to escort her from the hotel? Did he think she couldn't be trusted, that she'd do a runner as soon as she was out of his sight, or go to the police?

The gate was guarded by several soldiers—not in the traditional dress of the Swiss Guard but in smart khaki uniforms with black berets set at a jaunty angle. Hannah showed her passport and said she had an appointment in the Archives. She was braced for arrest, convinced that Hugo would have alerted the Vatican authorities after hearing the news from Berlin, but after a brief inspection they returned her passport and directed her to the second building on the right.

No guards here. Only a small nun, made even smaller by the massive reception desk. She scanned the screen in front of her. 'When did you make this appointment?'

'I emailed Doctor Lecci from Merano,' Hannah told her truthfully. Doctor Lecci was the Admissions Secretary. 'I was told to bring a note from my tutor at Columbia University in New York.'

She had it up on her phone. The outcome of protracted negotiation with Emily. The nun told her to take a seat.

Hannah sat on a bench seat beside a long, low table laid out with copies of *L'Osservatore Romano*, the Vatican daily newspaper, in several different languages. She picked up the English language edition, wondering if it might carry news of the murder in Berlin. It didn't but as she turned the pages a different story caught her eye—or rather the words 'Jesuit' and 'Sicily,' which made her think of the old priest Hugo had told them about. It referred to a 'terrorist attack' on a Jesuit study centre a month or so back. Six people had been killed or wounded in the attack, including five students *and a retired priest*.

She did not allow herself to get carried away. The number of retired priests in Sicily was probably quite large. None of the victims was named and she was about to google the story on her phone when her attention was caught by the photograph at the top of the page. It showed a man called Cardinal Seeburg, who was described as the Head of the Holy Office, visiting the scene of the attack with officials. But it was the man next to the cardinal who caught Hannah's attention. He was wearing a suit and tie but he looked remarkably like the cyclist she had met in Berlin, the man who had called himself Emil Brandt.

'Signorina?' Hannah went back to reception. 'I regret that Doctor Lecci is not here at present,' said the nun. 'Can you return at half past four this afternoon?'

'Are you sure?' Aiden was peering doubtfully at the picture in *L'Osservatore Romano*.

'No,' Hannah admitted. 'Not hundred percent. But I enlarged it on my phone and it looks a lot like him.' She kept her voice low. They were in a sidewalk café in the Borgo Angelico, just outside the walls of the Vatican.

'But what would he be doing in Sicily?'

Hannah told him to read the story that went with it.

'A retired priest?' He looked at her sharply.

'That's what I thought,' she said, 'but it wasn't Johann Winkler. I looked up the story on Google and they listed all the names. The priest who was killed was called Father Norbert. Father Erich Norbert. An Austrian.'

'What about the others?'

'All young, working in the fields.'

'Any suspects?'

'If there are, they're not making it public.'

Aiden stood up and fished his phone out of his pocket. But then he walked a little way down the street so she couldn't hear the conversation. She watched him with annoyance. Whoever he was talking to, it went on for some time.

'What was all that about?' she said when he rejoined her at the table.

'Old friend of mine,' he said. 'Works here in Rome—in the security services. I'm meeting him for lunch.' He picked up the newspaper. 'Can I show him this?'

'Help yourself,' she said coldly. 'I'll grab a sandwich.'

When he had gone she sat there, thinking things over. It didn't get her very far. Once again, she considered catching the next flight back to New York. Taking a cab to her apartment in Brooklyn, climbing into bed, and pulling the duvet over her head. Or she could go to the police here in Rome, or even to the US Embassy. That was probably the best thing. But how could she explain why she had not called the police in Berlin, as soon as she saw the body of Irma Ulbrecht?

She picked up the tab and wandered through the streets, going nowhere in particular. Eventually she found herself walking along the river until she came to a sign that directed her to the old Jewish Ghetto.

The school was still there. And still open by the look of it. With no great hopes, she presented herself at reception. The young woman at the desk listened to her request warily, frowning over Hannah's stumbling Italian. Halfway through Hannah almost gave up but then the woman said in English: 'You must speak to Signora Belmonte. She is *l'archivista*.'

'You have an archivist—at the school?'

'No—not here at the school. Signora Belmonte, she is the guide at *il Tempio Maggiore*. But she was a teacher—long time at the school—and she keep the archive. She may be able to help you.'

She wrote out the name and address on a sheet of the school notepaper.

Il Tempio Maggiore was not hard to find. It was the biggest building in the neighbourhood. Not only a synagogue, the sign told her, but a museum, a Jewish cultural and community centre, and the office of the Chief Rabbi of Rome. When Hannah asked for Signora Belmonte, the people on the desk said that she had just started another tour—but Hannah was welcome to join it if she wished.

She caught up with the group as they were being herded into the synagogue. The woman doing the herding was small and elderly with an air of brisk authority. She was heavily made up with bright red lipstick, a pair of carefully sculpted eyebrows that arched above the frames of her spectacles to suggest a look of permanently startled indignation, and a shock of Titian hair, clearly dyed—it would look quite extraordinary, Hannah thought, if permitted to escape from the head-scarf she had wrapped around it. The Bohemian effect was enhanced by several more scarves wrapped about her person and trailing in her wake, a long, brightly patterned skirt and brown leather boots with surprisingly high heels for a woman who must be in her seventies at least. There was nothing frivolous about her manner, however. She accepted Hannah's murmured apology for being late with a curt nod and a steely glare that made her feel there would be words spoken later, when she was made to stay behind, after class.

There were thirty or forty people in the group and the Signora addressed them in an excellent but somewhat toneless English, relating the history of the building and the Jewish ghetto in which it stood. This was interesting enough, but it only really came to life for Hannah when she gave an account of what had happened during the German occupation in 1943 when the SS began to round up the Jewish citizens of Rome for transportation to the death camps in Poland.

'There has been a Jewish community in Rome since, well, the time of the Romans,' she began. 'Jewish dignitaries were recorded at the mourning for Julius Caesar, and the community survived a number of pogroms and restrictions during the Christian era. When the Nazis arrived in September 1943, there were an estimated ten thousand Jews in the city and it was recognised as the oldest Jewish community in Europe. Within a month of the Nazi occupation they were rounded up for despatch to the death camps of Poland. A thousand were sent in cattle trucks from the main railway depot in Rome—the scenes will be familiar to you from a great many films and documentaries—but then something very unusual happened, one that did not happen in any other city in occupied Europe except, they say, in Copenhagen. There were protests from the citizens of Rome. Even in the streets they came out to abuse the SS. Many of the Jews were hidden in non-Jewish houses, even in the Vatican which was neutral territory. For some reason that we still do not know, the operation was suspended and the soldiers returned to their barracks.'

This was all new to Hannah, but there was a great deal more she wished to know, and when the tour ended, she approached the Signora and outlined her own particular request. The initial reaction was not encouraging and even bordered on the hostile, but then, surprisingly, she suggested Hannah join her for a coffee in her office.

'Is your grandmother still alive?' she asked as they walked through the dimly lit interior of the temple.

Hannah explained that she had died in the 1950s and gave her maiden name—Gabriele Fabel—in the outside hope that the Signora might recognise it.

'Ah yes. Gabriele. School prefect. Outstanding pupil. And a fine athlete. Very good at the long jump.'

'You *knew* her?'

A sideways glance down her nose and across her shoulder that must have quailed generations of pupils and that age made no less withering. 'I hope I do not look *quite* as old as that, my dear. I was not born until 1945 and I did not begin teaching at the school until the 1970s.'

Hannah stammered an apology as they walked on.

'People think I know everything,' the Signora complained. 'However, I expect there is something in the files. I will look her up in a moment, when I have sat down—and had my coffee.'

Hannah took this as another rebuke.

'I thought the files had been lost,' she ventured, 'or destroyed.'

'So they were. But I have made new ones. I interviewed everyone who is still alive and living within travelling distance. Teachers, pupils, even the caretakers. Others write to me and tell me of their experiences.'

They entered her office. It was small and dingy, and made even smaller by the large grey metal filing cabinets that filled every inch of wall space apart from a small window which offered a glimpse of the river. In front of the window was a desk, covered in books and papers, and there was a single hard chair for the convenience of visitors, and upon which Hannah was invited to sit by a cursory wave of the hand. Hannah looked in vain for a single frivolous touch or sign of individuality. Signora Belmonte's individuality was in her appearance, not her office. She sat behind the desk and opened a drawer from which she took a flask and two small but elegant mugs. The coffee she poured was as thick and black as treacle. There was no offer of milk and it probably would not have improved things much.

'So—your grandmother was here during the war years?' She gazed at Hannah reflectively. 'She would have been here in 1943 then, when the SS came.'

Hannah had just taken a sip of the coffee and was for a moment rendered speechless. She wondered where to put it. No surface had been provided for the mug, and it would not have been tactful to tip the contents out of the window. The Signora was looking at her like she was the dumbest kid in the slow-readers group. 'You do know the story of when the SS came?'

'Only what you told us during the tour.'

'I see. Yes, well, I cannot give all the details in the space of a sixty-minute tour. It is hard enough to keep people's attention as it is. However, as there are now just the two of us and there is only the window to distract you, I will tell you the whole story . . .'

She took a sip of the coffee and apparently found it as satisfactory as usual.

'The SS came to the ghetto at about nine in the morning. It was Shabbat of the holiday of Sukkot . . .'

CHAPTER TWENTY-FOUR

The Round-Up

Rome, October 16, 1943

She was barely awake when they came, enjoying the luxury of an extra half hour in bed, for it was Shabbat and there was no school that day. Her aunt's apartment was right next to the Octavia Gate, so they were probably among the first to hear them.

She ran to the window and saw the trucks pulling up on the cobbled piazza beside the Portico d'Ottavia, and the soldiers leaping down and spreading out into the surrounding streets. There were dogs with them, too, and men with whistles, and everyone seemed to be shouting. She heard her aunt screaming for the children to stay away from the windows and then her uncle's voice telling them to keep calm, and to put on all the clothes they could wear.

Then a loudspeaker van came into the square and a harsh voice in Italian told them to pack one suitcase per person and assemble in the street, outside their homes, and that if they did this, they would come to no harm.

It was not unexpected. People had been talking of this moment since the German occupation over a month ago. But some said they had enough on their hands, with the Allies at Salerno. Why would they take troops from the front line to round up a few thousand Jews in Rome? It was said that the Pope had obtained an assurance from the German High Command that none of Rome's Jews would be deported, but few in the ghetto believed it, and even fewer relied upon it. Then Kappler, the German commandant in the city, had demanded fifty kilos of gold from the Jewish community to save two hundred male adults from deportation and this had fostered a grim, but in its way hopeful, expectation that the Germans were only interested in money. But the ransom had been paid and still they came.

Gabriele was thinking about places to hide, but she had thought about that before, and there was nowhere. There were only three rooms in the apartment. No attic, no basement, not even a large cupboard. If it had been a school day she might have stood a chance. There were plenty of places to hide at the school. She wondered if there was a chance of getting there. It was only a block away. She chanced another look through the window. The soldiers were going into the houses and dragging people out into the street. Then, on the opposite side of the square, she saw a man on the roof. The soldiers saw him, too, and raised their rifles. He began to run along the ridge of one of the roofs, like a tightrope walker, and the soldiers started firing at him. Bits of tile were flying up at his feet, but he kept on running. But then he lost his footing and rolled down the steeply sloping roof. Gabriele saw him make one despairing grab at the gutter, and then he fell to the street below. It was four stories. Gabriele turned away.

When they were dressed her uncle assembled them in the kitchen, Gabriele and her aunt and her four cousins. They were all wearing at least two layers of clothing and they looked like fat little dwarves. Her aunt was emptying the shelves and the cupboards of food. There was not much, but what there was she packed into their pockets and bags. Gabriele's cousin Sarah was crying and Gabriele put her arm around her and tried to comfort her, but she had to fight back her own tears. Sarah was the youngest of them, she was only eight, and it was the fate of the children that upset Gabriele the most.

'Remember, at all costs, we must stay together,' said her uncle. His voice was still calm, but she saw the fear in his eyes. There is nothing we can do, Gabriele thought, absolutely nothing we can do. It was the helplessness that got her. If only they could fight.

Then they heard the hammering at the door.

They were herded out into the street at gunpoint. There were hundreds of people out there now, standing around with their pathetic little suitcases, so many old people, so many children, a lot of people crying.

There was so much noise, the barking dogs and the men with whistles, and so much shouting. Did they have to shout so much? No one was shouting back, there was no resistance at all. Gabriele had always hated shouting, or any loud noise. It bothered her more than almost anything else. If anyone started shouting at school she would clamp her hands over her ears, even if it was a teacher.

The trucks stood there with their engines idling and the soldiers began to load people into them. When they had crammed in as many as they could, they lumbered off towards the Octavia Gate. But what then? No one knew where they took people when they were deported, for the simple reason that no one ever came back, and there were no letters. There were only rumours. Vast concentration camps had been set up in the lands the Germans had occupied in the East, it was said, in Poland and Silesia and even Russia. It was said that the German plan was to move every Jew in Europe out to the newly conquered territories in the East. But the Germans had stopped conquering territories in the East, or anywhere else.

The loudspeaker van came back and Gabriele tried to catch what they were saying. Something about a holding station in a college in Trastevere, and then they would be moved out of Rome for their own safety. A squad of soldiers approached and ordered them into one of the trucks. Gabriele still had her arm around Sarah. She thought it was as much to comfort herself as the little girl. If she had someone to look after, she would not give in to her own fear. She was very, very frightened, but she felt angry, too. Not just that the Germans were doing this to them but that they were making such a noise about it. There was no need for all this shouting and whistling and the barking dogs. It wasn't helping at all. If they would just make one simple announcement, people would do what they were told. It did not need all of this.

But then she heard a different kind of shouting. It was coming from the direction of the Octavia Gate and she saw that a crowd had gathered. For a moment she thought they were Fascisti, *cheering the soldiers on, but they were not cheering, they were shouting insults in German and Italian, calling them cowards and bullies. The soldiers turned their guns on them, but for some reason they did not fire, perhaps because there were nuns and priests among the crowd, and even children, but when had that ever stopped them?*

There was a cordon across the entrance to the ghetto, but it was composed of a few Fascist police in their black uniforms and the crowd began to push past them and advance into the square. The German soldiers stopped herding people into the trucks and formed a line, levelling their guns. Gabriele let go of Sarah and began to walk towards them. It was as if she were sleep-walking. The soldiers did not see her coming and she walked between two of them, politely saying 'Excuse me' in German. Then she held her hands up to the crowd and addressed them in Italian.

'Thank you for coming,' she said. 'But please do not come any closer.'

Then she turned to face the troops and spoke to them in German.

'There is no need to shoot anyone,' she said. 'People will get into the trucks, if only you will stop shouting at them.'

A part of her knew that she was crazy to be doing this. She didn't even know why she was doing it, except that she wanted to stop the noise, and it was no good putting her hands over her ears.

And then something extraordinary happened. One of the soldiers came walking towards her. He wore a forage cap, not a helmet, and he had a pistol in his hand, so she knew he was an officer. She thought he was going to shoot her, but he stopped in front of her, and spoke to her instead. He seemed to be amused.

'Where did you learn to speak such good German?' he said.

'In Germany,' she said. 'I am German.'

'So what are you doing with this filthy rabble?' he said.

'They are my people, too,' she said.

He shook his head, either in sadness or bemusement.

Then he walked back to the line of soldiers, and they climbed back into the trucks and drove away, leaving the rest of the people, who had not already been driven off in the trucks, standing outside their homes in the square, weeping and hugging each other.

Her uncle looked at her in astonishment. 'What did you say to them?' he said.

'I just told them I was German,' she said.

She wondered if it had helped that she looked so German, or at least so like the image of a young German woman they had been taught to revere.

She learned later that there had been protests and resistance all over the city, that ordinary Roman citizens had come out onto the streets to make their views known, and that they had taken many of the Jewish citizens into their homes and hidden them there until the Germans had gone. Some said that there had been intervention at a 'very high level,' whatever that meant. So, it was not all down to her. But later she wished that instead of saying what she had to the German officer, that she was German, and that these were her people, too, she had simply said, 'I am a Jew.'

Chapter Twenty-Five

The Accident

'And then what happened?' said Hannah.

'To Gabriele?' said the Signora.

'To all of them, but to Gabriele, yes.'

'Well, I can tell you about the ones that were taken away. They were first taken to the military college in Trastevere and then two days later to Tiburtina Station, where they were loaded onto trains and deported to Auschwitz. One thousand and thirty-five people were taken. All but sixteen were exterminated.'

'And the others—the ones who stayed in Rome?'

'All we know is that many were hidden in people's homes, even in the churches and the convents. This was the action of individual priests and nuns. It was not official Church policy. Gabriele was one of those who were given sanctuary in the Vatican. So far as we know, she stayed there until the liberation in June 1944.'

'And what would have happened to her then? Or is that not something you would know?'

Signora Belmonte sighed as if this was the great burden she carried through life, this heavy weight of history. She placed her coffee mug on the desk with careful deliberation and crossed to the row of filing cabinets.

'F for Fabel,' she mused. 'What happens to her when the Allies came? I cannot have written it down or I would remember. I always remember what I write down.' She slid open a drawer, fumbling for the pair of spectacles hanging from a chain at her neck and which had become entangled with one of the scarves. She was a woman of many scarves and chains and strings of beads.

'Ah, here we are. Fabel, Gabriele.'

She removed a thin brown folder from the cabinet and brought it back to the desk. 'People say I should put it all on computer. When do I have the time for this? You should pay someone to do it, they say. How am I to pay someone with the pension of a schoolteacher? I say to the Chief Rabbi, why do you not pay for it if you care so much? And while you are about it, are you going to pay me for saving for you your precious heritage? He laughs at me. Oh, Signora Belmonte, she is so amusing. Ah yes, here we are.' She held up a small bundle of letters, written on thin blue paper and tied with yellow ribbon. 'The memoirs of Lisa Geisler. One of my most voluble—no, that is for talking, what is the word?— *prolific* correspondents.'

The name was vaguely familiar to Hannah. It took only a moment for her to remember. She was one of the three girls in the photograph David Gradowski had printed out for her. A schoolfriend of Gabriele's in Berlin. They must have come to Rome together, or at least around the same time and for the same reason.

'Is she still alive—Lisa Geisler?'

'Sadly not. If she was, she would have been, what—ninety-two? But she died a few years ago. If she was still alive I would not have room for all the letters she writes, we would need the whole Temple to make a store for them.'

She adjusted the spectacles on her nose and scanned the first sheet of paper. 'Yes. Here it is. After the war, Gabriele was interviewed by an officer of the British Army.' She looked up over her spectacles at Hannah, her expression fierce. 'Because she is a German, you understand, *an enemy alien*. This is all they know, these people, even after all that happened. She is a Jew. The Nazis murder the Jews. But now they would put her in a camp for being German.' Back to the letter. She read in silence for a moment. 'I see. This is good. This time is different. The officer falls in love with her.' She searched Hannah's face again. 'But you know this, yes. Your mother, she has told you about it.'

There might have been a touch of sarcasm in her tone. Certainly there should have been. All that Hannah knew was that her grandmother had been in Rome as a schoolgirl and that her grandfather had been in the British Army. Nothing of how they had met. But she nodded as if all this was familiar to her. 'Peter Ryder,' she said. 'He was a captain, I think.'

'Ryder?' The Signora frowned again and scrutinised the letter. 'No. His name is Rosen. A good Jewish name. Captain Peter Rosen. How is it you do not know this?' She looked at Hannah as if she must be an imposter.

'I always thought it was Ryder,' said Hannah lamely. 'It is the name my mother uses. I mean her married name is Harper, like mine, but she uses Ryder as a pen name. Ruth Ryder.' This all sounded very confusing, even to Hannah. Signora Belmonte obviously felt so, too. She was looking at Hannah as if she should get a grip. 'She's a writer,' Hannah explained. 'I always thought Ryder was her parents' name.'

'So she does not wish to use her Jewish name?'

Hannah looked contrite. On her mother's behalf, not that her mother had ever looked contrite in her life. Not while Hannah had been there to see it.

The Signora returned her attention to the file.

'He serves in North Africa, then Italy, where he is transferred to the Jewish Brigade.' She read for a moment in silence. 'I see. This is a special force of the British Army composed of Jews from Palestine, which was then ruled by the British.' She exposed Hannah to that fierce stare again. 'So was your grandfather from Palestine?'

'I don't think so,' said Hannah. 'I think he was from London.'

'Well, he seems to have stayed on in Italy when the war ended. Lisa writes that he was with the Allied Commission in Rome, investigating war crimes committed by the Fascist regime. That must have been a lot of work for him.' She turned the letter over. 'But in 1950 they move to London and are married. I wonder why it is they wait so long?'

Again, Hannah could not say, but Lisa Geisler knew.

'Ah—he was married before!' exclaimed the Signora after consulting the letter. 'To an Englishwoman. He has to wait for the divorce. But here is a picture of them after their wedding—Peter and Gabriele Rosen.'

She passed it across the desk to Hannah and there she was—Gabriele as a young woman, wearing a two-piece suit, heels, a hat—a face that reminded Hannah a little of her mother when she was younger, but only a little. It was not a great picture, monochrome, a little overexposed. And next to her, with his arm around her shoulder, was the man who had been Hannah's grandfather. He, too, wore a suit but no hat. Tall, dark, and handsome. A thin moustache. He looked like a 1940s film star, even in a poor print. They both could have been film stars. In the background was a fountain flanked by stone lions. There were lots of pigeons.

'Where did this come from?' Hannah asked her.

'Lisa Geisler, of course.' She turned it over. 'Yes. Trafalgar Square in London. 1950. Gabriele must have sent it to her.'

'Could I take a copy?' Signora Belmonte looked doubtful. 'A picture on my phone?' A picture on her phone was permissible. While she was taking it the Signora returned to her letters.

'In June 1956, they came to Rome with their little daughter, Ruth. That would be your mother, yes?'

Hannah was thinking about the date. It was the year of the accident. The Signora was still reading.

'They stayed with friends in Via Cassia, where many expatriates and diplomats live. An English family. They left the little girl with them while they went by car on a visit to the battlefields south of Rome where Captain Rosen had fought during the war.' Her expression changed. 'Oh. Oh, *che orrible!*' She looked at Hannah. 'But you know of this? On the road to Monte Cassino?'

Hannah did not know of this.

'They were on their way to the site of the battle. Monte Cassino. Where Captain Rosen had fought during the war.' She looked down at the letter. 'It seems they just went off the road. At a bend. The police say it is an accident. He was distracted, or maybe fell asleep.'

So. Not Hertford, Hereford, or Hampshire.

They sat in silence for a moment, the old papers spread across the Signora's desk.

'Lisa Geisler says it is the past that reaches out for people. The past we forget, but that never forgives.'

It was just after two o'clock when Hannah emerged from the Temple. She checked her phone to see if there was a message from Aiden. Nothing. She found a quiet café near the Octavia Gate and checked out the new name on Google.

Rosen, Peter and Gabriele.

And there they were, at last, if not as Hannah would have wished them. Their deaths had been reported in several English newspapers and there were obituaries of her grandfather in the *London Times* and the *Daily Telegraph*. The reports of the accident did not tell her much more than Signora Belmonte had, except that the car was a 1952 Alfa Romeo and that it had left the road at a bend and plunged into a ravine, bursting into flames. The couple's two-year-old daughter had been left with friends in Naples.

The obituaries were more informative—about Peter Rosen at least. There were references to his early life in London, taking part in anti-Fascist demonstrations in the East End, and then, when Britain and Germany went to war, joining the British Army as a private and making his way up through the ranks to lieutenant. In 1944 he had transferred to the Jewish Brigade with the rank of captain, serving as an intelligence officer in North Africa and Italy.

The ringtone of her phone recalled her to the present. It was a text from her father, asking if she was still alive. She said she was in Rome and that all was well. *E tutte bene*.

There was still nothing from Aiden.

Chapter Twenty-Six

Old Comrades

The restaurant was crowded but he saw Danny at once. He was hard to miss. Two metres tall and built like a buffalo with shaggy hair and beard, which he had always claimed enabled him to pass himself off as a Pashtun, though the advantages of doing so in Rome must be limited.

They had met in Afghanistan when Danny—whose full name was Daniele Zanetti—had been a captain in the 9th Reggimento d'Assalto Paracadutisti, the famous *Il Nono*. He had left the army a few years back and now he worked for the AISI, the internal security service, though in what precise capacity was something they had not yet discussed.

He stood when Aiden approached the table and opened his arms. Either his friends in Germany hadn't been in touch or he was putting on a good act. He stepped back, holding Aiden by the shoulders and searching his face.

'No more scars?'

'Not since you stopped looking out for me.'

'You think? Ha. Without me you would still be there, my friend, *un povoro vagabondo* on the Hindu Kush, bleating like a goat, "Which is the way to Herat?" I am amazed you find this place.'

By way of reply Aiden lifted up his phone with the map. In the service he was reputed to have no sense of direction. *'Give Aiden two ways to go, he always chooses the wrong one.'* Aiden didn't think this was true, but Danny liked to think it was.

They sat down and Danny filled his glass from a bottle of red.

'So, what brings you to Rome?'

'Just passing through on my way to somewhere else,' Aiden told him, which was as close to the truth as he cared to go.

Danny would know why he had left the service and in what circumstances, and he would know who he worked for now—or at least who he was supposed to be working for if he had not gone off on a quest of his own. In fact, he might very likely know a number of things that Aiden would prefer him not to know, but he did not suppose it would affect their friendship. So far, the signs were hopeful.

The restaurant served dishes from the Veneto, which was where Danny had been brought up and to which he had always claimed allegiance, rather than to the upstart Republic of Italy. Aiden wondered what his present employers thought about this, but they must be used to it. Regionalism was as much a part of being Italian as pasta and pizza, though doubtless Danny would say pizza was an atrocity inflicted on the world by the Neapolitans.

For the first few minutes they talked mostly of people and places— places they had served, friends they had made along the way, and what had happened to them since. Living and dead. These were friends they had made on active service. People they had come to know over a limited period of time and usually in one dark place. They were not like old schoolfriends, or neighbours, or people you worked with over a number of years or met up with regularly in a bar or a pub, or at a football match. But then Aiden often wondered what these kind of friendships were like. Certainly, he did not have them.

He knew Danny had a wife and two young daughters, but he had never met them. He knew he had an elderly mother, but he had never met her. He knew he had a house in Ostia, on the coast, within easy commuting distance of Rome, and another in a small village in the Dolomites where he went skiing, and he had been invited to both, but he had never been to either of them and probably never would.

When Danny asked him if he was okay, he said he was, most of the time. When Danny asked him if he had a steady girlfriend, he said no, not at the moment, with a shrug and a smile. When Danny asked about his family, he said he hardly ever saw them, which was true. He did not tell him about Michael.

While Danny ordered a second bottle of wine, Aiden reached down for his shoulder bag and pulled out the newspaper Hannah had brought from the Vatican Library.

'There is something I wanted to ask you,' he said.

'*L'Osservatore Romano*.' Danny eyed him warily. 'Tell me you read it for the football.'

'I picked it up in a church,' Aiden told him with no attempt at conviction. 'And I saw this.' He showed him the story about the terrorist attack in Sicily.

Danny glanced at it briefly. There was no change in his expression. 'So, what is *your* interest in this?' he enquired.

Aiden indicated the man Hannah thought she had recognised. 'Any idea who this is?'

Danny studied it more carefully for a moment, but then shook his head.

'I met him in Berlin,' said Aiden. 'At least I'm pretty sure it was him. He told me he was a press officer for the German Embassy in Rome. So, what's he doing with some cardinal at the scene of a terrorist attack in Sicily?'

The dark eyes were now fixed on Aiden, their expression wary. 'You are not shitting me?'

'I swear to you, Danny, I have no interest in this other than wanting to know who he is and why he tells me some bullshit about being a press officer.'

After a moment's further contemplation of his friend's face, Danny dropped his eyes to the newspaper again. 'Well, I do not know the identity of your friend from Berlin, but the man in the centre of the picture is Cardinal Emerson Seeburg, the head of the Holy Office.'

He looked to see if this meant anything. Aiden's expression suggested it did not.

'You maybe know it by the old title. The Holy Inquisition. In the old days they burn people like you and the world is a much safer place. Seeburg is the first priest from the US to hold this office. Emerson Seeburg, the cardinal from Kalamazoo, the man they say is the next Pope. When they get rid of this one.'

Aiden took the paper back and focused on the cardinal—a tall, imposing figure in a black cassock with red piping, a simple red skullcap showing what appeared to be a crewcut, greying at the edges. His features were almost movie-star handsome, with a hint of George Clooney, not the most obvious casting for the head of the Holy Office, and he gazed at the camera as if he was staring down the Devil. He was probably in his fifties or early sixties, on the young side for a cardinal. 'Seeburg?' he repeated thoughtfully, though it meant nothing to him.

But Danny had taken his phone out.

'What are you doing?' Aiden asked him.

'I am searching online. For the photograph. So I can send it to some one who will find out for you.' He looked sharply at Aiden. 'But if this is why you came to Rome . . .'

'What—to find out about some shooting in Sicily? I only saw this an hour ago.' He did not like the way Danny was looking at him. 'Okay.' He raised his hands in mock surrender. 'I've come to shoot the Pope. But I thought we'd have lunch first. I always like a decent lunch before I kill someone.'

'This is what I was thinking,' Danny confirmed. 'This is why I just text the GIS. They arrive in a few minutes. You have time for dessert. I recommend the *affogato*.'

The GIS was the *Gruppo di Intervento Speciale*, the special forces of the *Carabinieri*. Aiden was not unduly alarmed.

'Why would I want to shoot the Pope?' he asked.

'They will ask you this when they put the electrodes on your testicles if they can find them. The *fritole* also is very good. They make it with raisins soaked in rum and pine nuts. And for wine, we have the *moscato d'arancio*.' He kissed his fingers and signalled the waiter.

'Sorry, I didn't mean this to be a downer,' Aiden said, when Danny had placed their order and they were alone again. 'I just don't like it when people bullshit me.'

'None of us do, my friend.' But he leant across the table and squeezed Aiden's hand. 'Okay. Is fine. We do what we have to do. But this is what you call a sensitive area.'

'This thing in Sicily?'

'That. And anything that is to do with the present Pope.' Danny picked up his phone again. 'This is a search I make on Google a week or two ago. Nothing official. Just curious. Like you.' This was a dig, but Aiden let it pass. He handed the phone to Aiden. 'Scroll down, see how much there is, it goes on and on. See? All these blogs and websites. All about the Pope—how bad he is for the Church, for Italy, for the world, for God. What are we going to do about him? How do we get rid of him?'

It was mostly in Italian, but Aiden got the message. The vitriol and the hatred practically leapt out of the screen at him, in whatever language it was in. He wondered why Danny had this on his phone. 'Who are these people?' he said.

'Most of them are American, but there are plenty in Italy. Everyone who thinks the present Pope is an offense to God and to man. *L'Anticristo*, they call him. Or a Communist, which is worse. The latest offence, from their point of view, is that he has opened the Secret Archives so people can read the private letters of the Pope who was in the Vatican at the time of the Nazis. Pius the Twelfth. What deals he makes with Hitler and Mussolini and all the other *Fascisti*.'

'And what is wrong with that? I mean, opening the files.'

Danny laughed. 'You ask me? You should ask them.' He pointed a finger at the phone.

Aiden looked at him curiously. He knew nothing of Danny's politics or his religious beliefs. He knew he was a Catholic, of course. He'd seen him cross himself before going into action, but he'd thought it was like a footballer crossing himself when he went onto a soccer pitch. For luck.

'Okay. I tell you what they think is wrong. For years, all the left-wing journalists and historians, the Jews, all the enemies of the Church, they are saying that the Pope—Pius the Twelfth—during the war, he knew about the Final Solution, Hitler's plan for the Jews, and did nothing to stop it, not even a quiet diplomatic protest. That this makes him the accomplice of Hitler and the Nazis. And now this Pope we have now, the one they call the anti-Christ, he throws open the doors of the Church and says to all its enemies, come in, take what you like, find the evidence and publish it wherever you please, do the Devil's work for him, drive another nail in the cross. Cover the Church in shit, I give you my blessing.'

Aiden considered him carefully, wondering whose side he was on in this. 'Maybe there is no evidence,' he suggested.

'Well, that is the question. But it is not really about that. Nor is it about the past. The *Fascisti* are on the march again. Here in Italy, in America, Poland, Hungary, maybe France—and the last thing they want is for the Pope, the man they think should uphold everything they stand for, he now opens up this can of worms, to remind people of the fuck-up they make of the world the last time they are in charge.'

Aiden could not remember seeing Danny so serious, except perhaps when people were trying to kill him, or even then. He gave him his phone back.

'There's a lot of crazy people on social media,' he said. 'Does it bother you that much?'

Danny thought about it. 'More than before. Besides, it is not just them. It is the people behind them.'

'And they are?'

Danny laughed. Or a noise in the throat that could have been a laugh or the beginning of a growl. 'The big question. You have heard of the dark money?'

Aiden nodded. 'I'm not sure I know what it means. Or even if it exists. But why would the dark money be interested in getting rid of the Pope?'

'I do not know for sure. All I know is that he bothers them. Maybe he shames them. Maybe it is because he is not one of them. And he says stuff they do not want to hear. Or anyone else to hear.'

'Who will rid me of this turbulent priest?' said Aiden distantly. It was a line from a film or a play he had seen set in a time when priests and Popes were men of power and influence, whose opinions mattered, even to kings and emperors. But not now, surely.

Danny's phone went. He read whatever was on the screen, then shot Aiden that look again, with perhaps a little more menace in it.

'What?' said Aiden.

'Okay, this is your man.' He showed Aiden the picture, a different one than the one in *L'Osservatore Romano*, but definitely the same man. 'His name is Eissen. In German it means the Iron Man, but he is Swiss— and a senior officer of the Swiss Guard, recently appointed to the command of the Pope's personal bodyguard. Major Kurt Eissen. So why is he telling you he is a press officer in the German Embassy? And why are you here in Rome asking questions about him?'

CHAPTER TWENTY-SEVEN

Our Lady of Miracles

It was a different nun this time, but she'd clearly been to the same charm school.

'Doctor Lecci has been informed of your request,' she told Hannah, 'but the documents you requested are not available for study.'

Hannah expressed surprise. 'Could you tell me the reason for this? I mean, I thought the archives were available for legitimate research . . .'

'Only certain documents,' the nun informed her. 'And in this case, only up to the year 1939. The documents you have requested are from a later period.'

'So I cannot see *any* of the documents relating to the Bishopric of Merano?'

'Not for the year that you have requested. If you wish for a different year, you must make a new request.'

Hannah left the building. She checked her phone again to see if there was a message from Aiden. Surprisingly, there was. He would meet her at six o'clock at the statue of Garibaldi in the Borgo.

Hannah swore to herself. She was tired and hungry, and she needed a shower. She checked the time. Half five. Then she found a map on her phone.

It was only a short walk from the Vatican to the Borgo but rush hour was in full swing, the streets an anarchy of unruly traffic, with a murder of motor scooters that came hurtling at you from all directions. Pedestrians were like holes in the road, to be avoided if possible but not if it meant losing face. Hannah fought her way through the mayhem into the relative serenity of the Borgo, which was mostly parkland climbing steeply to the tall equestrian statue at its crest. Garibaldi, the founder of modern Italy, his long hair tied with a bandana and a rifle across his saddle. If America's founding fathers resembled bewigged preachers and lawyers, this was the hero of the nation as Apache, mounted on a pony, carbine in hand, a pair of pistols in his belt. Geronimo with a beard.

There was no sign of Aiden, of course, and the sky was heavy with the threat of rain. She tried ringing him—voicemail, of course—and left an irascible message to say she'd given up waiting for him and would see him back at the hotel.

On the way down to Trastevere it started to rain. She pulled up the hood of her parka, but then it started to bucket down. To make matters worse, she had lost her way. There was no sign of a cab rank and the only people she saw were hurrying out of the rain. She stopped under a streetlight to find directions on her phone, but it wasn't responding to her touch, possibly because her fingers were so wet. It seemed grimly appropriate to her current state of mind that she had managed to get lost in a labyrinth, with darkness falling and the rain coming down in sheets. She battled on, feeling more and more angry—with Aiden and her phone, with the world, with herself, and, of course, her mother, though how her mother was responsible for her present situation was hard to put into words, even in Hannah's head. It would be there somewhere though.

She came out of yet another back street onto small square with a couple of restaurants, both apparently closed, and a church. This at least offered the possibility of shelter if not warmth and a drink, which is what she really wanted. She tried the door which, surprisingly, was unlocked, though it was off the beaten track for tourists and past closing time, if churches had a closing time. It was quite a small church, as they go, lit by one small red light and a few flickering electric candles. Lots of statues but no apparent human presence. There was a selection of guidebooks on a table near the door which told her that it was the Church of Our Lady of Miracles, built 1346.

She moved closer to the altar, where most of the light was coming from, and sat in one of the pews to see if she get some response from her phone. She heard the sound of a door closing and turned to see that someone else had come in. For a moment she thought it was Aiden. Certainly he was as big as Aiden and he wore a black leather jacket with a hood. But he showed no sign of having recognised her and sat down at the back near the door.

The logical thing would be to go up to him and ask for directions—she had enough Italian for that—but something held her back. Perhaps because it was a church and he might be praying, but more likely because of the hood. Why would he keep the hood up *inside* the church? She was probably being paranoid, but nothing in her recent experience encouraged her to be anything but.

She stood up and moved closer to the altar, taking her time, pretending to be looking at the stuff on the walls like a typical tourist. Images of Death for the most part: dancing skeletons engaged in lewd and sinful practices. It was practically pornographic, if you could do porn with skeletons. Grinning skulls, mocking her fears, laughing at her predicament. Then she saw a small door to the right of the altar. Trying not to appear hurried or anxious, she walked over and gave it a try, thinking it might offer an alternative way out. The door opened into a small room resembling a vestry, lit by a single electric candle. There was a strong smell of beeswax and incense, a table, and several large cupboards from floor to ceiling. The ceiling was painted with faces of old men with beards, possibly prophets. Of more interest to her at this present moment was the door opposite. She crossed swiftly towards it, hoping it would lead to the street. It might well do, but it was locked.

Hannah took a deep breath and decided she was being foolish. She would have to go back into the main body of the church and leave the same way she came in.

She had almost reached the door when it opened towards her to reveal the man in the hood. She could see nothing of his features. He might not have had any. The horror of Mystic engulfed her. In a blind panic she hurled herself at him. Rather to her surprise she met with no resistance and dashed up the aisle to the door by which she had entered. She had almost made it when another man came in. He, too, wore a black leather jacket and a hood.

The absurdity of the situation was not lost on Hannah, but she would share the joke later. She let out a yell and charged him, swinging her shoulder bag at his head.

CHAPTER TWENTY-EIGHT

Say Three Hail Marys

Aiden raised an arm to take the blow and was about to return it when he saw who his assailant was. He grabbed the strap of the bag and spoke her name. He saw a brief flicker of response, then she looked back over her shoulder and he saw the other man. He was standing about halfway down the aisle, but when Aiden looked in his direction he made a dash for the door. Aiden let go of Hannah and grabbed him instead, and in a moment they were both rolling on the floor.

Aiden wished he had not had such a large lunch. He was working on his options when there was a sound like breaking crockery and his opponent went limp.

He climbed to his feet and looked down. The man was out cold among the broken pieces of what appeared to be a statue. Hannah was holding what was left of it in both hands.

Aiden swore. He bent down to check his pulse.

'Is he dead?'

'He'll live,' Aiden said, though he was by no means sure of this. He pulled back the hood. He was youngish, clean-shaven, close-cropped hair, long jaw. A predatory face, even in repose.

'I think he was following me.'

'I know he was following you,' said Aiden. 'I followed you both from the Vatican. Then I lost you both. What were you doing in here—praying?'

'I was just getting out of the rain—what do you mean, you were following us?'

'Can we talk about this later?' Aiden turned back to the man on the floor and knelt down and went through his pockets. He found a phone and a wallet. When he opened the wallet the first thing he saw was his ID. He swore the same single oath as before.

'What is it?'

'Nothing.' He stood up. She was still holding the statue. It might have been Our Lady, but this was a small detail. He supposed he should be glad it was plaster. If it had been anything heavier, he would almost certainly be dead. 'We better get out of here,' he said.

'What about him?'

'What about him?'

'We can't just leave him here. Can't we phone someone?'

'Like who? The Swiss Guard? There's one of your blokes lying in a church in Trastevere, do you want to come and collect him?'

'The what?' He hadn't meant to tell her that, but the situation had thrown him slightly.

'They're a kind of—security force . . .'

'I know what they are! Fuck!' She stared down at him. 'What is he doing *here*?'

A sound came from the figure on the floor. It might have been a sign of returning consciousness or a death rattle. Either way it was time they left.

He took Hannah's arm. 'Come on.'

She pulled away. 'I'm not leaving him like that,' she said firmly. 'He could die.'

'You should have thought of that when you smashed his head in with a fucking statue.' He had been brought up not to swear in church, but the circumstances were exceptional.

'We need to phone an ambulance,' she insisted.

He sighed. 'Do you know where we are?'

'Our Lady of Miracles,' she told him.

He looked at her disbelievingly. 'Seriously?'

She rolled her eyes and pulled out her phone.

'Don't use your own phone,' he reproved her. 'Use his. If you must.' He handed it to her. 'It's one-one-eight for an ambulance. Tell them there's a man lying on the floor of Our Lady of Miracles in Trastevere and you think he's had a knock on the head. Then end the call. Don't give them your name.'

'Why me? Why don't you do it?'

He counted to three. 'Where do you want me to start? A, because you laid him out, B, because it's you who wants to call an ambulance, and C . . . I don't know—because you speak Italian?'

'I don't speak Italian.'

'You speak more than I do.' He was still holding the phone out.

There was another sound from the figure on the floor. He opened his eyes and looked at them. He didn't look all there, but enough for it to be a concern.

'Go,' said Aiden, turning her in the direction of the door.

They ran through the empty streets. The rain was coming down harder than ever. They ran until they came to the river. Then Aiden stopped to check for directions on his phone. He saw that Hannah was glaring at him from under her hood.

'What have I done now?' he said.

'You set me up, didn't you?' she said. 'You used me as bait.'

'I didn't set you up,' Aiden assured her wearily, though she had a point. 'I didn't know you were going to drop into church. I wanted to see if anyone was following you. And I'd have found out *why* he was following you if you hadn't bashed him over the head with Our Lady of Miracles.'

She was still clutching it to her chest like it was her favourite doll, what was left of it.

'How did you know we were in there?'

'I didn't. I was just looking. Give me that.' He held his hand out for the statue. She resisted for a moment but after a brief tug-of-war he wrenched it off her and crossed to the parapet and threw it into the river. Then he tossed the man's wallet and his phone after it.

They headed back to their hotel. They were both silent, Hannah lagging a step or two behind with her head down. Aiden was working out what to do next when he heard a ringtone. It was Hannah's. She answered it before he could stop her.

'Hugo?' She covered the mic. 'It's Hugo von Stahlberg,' she said to Aiden. 'He wants to know if it's a bad time.'

Aiden lifted his face to the heavens. It didn't help. Hugo must have heard about Irma, he thought. He reached for the phone, but she backed away, frowning furiously.

'What priest?' she said. 'Oh *him*. Right.'

She listened for a moment. 'Yes, we're still in Rome,' she said. 'Yes. He's with me at the moment.' Like a disease she couldn't get rid of. Aiden drew a finger across his throat. 'He sends his regards.' She looked at Aiden, who was staring at her in something beyond disbelief. 'He sends his.'

She listened again, saying little beyond 'Really' and 'O-kay' in a tone that was expressive of surprise and concern, looking directly at Aiden as she spoke. He wondered if Hugo was talking about him. But at least they didn't appear to be talking about Irma Ulbrecht.

'O-kay,' she said again. 'Look, Hugo, I better go now. I'll call you back.'

'He's found the priest,' she said. 'Father Johann. You know, the boy who was with the partisans?'

'So where is he now?'

'In Sicily. But—' the frown was now more puzzled than angry— 'he said he'd already spoken to you.'

Now Aiden was confused. 'Who already spoke to me?'

'The Monsignore—about Father Johann.'

'To me? When?'

'A few weeks ago. He said he told you to try the Jesuit Information Centre in Palermo.'

'How many weeks ago?'

'He didn't say but—he remembered the name Blake. Do you think...'

'It'll be Michael,' Aiden said. 'Christ.'

He pulled out his phone again.

'What are you doing?' she said.

'Checking the flights to Palermo,' he said.

Chapter Twenty-Nine

Palermo

They made it five minutes before they closed the flight.

'How you feeling?' Aiden asked her as they waited in departures. He sounded unusually solicitous.

She gave him a look that was probably ungracious, but she was past being gracious. Grace under pressure, was that the expression? Well, fuck that. She felt bullied was how she felt. There were probably a few more words she could add to that without much help from a thesaurus, but she was too weary to try. She supposed she was in shock.

'Were you serious about the man in the church?' she said.

'Serious about what?'

'Being in the Swiss Guard.'

She kept her voice low but departures was almost empty at this time of night.

'Well, that's what his ID said. Corporal.'

'I thought they just stood around with pikes.'

'It's a halberd,' he said. 'They're halberdiers. Technically speaking.'

'What?'

'That's just for ceremony. They're like any other army, except that there are not so many of them. They normally have the same weapons as the Swiss Army.'

She didn't want to know about their weapons or anything else about them except why one of them had followed her into the church. 'Do you think he was off duty?'

'What do you mean?'

She spelled it out for him. 'Not on active service. Not *operative*. *Off duty*.'

'You think he was following you for the fun of it? Trying to pick you up?'

'No, I don't think that, but—he didn't stop me making a break for it. In the church.' She had been thinking about this. She might have taken him by surprise when she pushed past him in the doorway of the little vestry, but she didn't think so.

'He was probably told to follow you,' he said. 'Not kill you.'

'Told by who?'

'Whoever is next in the chain of command. Or even a bit higher up.'

'But why?' she almost wailed. He told her to keep it down. 'Why are the Swiss Guard the slightest bit interested in me? Because I asked to see the archives from Merano?'

'I'm not saying they *are* interested—officially.'

'Then what are you saying?'

He sighed. 'Well, I don't want to alarm you—'

'Really?'

'—but that bloke you met in Berlin. Apparently, he's also in the Swiss Guard. A bit higher up in the pecking order.'

She stared at him, trying to take this in. 'Emil Brandt?'

'Yeah. Except that's not his name. His name's Eissen. Major Kurt Eissen.'

'Oh shit.' She put her head in her hands.

After a few moments of trying to sort out the thoughts that were whirling through her mind and not getting very far, she came up for air.

'How do you know that?'

'Because my friend told me. Eissen is one of the top men in papal security. I mean, protecting the person of the Pope.'

'You think he thinks we're a threat to the Pope?'

'It's possible. But I doubt it. I think it's probably a bit more complicated than that.'

'Why are they doing this?' This was close to another wail. 'Do you think they're all in on it?'

'All who?'

'The Swiss Guard.'

'Oh, no, no. No, this will just be a kind of—rogue element.'

'Well, that's a relief.' She meant this to sting. But after a moment she added hopefully.

'So you think it could just be the two of them? Brandt or Eissen or whatever his name is and the guy in the church?'

'It's possible, I guess, but what happened to Irma suggests more of a team.'

Hannah sank into a stricken silence.

Then he said: 'Did you know the Pope was in New York when Michael was killed?'

She looked at him in surprise. 'No. I knew he was in the States but . . . But what's that got to do with it? You think the Pope killed Michael?'

'No, I don't think that.' He rolled his eyes. 'He was there to address the UN. I don't suppose he had the time. But it's very likely Eissen was there, too. And we know he was in Berlin when Irma was killed.'

This was unusually forthcoming. She gave it some thought.

'So—you think Eissen is behind all this?'

'Or someone behind *him*.'

Before she could pick him up on this their flight was called.

It took just over an hour to Palermo. Aiden slept through most of it, making small puttering noises that were not quite snores, more like a large dog dreaming of rabbits, or other dogs. She felt like kicking him. He only stirred when they began their descent. She had never been to Sicily, but she looked at the lights below without curiosity or even fear, only a weary fatalism. One door closes, another opens—and leads to an even darker place than you were in before.

They took the shuttle into Palermo 'They skin you for a taxi,' Aiden said, but she thought it was probably because there was less chance of the driver remembering them. He'd obviously been here before, but she didn't ask him whether it was on business or pleasure. If he had even bothered to answer she would not have believed him.

He'd found them a hotel near the Opera House, which he said was 'touristy.' She was just trailing along now, usually with her head down, and no clear idea of what they were doing or why, except running away from somewhere else. It was gone eleven by the time they checked in, but Aiden was keen to eat. One thing she could count on, he was always keen to eat. She was amazed he wasn't as fat as a pig. There were a number of bars within walking distance that would still be open, the man on the night desk told them, though he wasn't sure if they'd be serving food.

Hannah declined to join him. She had a terrible headache and all she wanted was sleep. It didn't come easy and when it did it was filled with men in hoods. She'd wake on the edge of a scream, sitting up and staring into the dark, clawing at imagined faces. Finally, she took a couple of pills she'd bought at the airport and they knocked her out until morning. She awoke to the sound of her phone. Aiden. He said he was just leaving for the Jesuit Centre. She checked the time. Just after nine. The headache had gone but her head felt like it was stuffed with cotton wool.

'You want me to come with you?'

'No,' he said. 'I'll be all right. You have a lie in.'

She was used to this by now, she didn't even have the energy for a spirited response.

'Okay,' she said dully. 'Good luck.'

She supposed the Jesuits would speak English and if they didn't that was his problem. Her Italian wouldn't have helped much anyway. It was just about up to asking directions and calling the emergency services, though this could be quite useful, she thought, when you were with a man like Aiden Blake.

She had breakfast in an open courtyard at the back of the hotel. The sun was shining, flowers sprouted from terracotta pots, small birds pecked at crumbs, and a small fountain splashed away in an ornamental pond. It almost gave her an illusion of peace and tranquillity. But she knew by now that it *was* an illusion. Nowhere was safe. And this being the case, she might as well be in Brooklyn. She would tell Aiden as soon as he came back. She didn't think he'd mind. He didn't need her to translate for him anymore. He'd probably be glad to see the back of her.

She checked the flights to New York on her phone. There was an Alitalia at 11:55 that would have her in JFK by seven that evening, given the time difference. They still had seats. If she left now she could just make the check-in. But she felt bad about leaving Aiden without telling him first. She was surprised she felt this obligation, but there it was, it was the way she had been brought up, though she blamed her father for once, not her mother. The next available flight was in the evening, with a stopover at Rome. She was thinking about this and whether it would be wise to go anywhere near Rome after what had happened in the Church of Our Lady of Miracles when she became aware that there were two men standing at her table and they didn't look like waiters.

'Miss Harper?'

It was what she had been braced for since leaving Berlin.

Chapter Thirty

Into the Hills

They picked Aiden up on his way to the Jesuit Centre, but unlike Hannah he did not take them for police. He had been cutting through the back streets behind the Opera House, following the directions on his phone. It was a little before nine in the morning, the streets were crowded, and there were a number of delivery vans dropping stuff off at the shops. One of them came up behind him and he had to move into a doorway to let it past. But then it stopped in front of him, blocking the road, and three men jumped out. They wore the kind of clothes workers might wear on a building site, or roadworks—denims and dirty yellow jackets, yellow helmets, heavy boots—but he knew that whatever they were, they were not mending roads. The handguns would have ruled that out, even in Sicily.

One of them told him to get into the back of the van. His English was poor, but his meaning was clear. Aiden got into the back of the van. They pushed him to the floor and secured his hands behind him with what felt like plastic tags. Then they put a hood over his head. It was made of hessian sacking and smelt of animal feed. The van was already moving. After a few minutes and a few sharp turns he was dragged into a sitting position with his back against the side of the van and his feet stretched out in front of him. He was laying on what felt like bags of cement or plaster. One of the men searched his pockets and took his phone, his wallet, and his passport. He heard a brief exchange in Italian which he did not understand. He did not attempt conversation. Whoever they were they must have known he was coming. This could mean a number of things, but the most likely was that someone had been watching their hotel in Rome and followed them to the airport before alerting their friends in Sicily. This conclusion was of little comfort to him. The only thing that gave him grounds for optimism was the hood they had put over his head. If they didn't want him to see them, or know where they were taking him, it could only be to prevent him from identifying them in the future—which implied that he had a future.

But he would not count on it.

After turning a few corners the van reached a more or less straight stretch of road and then stopped. He heard someone get out—from the front of the vehicle—and then after a few minutes come back. There was a smell of bread and coffee and he assumed they were having breakfast. No one offered him any. The journey continued and from the speed they were going and the straightness of the road he assumed they were on the autostrada out of Palermo. After a while he fell into a shallow doze. He had always been able to sleep when there was not much else to do.

He awoke when they came off the motorway and onto a road that was much less comfortable to someone sitting on the floor of a van with a hood over one's head. There were a lot of bends and they were constantly climbing. After about a quarter of an hour of this, as near as he could guess, they turned onto a much rougher track, also climbing. For a while all he could think about was bracing himself against the side of the van to avoid being thrown about, but finally it came to a halt, the doors were opened, and he was dragged out. He could hear dogs barking—probably big dogs and at least two of them, but not too close for comfort. The ground underfoot was hard, packed earth, not paved, and the air was cool—cooler than it had been in Palermo—but the sun was bright enough for him to know it was there, even through the hood.

His head was pushed down and he felt himself being guided through a narrow doorway. The packed earth changed to stone paving and there was less light coming through the hood. He heard the sound of a television—a frenzied commentary which didn't tell him much except that it might be a football match. One of the men told him in his poor English that there were stairs. Aiden stumbled his way up them. Then there was another door and they sat him down on what was either a bed or a couch. His hands were untied and he heard a door being shut, then locked. He pulled off the hood. He was in a small plain room with one shuttered window, which let in splinters of sunlight. The bed he was sitting on was the only furniture in the room unless you counted the plastic bucket in a corner. There was no carpet on the wooden floor and nothing on the walls. The bed had a pillow but no pillowcase, and a blanket but no sheets.

There was a dirty-looking sink in one corner, with one tap. He walked stiffly over to it and turned it on. A dribble of brown water, but then after juddering for a few moments, it ran fast and clear. He splashed some of the water on his face and drank a little. He doubted if polluted water would kill him, given the competition. Then he moved to the window. It was a sashcord with what looked like a new lock at the top so you couldn't raise it without the key. He supposed he could smash the glass but it would cause a lot of noise and he'd still have to get to the ground. He had counted sixteen steps on the stairs—what was that: four metres? He pressed his head against the glass, trying to peer through the cracks in the shutters, but the glass was too dirty and the sunlight too bright.

The dogs had stopped barking but he thought he could hear hens—and bells, the kind of tinkling bells you put on sheep or goats. He sat on the bed. He wished he knew the time. He didn't have a watch—he normally relied on his phone—but he figured that it had taken over two hours from Palermo, maybe two and a half, so it must be about midday. Judging from the brightness of the sun, the room was facing south. He saw the way the beams fell on the floor and took off his belt and used the buckle to scratch a mark. That was midday. As the sun set to the west the angle of the beams would change and he could mark them accordingly until sunset, which he figured must be just after seven. Of course, he didn't know what buildings or trees might be in the way, and the sun might vanish behind cloud, and knowing the time wasn't going to help him much anyway, but he felt slightly better for having done something. They should not have left him the belt—there were other uses he could put it to—but it was worth finding out what they wanted from him first. It was a good sign that they had untied his hands.

He inspected the pillow on the bed. It wasn't that clean but not that dirty either. He had been in worse places. In fact, compared to some places he had been, this was a four-star hotel. He stretched out on his back, crossed his legs at the ankles, and settled down to sleep. It was a long time coming. It had been easier in the moving vehicle. Perversely, he had no trouble sleeping on the move, but lying still, on a bed, it was sometimes a problem for him. Also, he was hungry. He got up and walked about a bit. Did some press-ups and then lay down again. Eventually he drifted off and was awoken by the sound of a bolt being drawn. Then another. He swung his feet down to the floor and sat there, waiting for whatever was coming. The light had shifted and softened. There were more shadows. He figured from his sundial that it was about three o'clock. The door opened and a man stood there, looking down at him, smiling. Unlike the men in the van, he was clean-shaven and wore a suit.

'Mr Blake,' he said. His tone was weary. 'I am sorry it was necessary to bring you here. I hope it will not be for long.' He spoke in almost perfect English with just a trace of an accent. Aiden thought he had seen him before but he could not think where exactly. His features were sharply defined, as if his face had been chiselled from something more solid and enduring than mere human flesh. There were other men on the landing behind him.

'And you are . . . ?'

'That would mean nothing to you,' said the man, 'but you can call me Franco.'

But Aiden remembered now where he had seen him before. It was in *L'Osservatore Romano* and according to Danny his name was Eissen. Iron Man Eissen. The bodyguard of the Pope.

CHAPTER THIRTY-ONE

The Banker and the Biker

THEY TOOK HANNAH TO POLICE HEADQUARTERS IN PALERMO FOR questioning. She was not under arrest, she was informed, just helping with inquiries.

Inquiries into what, she said.

An incident, he said. A *serious* incident. He declined to say more.

Naturally she assumed he meant the incident in the church in Trastevere, or possibly the death of Irma Ulbrecht in Berlin, though surely he would have called that a murder inquiry. Either way, she had problems. This was the main reason why she did not make more of a fuss, even when they took away her passport and her phone. But she had been left alone in the interview room for well over an hour now, and she felt this was a bit much. There was a long mirror running the length of one wall and a camera on the wall opposite, and she assumed she was being monitored by one or the other, possibly both.

A few minutes later, the door opened and two men came in. They were not the same two men who had picked her up from the hotel. One of them was tall, slim, and clean-shaven, with a white shirt and tie, and a dark suit. The other was a man of considerable bulk with a mass of dark curly hair and a beard. He wore a leather jacket with jeans and a T-shirt. The Banker and the Biker, she thought.

The younger man gave Hannah other names but they did not stick in her mind. The Banker and the Biker was easier. He also told her they were members of the state security service, and that they were investigating a major terrorist incident in Sicily in which five people had died.

Hannah expressed bewilderment. She knew nothing of this, she said, and she could not possibly imagine why they thought she could help with their inquiries.

Her interrogator offered no further explanation but asked her to explain what she had been doing in Rome, and why she was now in Sicily.

Hannah did briefly consider telling the truth, but it did not make a great deal of sense, even to her, and inevitably the truth would lead back to Berlin and Irma Ulbrecht. So she told them a different story, one that she hoped would be a great deal more plausible.

It was basically the same story that Aiden had told Hugo von Stahlberg, with certain adaptations of her own. She was working on a television documentary about the closing stages of World War Two in Europe, she said, and she was particularly interested in certain events that had occurred in Northern Italy after the German surrender. She had come to Sicily, she said, in search of a man who had witnessed these events while working as a courier for the partisans in the mountains above Merano when he was a young boy.

When she had finished she almost believed it herself.

There was a brief exchange of Italian. Then the Banker asked her about Aiden Blake.

'Oh—Aiden? He's the producer,' she said. 'Of the documentary. In fact, I believe it was his idea.'

'Aiden Blake is a television producer?'

'Yes.' She looked surprised he should ask. 'Why? What else did you think he was?'

They gazed at her in silence for a moment. She felt like a stand-up with an unreceptive audience.

'How long have you known Mr Blake?'

'Not long,' Hannah admitted. 'About a month, I suppose. We met in New York, when he interviewed me for the job.'

'Did you check on his credentials—as a television producer?'

'No.' Hannah contrived to look puzzled. 'But I'd heard of him through a friend. I'm freelance,' she added helpfully. 'It's the way it works.'

'Did he tell you of his time in the British Royal Marines?'

'I think he might have mentioned it, yes. Subsequently.'

'Did he also mention that since he left the Marines he had been working as a security consultant—mainly in the Gulf states?'

Hannah expressed surprise and a degree of incredulity, though in fact it did not surprise her at all. Had they got the right Aiden Blake? she demanded.

By way of a reply the Biker showed her some pictures on his phone. Aiden in combat uniform with a group of other men, also in combat uniform. Mountains in the background. Aiden in a chequered cotton keffiyeh sitting in a jeep with a machine gun, possibly in the desert. Aiden in swimming shorts sitting at a bar on a beach. In all of the pictures he looked younger and happier than the Aiden she knew. In one of them he was actually smiling.

'He has changed a bit since then,' she observed, 'but yes, I think that's him.'

'And did he appear to know a lot about television?' she was asked.

'Not a lot,' she said. But this was not unusual in a television producer, she said. It was largely a question of bluff and pretence—and who you knew. She kept this quite light.

So who did Aiden know, in the television industry? And had she met any of them?

She admitted that she had not.

'Moving on,' said the Banker, whose manner had become noticeably more sardonic. 'Have you any idea where he is now?'

She assumed that he was at the hotel in Palermo, she said.

'Not when our colleagues were there this morning,' he informed her. 'Nor has he been back since. We have people there waiting for him.'

People. How many people? she wondered.

'Well, I don't know where he's gone,' she said. 'Maybe he's gone for a run. He sometimes goes for a run in the morning. Or a swim,' she added helpfully.

This rachetted things up a notch. They were not playing games, they told her. They were investigating an attack in which five people had died and they had powers to detain her under the Prevention of Terrorism acts. This would involve being strip searched, wearing a prison uniform, and being locked in a cell until she decided to cooperate with them. That sounds fun, she thought of saying, who will do the strip search? But she didn't, of course. Her sense of humour didn't travel well. It worked better in Brooklyn.

'I *am* cooperating,' she said. 'I've told you the truth.'

She wondered if being tearful would help, but it was so humiliating, she decided to keep it in reserve.

'That Aiden Blake is a television producer?' Mr Sarcasm the Banker.

'But what makes you so sure he isn't?' Hannah retorted.

'Because Aiden Blake has been many things, Miss Harper,' he said, 'but never, so far as we know—and we know quite a lot about him—a television producer. He is a man of the shadows, but what we do know is that he is a trained killer and very possibly an assassin and now we need you to tell us where he is.'

'An assassin?' Hannah expressed more incredulity. She thought the Biker did not look especially happy with this description. There were a few more words in Italian. The Biker leant forward with both elbows on the desk and fixed her with the textbook stern gaze. Now he put her in mind of the Gruffalo, one of the monsters of her childhood, though by no means the worst. She felt like Little Mouse. She would have to be at least as clever.

'Okay. Let me level with you.' She gave him a nervous but appreciative smile. 'Aiden Blake is my friend. We served together in Afghanistan when he was in the Special Boat Service—do you understand what this is?'

'Boats?' she frowned. 'In Afghanistan?'

He let this go. 'It is the counter-terrorist force of the British Marine commandos. Elite of the elite. I think he would be a little wasted in television.'

Hannah made no comment.

'We are good friends. We met yesterday, in Roma.'

'Ah! You were the friend he met for lunch.' She regarded him with more interest.

'He told you this?'

'He said he was meeting someone, he didn't say who.'

'Did he say why?'

'No. I assumed it was a social call.'

She maintained an expression of amiable curiosity. His own remained stern. His eyes might have narrowed a little. Push me too far, they said, and you will regret it.

He kept his eyes on her while he reached into his pocket for his phone. After a brief search, he showed her a video.

She recognised it as the exterior of their hotel in Rome. Night. Rain. Two hooded figures were approaching. They went in. Cut to another shot, still an exterior but this time it showed an interior of the hotel through the glass doors. The same two hooded figures at the reception desk picking up their keys. But then one of them pushed back the hood.

'This is you, yes?'

There was little point in denying it.

'What of it?' she said. She contrived a level of indignation. 'Did you have us followed?' She was wondering where they had been followed *from*. The church in Trastevere?

'Unfortunately not. Not until this point, at least. I knew where Aiden was staying so I had people waiting at the hotel.'

'I thought you said you were his friend.'

'I am his friend. That is why I look out for him. Aiden is not always so good at picking his friends, or the people he works for, you understand?'

Hannah thought this could well be true, but then she had no idea who he worked for. 'So I think it is better maybe to find out what he is doing in Rome and who he plans to meet.'

He showed her another exterior of the hotel. Same night, same rain. And the same couple, so far as it was possible to tell, coming out of the hotel with suitcases and getting into a taxi.

'Only then do we follow,' said the Biker. 'To Rome airport where you catch a flight for Palermo. So—' he spread his arms, 'why are you here?'

'To look for locations,' Hannah said. He made a rude noise and turned away. 'I'm sorry, but I don't see the problem,' she said.

'No? The hotel in Rome says that you had reserved rooms for two nights, so why the sudden departure?'

'Change of plan.' Hannah shrugged. 'It happens. DFI they call it in the film business. Different Fucking Idea. I've told you . . .'

'I know what you told me. Most of it is bullshit. Fortunately, when I know that you are heading for Palermo I am able to place you under a proper surveillance. At least, this is what I thought. When Aiden left the hotel this morning he was followed for several blocks until picked up by a van. It may have been that he was forced into the van—at gunpoint. After that—' he shrugged, 'we do not know.'

Hannah gathered that this had caused the Biker serious displeasure and was possibly the reason for his present ill temper. Or at least one of the reasons, beside her.

'So now we do not know where he is, and I think it is possible he is in big trouble. So, I will ask you again, why did you come to Sicily? And if you know where Aiden is—or who he was planning to meet here in Palermo—now is the time to tell us, before it is too late.'

CHAPTER THIRTY-TWO

The Iron Man

AIDEN SAT ON HIS BED AND WATCHED THE FILE OF MEN ENTER THE room. The first carried a small table, the second a pair of folding chairs, a third carried a metallic silver case, and the fourth a shotgun.

They did not look like the Swiss Guard.

The table and chairs were set up in the centre of the room. The metal case was placed on top of the table. The man with the shotgun stood at the door. The other men stood against the wall, their arms held in front of them, crossed at the wrist. The room was suddenly crowded. Eissen was still looking at Aiden, still smiling.

'I am sure you are wondering why you are here,' he said. Aiden made no comment. 'Well, the fact is we would like you to do something for us.' He sprung the clasps on the metal case and opened the lid. 'You will be familiar with the Glock 17, of course. This is the 43.'

Aiden looked at the pistol nestling in the foam rubber padding.

'Much the same as the one you will be familiar with from your time in the Special Boat Service. Nine millimetre, semi-automatic, takes a six-round mag.'

'I'm not really in the market for firearms at the moment,' Aiden told him. 'What else are you selling?'

'Feel the grip,' Eissen invited him.

After a moment's hesitation, Aiden lifted the gun out of the case and turned it over in his hands. It was, as Eissen had said, familiar.

'See what it is like with the magazine.'

Eissen held the case out to Aiden like a box of chocolates. Aiden took it and slotted it into the breech.

'In case you were wondering, it has just one round in it,' Eissen advised him.

'For me?'

Eissen's laugh was overdone. It was not that good a joke. In fact, it wasn't entirely a joke.

'I do not think it has come to that yet, has it? Should you attempt to use it on one of us, however . . .'

'Who *do* you want me to use it on then?'

'A hen,' said Eissen. He said something in Italian to one of his men, who took a key from his pocket and opened the lock on the window. Then he slid the sash up. Eissen crossed over to it and opened one of the shutters a little. He looked out for a moment and then made a gesture with his head for Aiden to join him.

'Take a look.'

Aiden peered through the narrow gap Eissen had left between the shutters. Down below was what looked like a farmyard. And indeed, hens. About half a dozen of them, clustered around a feeder.

'You want me to shoot a hen?'

'If that is not a problem for you. The white one, perhaps.'

There was only one white hen. The rest were brown or black. Aiden considered. He looked at the men standing between him and the door. One round. He could take out the one with the shotgun and smash the grip into Eissen's face, but that still left three of them. And that assumed Eissen was telling the truth about there being a round in the magazine. He probably was. The other men did not look anything like as relaxed as Eissen was.

Aiden put his eye to the crack of daylight between the shutters. The range was about thirty yards. An easy enough shot, in theory, but once you stepped back you would have a very limited field of vision.

'Why would I want to shoot a hen?' he said.

'To show me that you can?' Eissen suggested. 'Why, what is the matter? Are you a vegan?'

'No,' said Aiden. 'But what have they ever done to me, these hens?'

Eissen swore. In German. He shook his head and moved Aiden aside and pressed his eye to the gap. 'Very well,' he said. 'Shoot at the feeder. If you have no objection to that.'

The feeder was a little bigger than your average hen but not much.

Aiden knelt down and raised the pistol. It had been fitted with sights. He examined them more carefully. Hackathorn sights. Only the best for Iron Man Eissen. He adjusted them slightly. The gap between the two shutters was very narrow, not more than about ten centimetres he reckoned. It wouldn't stop him from making the shot but now that he was leaning back, the shutter on the right distracted him a little. He reached out to open it a little wider.

'No.' Eissen's tone was sharper than it had been. 'Leave it where it is.'

Why was Eissen bothered about the size of the gap? Did he not want the hens to see them?

Aiden took aim again. He didn't know what Eissen's game was, but he supposed he would have to play it for a little while longer to find out. He squeezed the trigger. The feeder may have moved slightly and there was a bit of a clang. The hens moved a lot more and made a lot more noise about it. Aiden could see the hole about halfway down the feeder, exactly where he had meant it to be. He moved aside for Eissen to look.

'Very good,' said Eissen. 'The hen would have been better. We could have had it for dinner.'

They sat down at the table together. Just Aiden and Eissen. One of the men had brought in a tray with several bowls of food, a jug of wine, and two glasses. There was bread and olives, anchovies and burrata cheese. The man with the shotgun still stood at the door but the rest of them had gone.

Eissen poured the wine.

'*Cin, cin,*' he said.

'Cheers,' said Aiden.

He took a good mouthful of the wine and ripped off a hunk of bread to dip in the cheese. Eissen let him eat for a minute or so. Then he took out his phone.

'So,' he said, 'why you are here.' He showed Aiden a picture. 'Do you know who this is?'

Aiden looked at it. An old man in a clerical collar. 'No. I don't think so. Should I?'

'His name is Father Johann Winkler,' said Eissen. 'And he is the reason why your brother was murdered.'

Aiden looked from the picture to Eissen. His face was serious for once, but that did not mean he had stopped playing games.

'Go on.'

'Winkler is a paedophile. A notorious paedophile who should have been put away a long time ago. However, you know what it is like.' Aiden gave no indication that he did, so Eissen told him. 'Well—Father Winkler has the protection of some very senior men in the Vatican. Has done for many years. Your brother seems to have discovered this. At the time of his death he was pursuing a line of enquiry that was of concern to these people, which is why they took the action they did.'

'You're saying they killed him.'

'I am saying they had him killed. By men more practised in the art than they are.'

'How do you know this?'

Eissen reflected. 'Let's say I move in the same circles.' He indicated the picture on his phone. 'He is an old man now, well into retirement, but he has had a long and distinguished career in the Church. At one point he was private secretary to the Vatican Foreign Minister. Then he became director of a seminary in Rome which trains many of the top men of the Church. And in his later years he was director of a youth project here in Sicily. The number of young boys he abused in the course of this long career is unknown, but it was a very great many. And even worse, he became, what is the word in English? In German it is *vorfahr*. The *creator* of abusers. One might say, their mentor.'

'And how did my brother know this?'

'That I cannot say. Possibly it is something he stumbled upon in the course of other work. He was a historian, I believe.'

'And you say he planned to expose him?'

'Along with his protectors in the Vatican.'

'But my brother can't have been the only one who knew of this,' Aiden objected.

'This is true. And some of those who knew of it tried to bring him to justice. But always his protectors were too powerful. So a few weeks ago, some people here in Sicily took the law into their own hands. Unfortunately, it was badly planned and even worse executed. A number of innocent people died, while the guilty one escaped without harm. However, this is why the people who are protecting him decided to target your brother.'

'You're saying my brother had something to do with what happened here in Sicily?'

'No, I am not saying that at all, nor do I think it. It was probably intended as a warning to your brother's informants. I think the expression in English is "Don't fuck with us."'

Aiden thought about it. A lot of this sounded like bullshit, but maybe not all of it.

'Why are you telling me this?' he said.

'Because there is—what do you say?—a small "window of opportunity" to send this man to Hell, where he belongs.' He showed the width between his finger and thumb. 'As small as the gap you have just fired through. And we believe you are the man to do this.'

CHAPTER THIRTY-THREE

A Secret Never to be Told

IF ALL ELSE FAILS, HANNAH'S MOTHER HAD ONCE ADVISED HER, TRY telling the truth. Hannah was about seven at the time and it might have been a sardonic response to some minor evasion on her part. Even so, it probably counted as one of the most useful pieces of advice her mother had ever given her.

So, all else having failed, she told her interrogators the truth at last, give or take a few careful edits. She cut the scene in the portacabin in Berlin where they had found the body of Irma Ulbrecht, along with the incident of the mysterious exploding houseboat and the encounter in the Church of Our Lady of Miracles in Trastevere. It was not such a good story without them, but it made her own role considerably less reprehensible. Besides, she felt that these scenes properly belonged to Aiden. But otherwise, she gave them a reasonably accurate account of her life and movements from the moment she had found Michael Blake's body in the beach house on Long Island to her arrival in Palermo. She told them that Aiden was convinced there was a link between his brother's death and the research he had been doing for his next book and that he had employed Hannah to find out what it was. She was far from convinced, she told them, that there *was* a link.

The death of Michael Blake was clearly a shock to them and they asked a number of supplementary questions, only some of which she could answer. She advised them to check with the police on Long Island. They said they would. They exchanged what she took to be meaningful glances and then stood up. They must talk about this, Hannah was informed, and make some enquiries. They would be back shortly.

They were gone for more than two hours. In the meantime, one of the women brought Hannah a coffee and a panini, and a couple of women's magazines—in Italian. They had taken her phone so she couldn't call anyone, even if she had wanted to.

It was just after three in the afternoon when they came back. Their expressions were grim, but then they had never been especially cheering. She wondered if they had spoken to the police in Berlin. It seemed likely.

The Biker showed her another picture from his phone gallery.

'Do you know this man?'

An elderly man wearing a clerical collar. She shook her head.

'His name is Father Johann Winkler of the Society of Jesus. He is the man you came to Sicily to see, yes?'

Hannah said nothing, though it seemed pointless now to deny it, not if they had seen the texts and emails on her phone.

'We have just spoken with him. He wants to meet you.'

This was a surprise. 'Did he say why?'

'Apparently he spoke with Doctor Michael Blake shortly before he died. You were this man's assistant, yes? Or is that another piece of fiction?'

'Did he say what they spoke about?'

'He will tell you that himself. He is here in Palermo. In hospital. He suffered a mild stroke during the attack on the Jesuit retreat near Erice.'

He had been outside the centre when the attackers arrived, the Biker told Hannah, sitting in a chair among the olive trees, watching the sun go down. He had seen two cars arrive and four men get out, carrying guns. They shot a young woman who had just emerged from the building, but they did not see the priest in the shadows of the trees. It was then that he suffered his stroke. It probably saved his life.

'So, the attack on the *Gesuiti*, the murder of Michael Blake, the assault made on you at the house of your mother—they were almost certainly linked. And now this woman in Berlin—Dr Irma Ulbrecht.'

Hannah tried to look puzzled.

'Yes, we know about her, and your meeting with her two days before she died. Did you forget to mention that, or did you not think it was important? And now Aiden.'

Hannah thought for a moment that he had been the next victim, but no, they were still looking for him.

'But already there are enough bodies, I think, for you to cooperate with us,' the Biker pointed out. 'In case you are the next.'

'I thought I was,' said Hannah. 'Cooperating.'

'But you did not tell us about your meeting with Doctor Ulbrecht in Berlin. What else have you not yet told us?'

Hannah considered telling them about the incident in the church in Rome, but she had taken enough of her mother's advice for one day.

They stood up again.

'*Andiamo,*' said the Biker.

They had a car waiting in an underground carpark. Hannah sat in the back with the Biker and the Banker sat in the front with the driver. As they were getting in, she thought she heard the driver address the Biker as *Colonnello*.

'Did he call you colonel?' she asked as they drove off.

'This is a surprise for you? Do I not look like a colonel?'

There was a small noise—it might have been a snigger—from his colleague in the front.

'But you say you are a friend of Aiden's?'

'This is true.'

'And he was only a sergeant?' She knew enough about the armed forces to know that friendships between a sergeant and a colonel were rare.

'Is this what he told you?'

'So is he a colonel, too?'

This merited a smile. 'Not quite. Something between the two. Did he ever mention me?'

'I'm afraid I've forgotten your name,' she said.

'Daniele Zanetti,' he told her. 'But you can call me Colonel. That was a joke,' he said. 'Call me Danny if you like. And I can call you Hannah, right?'

Hannah, right? A brief flash of a black mask and her head forced under the water. But he was too big and it did not look as if anyone had been sticking scissors in his face, not lately at least.

'OK,' she said. 'Deal.' She found she quite liked this man. She could not think why, but there was something about him she could almost bring herself to trust. She realised this would probably be a mistake.

It was dark outside, but the streets were crowded. They were passing the Opera House.

'When we met in Afghanistan he was a captain,' said the colonel suddenly, as if he had been thinking about it. '*Acting* captain,' he corrected himself. 'Promoted from the ranks. But there was an incident.'

'What kind of an incident?'

'I was not there. I have only read the report. But it was in Helmand province. There was a report of Taliban in a village in the mountains. Aiden was second in command of a special forces unit, composed of different regiments, different nationalities. The commanding officer was an American. A major on his first tour of duty. On their approach they came under small arms fire. No one was hurt but the commander called for air support. Aiden was opposed to this. He considered the resistance to be light and advised a ground attack. But the commander had his way. The planes came and went. When the unit entered the village there was no further resistance. Everyone was dead. Most of them women and children and old men. Aiden was very angry. The major says Aiden assaulted him, knocking him down in front of his own men. Several witnesses say that Aiden only pushed him aside. Either way, the major ordered Aiden's arrest. Then all hell is let loose. It involves a number of men of different nationalities. Mostly pushing and shoving, maybe a punch is thrown. The result is a major enquiry. The findings were hushed up to avoid any political embarrassment but—Aiden was reduced to the ranks. Soon after this he left the service. He has not spoken to you of this?'

It was clear that he hadn't. He sighed. 'Well, Aiden has, what can I say—a strong sense of justice? Or perhaps the word is injustice. This combines with a strong—what is the word?—*tendenza* to take the law into his own hands. He does not always stop to examine the evidence, or what happens as a result. He would never make a policeman. But I suppose that has never been an ambition with him.'

So that ruled out one possibility she had considered. 'What does he actually do these days?'

'Good question. It is what we are all asking.' He glanced at his colleague, though all he could see was the back of his head. 'Officially he is a security consultant to one of the ruling families in the Emirates, but some will tell you that is a cover for less lawful activities.'

They turned into the hospital.

The priest was in a private room on the third floor with a police guard outside. Hannah had anticipated a sick, frail old man and was startled by how fit and well he looked. He was seated in an easy chair by the window reading a book, but on their entrance he stood up and gave Hannah a quick look of curiosity. There was no sign of the stroke in his face or his movements, but she noted the wheelchair behind the door.

The colonel—Danny—introduced them. Then he and his colleague left. '*He will talk more freely, I think, if you are alone with him,*' Danny had said. But she wondered if their conversation was being recorded. There was no obvious sign of it, but it seemed likely.

The priest indicated the one other chair in the room, beside the wheelchair.

'I am very sorry to hear about Doctor Blake,' he said with apparent sincerity. In fact, it looked as if it troubled him a great deal. He spoke a near-faultless English with just a trace of a German accent. 'Do you know what happened?'

She shook her head. There was no point in telling him what the police thought. She assumed he had already heard from Danny or one of his colleagues.

'There's a thought that it might have been to stop him writing his next book,' she said.

He looked shocked. 'But what was he writing that could be so important?'

Good question. 'You spoke to him, I think, not long before he died. Did he not tell you?'

'He said it was about the end of the war. The war in Europe, that is. It did not seem to be anything anyone would kill him for. Were you very close to Doctor Blake?'

'We had only just met,' she told him. 'But he was very interested in what happened in Merano in the spring of 1945.'

This was pure supposition. Michael had never so much as mentioned Merano to her. The old priest seemed to be puzzling over this, his expression tense. Hannah did not know if it was the strain of remembering or because he did not want to.

'Was it this that you and Michael talked about?' she prompted him gently.

He nodded. 'It was one of the things. But he seemed to know more about it than I did.'

Then suddenly his face brightened. 'You would like some coffee? *Kaffe und Kurchen?* They treat me very well here. I have never been so comfortable in my life. And they tell me there is an armed guard outside in case anyone else tries to kill me.'

He lifted the phone next to his bed and ordered coffee and cake for two. Hannah gathered that this was not accomplished without some opposition. When he had finished, he asked Hannah if she would mind speaking in German, as his hearing was not so good, and it would enable him to concentrate on remembering things other than the right English word to use. 'Besides, I like to hear German spoken by a beautiful woman,' he said. 'It is a much more seductive language than some people credit. I blame Adolf Hitler. They should remember Marlene Dietrich.'

Hannah took this graciously, making an allowance for his age. She wondered how he knew she spoke German, and what else they had told him about her.

'We were talking about your conversation with Doctor Blake,' she reminded him. 'Can you recall him asking you about a man called Bechmann? An SS officer who came to Merano at the end of the war. *Sturmbannfuhrer* Heinrich Bechmann?'

He bowed his head a little as if in thought, or he might have been praying.

'He was one of Hitler's bodyguards,' Hannah said. 'The most senior, I think. He was with him in the bunker in Berlin. And then in the last days of the war he came to Merano. To *Schlossraben*, in fact. Doctor Blake was very interested in this man. He did not mention him to you?'

He did not answer directly.

'Was he an important man, this Bechmann?' he asked her. 'I mean, what was the nature of Doctor Blake's interest?'

'Well, it was not so much him, personally, as what he might have brought out of the *Fuhrerbunker*.' He stared at her without expression. 'He had some papers with him,' she said. 'Documents. From Berlin. Relating to the Vatican.'

'And it is these papers that are of interest to you?'

There was a knock on the door and a nurse came in pushing a trolley and bringing a strong smell of coffee. Hannah suppressed a sigh of irritation.

'Ah, *Kaffe und Kurchen*!' The old priest was now rubbing his hands together, his eyes gleaming.

'You know you must not have coffee,' the nurse scolded him in English. 'I make it very weak and you are to have only one small cup.'

She insisted on taking his pulse and looked sharply at Hannah. 'How much longer will you take?'

'Not long,' said Hannah. She had barely started. 'I'll just be a few more minutes.'

'Well, do not get him too excited.'

'I am afraid those days are long gone,' said the priest sadly, but he winked at Hannah. His manner suddenly seemed more relaxed.

When the nurse had gone Hannah poured coffee for them both and carried his cup over to him with the slice of cake.

'Very well, I will tell you it all I can remember,' he said, when he had thanked her and taken a satisfying first sip of the coffee. His voice was stronger now and more confident. 'As I told it to Doctor Blake.

'It was the first week in May 1945. Hitler was dead by then, but I am not sure if we knew about that. We had a lot of other things to think about. Italy was in ruins. The Germans were fleeing north, leaving devastation behind them and taking whatever they could carry. The British and Americans were advancing from the South. The partisans were everywhere, settling scores. Especially in the North. Mussolini was on the run with his mistress, what was her name?'

He looked at her as if she could help him out. She shook her head apologetically.

'Clara. Clara something. She was with him in Salò, on Lake Garda . . . ?'

'Sorry,' she said. She wondered if this was a deliberate prevarication, but that was ridiculous. He was nearly ninety. She would have to accept a certain amount of rambling. 'And what was it like in Merano?' she said, trying to nudge him back on track.

'Ah, in Merano.' He smiled. 'In Merano, it was business as usual.'

She was startled, for this was the expression Hugo had used of *Schlossraben* when the SS were there.

'Merano was the Great Souk,' he said, 'the marketplace. A place of power brokers, wheelers, and dealers—*Geschäftemacher*—the place where the deals were made, fortunes exchanged, loot was traded, documents forged. Fascists, Communists, Axis, and Allies all mingling together, as if they had not been killing each other for six years, and still were. And in the middle of all this was *il Vescovo*.'

It was as if it was yesterday and not halfway through the last century. And also, as if a dam had opened. She wondered what had made such a difference from the first few minutes of their conversation. It could surely not have been the coffee.

'It is hard to imagine now, but in those days a bishop was like a prince—a prince of the Church of Rome—with great power. And I am talking of earthly powers. Senner, he was like the prince in Machiavelli. *Il Principe.* You know? A master of the *Realpolitik*, playing off one side against the other. There was so much distrust, you understand, even enmity between the Communists who answered to Stalin in Moscow and the British and Americans. Everyone is playing for the future, even if the past is not yet over. And into all this comes Major Heinrich Bechmann with these papers that he has brought from Berlin.'

She looked at him in surprise. A moment ago he had given the impression he had never even heard of the man.

'You knew about this at the time?' she said.

'Did I? How could I know of such things? I was only a child.' He looked at her as if she could tell him.

'But—you were a courier, were you not, between the bishop and the Communists?'

'*Kurier?*' He smiled at the word. 'That would be to exaggerate my importance, I think. I was an errand boy—one of many.' He used the word *Laufbursche*, a legman, a runner. 'I was not the confidante of *il Vescovo*.'

'But you spent some time in the Bishop's Palace?'

'It was more comfortable than on the streets. Or fighting in the mountains with the partisans. I was not paid, but there was always something to eat in the Bishop's Palace. I was something of a street urchin in those days, finding a refuge where I could.'

Ein Strassenkind. She could see the street urchin in him even now, the survivor. She wondered what had happened to his family, but she was not going to ask him now.

'So, when did you find out about all of this—Bechmann and the papers from Berlin?'

He considered the question with his head to one side, frowning with the effort of memory, like an old crow, she thought, or a magpie. 'Perhaps it was the bishop who told me. But not then. Years later perhaps when I knew him in Rome.'

'You knew Bishop Senner in Rome?'

'Yes. But he was a cardinal then, and the Vatican Foreign Minister. I was a lowly cleric. But we reminisced sometimes about the war. He may have told me then.'

He looked at the cake on the little plate as if he was trying to remember how it got there.

'Did he say why Bechmann came to him, rather than anyone else?' Hannah prompted him.

'I do not think so. Perhaps it was because they both came from the same part of the Sudtirol—and of course they may have met again in Rome when Bechmann was there during the war.'

'I did not know that Bechmann was ever in Rome,' Hannah said. And how did Father Winkler know?

'Oh yes.' But he was looking vague again. 'How do I know that? I am sorry, people tell you these things, and you forget who it was.'

Hannah thought she had better stick to Marcus Senner for the time being.

'There is a suggestion that the Bishop of Merano was a close confidante of the Pope,' she said. 'Pope Pius that is. That they had known each other pretty well in Berlin when he came to make a deal with the Nazis.'

'Yes, I have heard that. But again, it was not something I thought about at the time.' He smiled at the very idea. Then he looked sharply at her as if she had triggered a memory. 'You think this is why he came to Merano—Dechmann!'

'I think it might have been,' she said, keeping her voice gentle, the bedside manner. 'I think they would have known of this connection in Berlin. They would have known that the bishop would have been very interested in these documents and that he would have had a direct line to the Pope.'

The priest was shaking his head doubtfully. 'Everything was very confused at the time,' he said. 'I am not sure there were any lines. And besides, the Pope would have had a lot of other things on his mind.'

'But if they reflected badly on the Church?'

'In what way?'

She was struggling here, at least as much as he was. 'Well, in terms of complicity—with the Nazis. You said yourself, the past was in ruins, and everything was to play for. Italy might go to the Communists. All Europe for that matter.'

'Oh yes,' he said. 'The Church was the great ark in the flood. The only refuge in a hurricane.'

'So—these papers could have been very important,' she prompted him again. 'Especially if the Communists got hold of them.'

'Perhaps. Though it is hard to think what can have been in them that was so important.' He looked up at her, his face a picture of innocence. 'Is that what happened?'

'You tell me,' she said with a smile. 'You were there.'

'Was I? Where?'

'Merano,' she said, trying to keep her voice calm. '*Schlossraben*. You were there when Bechmann was shot, remember? On the night of May sixth. By the partisans.'

'May the sixth?' he repeated. 'Was I there on May the sixth? What day would that have been?'

There was another knock on the door and the nurse was back. She took one look at her patient and told Hannah in English: 'I think is time you leave.'

Hannah repressed a sigh. 'Well, thank you, Father,' she said. 'I am very glad to have met you and had this time to speak with you. Maybe when you are feeling a bit more recovered, we can meet again.'

'It is I who must thank you,' he said to her in English. 'You have taken a great weight off my mind.'

She nodded politely but had no idea what he meant. Although she knew she should make allowances for his age and his state of mind after the stroke he had suffered, she had a distinct feeling that she had just been taken for a ride.

'So—no "smoking gun,"' said Danny Zanetti when Hannah reported back to him. 'No *incriminanti documenti*.'

'You think he was telling the truth?' She imagined he had heard every word as clearly as she had. But maybe not. And they had been speaking German.

'A priest of Mother Church lying?' The Banker obviously thought this was not beyond the bounds of possibility.

'He is a Jesuit,' said Danny simply. 'One of the old ones.'

'So what do *you* think happened?' Hannah asked them. The three of them were back in the car, on their way back to police headquarters—she assumed.

'Well, I know what I think happened,' said Danny. 'They have Bechmann killed and throw the papers on the fire. Or bury them in the deepest, darkest hole in the Vatican, never to see the light of day.'

'Until now,' she said. A puzzled frown. 'If the Secret Archives are to be opened at last,' she clarified. 'Isn't that the plan?'

'Ah. Well . . . It is the plan of the Pope, maybe.'

'You don't think they'll let him?'

'We will see.'

'So—a secret never to be told.'

Another frown, though he hadn't finished with the first one yet.

'It's an old English nursery rhyme,' Hannah said, 'about magpies.'

He seemed at a loss. She was giving him a lot of work here.

'Birds,' she said. 'Black and white ones. Like crows.'

'Gazze,' said the Banker.

'One for sorrow, one for joy, three for a girl, four for a boy . . .' Danny looked at her as if she had lost it. Maybe she had. 'Five for . . . I don't know what five and six are for—but seven is for a secret, never to be told.'

'Okay. Thank you for that. But I think this is a secret they will keep, these magpies, whatever *il Papa* has to say about it.'

'You mean the Church? Even if they have to kill to keep it? Michael Blake, Irma Ulbrecht, their own people here in Sicily . . . ?'

'You could say it was in the finest traditions of the Vatican,' said the Banker.

'Well, that is what Aiden thinks,' Hannah confirmed.

'And you?' Danny was regarding her curiously.

Hannah gave a little shrug. 'It is so long ago. Who would care? Really? With all the other things to worry about in the world.'

'But people do,' said Danny.

'Especially in the Eternal City,' the Banker added, 'where seventy-five years is the blink of an eye.'

The car drew to a halt. They were outside her hotel.

'You are dropping me off?'

'*Dropping me off?*' Clearly, the expression was not familiar to him.

'Leaving me here.'

'Ah, no, I am sorry. This is to pick up your luggage. My friend will accompany you to your room, if you do not mind. While I wait in the bar.'

She was not amused. 'Where are you taking me?' she demanded.

'To a safe place.'

'Do I need a safe place?'

'We think so. For a day or two.'

'Why only a day or two?'

The two men exchanged glances.

'Until His Holiness has been and gone,' said the Banker.

'His what?'

'*Il Papa*,' said Danny. 'He arrives in Sicily tomorrow. Did Aiden not tell you this?'

'No.' She was startled. 'The Pope coming to Sicily. But why would Aiden . . . ?' She stopped herself from saying any more. 'What has the Pope got to do with Aiden?'

'That is another one for the magpies,' said the Banker.

'But—' Hannah could not make any sense of this. 'Why is the Pope coming to Sicily?'

'Good question. Because he is a Jesuit? Because he is who he is? *Per fare un punto?*'

'To make a point,' the Banker translated helpfully. It didn't help that much. 'He is coming to attend Mass at *il Duomo*—the cathedral in Erice,' he explained. 'To give Communion to the survivors of the attack on the *Gesuiti*. Your Father Winkler will be there—against the advice of his doctors—to pay his last respects to those who were killed.'

'It is *una Messa di Requiem*,' said Danny.

'A Mass for the Dead,' said the Banker, in case she hadn't got it.

CHAPTER THIRTY-FOUR

The Mass for the Dead

AIDEN HAD ATTENDED MASS JUST THREE TIMES IN THE PAST TWENTY years, and in each case death had been the prime, if not the sole, motivator. The first two had been funerals, one for a friend killed in Iraq, the other for his brother Michael. The difference this time was that there was no corpse. The dead had already been buried. This was their requiem.

He stood in the aisle to the right of the altar with his back to the wall, hands crossed in front of him in the traditional stance of the security guard. He wore a black suit with his ID card on a scarlet ribbon about his neck, and a radio communication device was plugged into his right ear. One of the men at the farmhouse had shaved not only his beard but the hair on his head to reduce the risk of his being recognised, and he looked far more like a professional bodyguard than when he had played the part for real. All he lacked was a gun.

'That will come later,' Eissen had told him.

The little cathedral was packed to capacity. Most of the congregation were priests or nuns, but the local community had been allocated several pews near the back. Nearer the front there were a number of dignitaries from Palermo and even Rome. At the very front sat the survivors. Seven of them in the pews—and Father Winkler, in his wheelchair in the side aisle, flanked by security guards. Aiden was at the far side of the nave, almost directly opposite him. If he had been armed he would have had a clear shot, though it might have been difficult to make his escape afterwards.

And that was not part of Eissen's plan.

He had explained it to Aiden in the kitchen of the farmhouse, with the photos and the plans of the cathedral spread across the table and dark clumps of Aiden's hair all over the floor.

'To the left of where you will be standing you will see a closed door.' It was to the left of Aiden now. 'This leads to a short transept and another door—a side door leading to the street. Officially, your job is to prevent anyone from coming in through that door during the service. However, when the survivors move to the altar rail to receive Communion, you will go through it and into the transept. On your left you will see a narrow staircase. This leads to the console where the organist usually sits. But at this service there will be no organist—not there—because the pipes for the organ have been removed and sent for renovation.'

This was the key to Eissen's plan. The pipes at the front of the organ, facing the church interior, had been replaced by vertical wooden slats, like a louvred shutter or blind. The angled gap between them, according to Eissen, was a mere seven centimetres—the same as the gap he had left in the shutters at the farmhouse for Aiden to shoot at the hen feeder—but they provided a restricted view of the altar rail, and the people who would be kneeling there. The handgun was presently concealed beneath the pedalboard in the organ console, now fitted with a silencer and a spring-loaded shoulder brace. Eissen had made him practice with them. They more than doubled the length of the weapon but the brace made for a steadier shot. All Aiden had to do was pick it up, take aim, and fire. Then he was to go down the stairs and out of the other door at the far end of the transept, which would be left unlocked for him. Outside would be another of Eissen's men, who would conduct him to a house in the city where he would be relieved of the gun and handed a bag containing his passport, his phone, and 200,000 euros. He would also be given the keys to a hire car parked outside the Porta Trapani. From there he was free to go wherever in the world he pleased.

It all sounded quite simple. And it was complete bollocks, Aiden had decided, from start to finish.

Even if the story about Father Winkler was true and even if Eissen meant Aiden to kill him, he would never let him walk away from it. With or without 200,000 euros.

If Eissen really meant Aiden to kill Winkler, he would have put him in place before the service began, not make him stand around until the target was wheeled up to the altar rail and have to do everything in a rush. The only reason he could have for not doing so was because he had no intention of letting Aiden anywhere near a loaded gun. If he did plan to kill the priest, he would have someone else do it and the assassin would be in position already. Aiden had a different role, if only a little less vital. His prints were already on the gun. That was why Eissen had made him go through the pantomime of practising at the farmhouse. Sometime in the next hour or so Winkler might very well die, but so would Aiden, probably in the chaos that would follow the shooting, and the police would find all the forensic evidence they needed.

Aiden glanced up at the louvred shutters, but he could see nothing behind them. It was impossible to tell if anyone was up there—unless he went up there himself. He looked around the interior of the cathedral. There were men stationed at intervals of a few metres along both of the side aisles, dressed as he was in dark suit and tie but doubtless, unlike him, all armed. None of them resembled the men from the farmhouse, not the ones he had seen at any rate. He guessed they were the special detachment of Swiss Guard whose job was to protect the person of the Pope. The one standing nearest to him bore some resemblance to the man he had encountered in the Church of Our Lady of Miracles in Rome. Aiden wondered what would happen if he moved from his present position before he was supposed to, but not enough to try it.

No wrong moves, Eissen had told him; everyone's on edge, I don't want you shot because you needed to have a pee.

They probably wouldn't want to make a scene in the cathedral itself, but the moment he stepped outside they would be all over him. He put a hand in his pocket and felt the buckle he had taken off his belt. The only weapon he had, and even if he could fight his way out of the cathedral, he still had to get out of the country—with no passport, no ID, no money, and no phone. The best thing he could do was give himself up to the Italian police and hope they would listen to him, and understand a little more English than he did Italian.

But he wasn't ready for that yet.

He heard a clipped voice in his earphone—*Tenersi pronto!*—followed by the opening chords of what the Order of Service told him was the Introit, played on a small chamber organ at the front of the choir. From the back of the church a solemn procession advanced down the central aisle led by a white-robed figure carrying a cross. There was a shuffling of feet as the congregation stood, then the first bemused stirrings as the people at the back took note of the individual immediately behind the man with the cross. An elderly, bespectacled man of average height, wearing a simple white chasuble and white zucchetto, with nothing particularly distinctive about his appearance . . . And then it dawned. By the time the procession had reached the choir the whole congregation was in a subdued frenzy as a thousand voices murmured *il Papa* in varied tones of astonishment and awe and adulation.

Even Aiden, despite his present concerns, was moved. It was probably not a latent religious fervour—he had not even felt that as a kid in Liverpool, when he had attended Mass every Sunday—and he had been a nonbeliever for many years. But there was something about this Pope that reached out even to nonbelievers. Aiden liked his style. He liked his non-conformity and his apparent conviction, his insistence on humility and simplicity—and his rejection of the trappings of office, including the famous red shoes. He liked the fact that he had once been a bouncer at a nightclub, and had danced the tango. But above all he liked his *contrariness*. For someone who had spent the best part of his life fighting insurgency, Aiden maintained an odd respect for rebels, and he felt that the benign, bespectacled presence walking down the aisle, smiling slightly, almost shyly at the stir he was causing, had something of the rebel in him, even if he was not an out-and-out insurrectionist, and that this was a quality he shared with Christ.

He had been alerted to the Pope's likely presence by Eissen shortly after they left the farmhouse. His Holiness wanted to pay his respects to the dead, Eissen had informed him, and to give Communion to the survivors, but the visit had been kept from the media in the interests of security. His presence was an added complication, Eissen admitted, but it might work to their advantage. There were four different agencies responsible for security—the police, the *Carabinieri*, the internal security service, and the Swiss Guard—and as usual the right hand did not always know what the left was doing. This would make it a lot easier for Aiden to pass undetected into the building and take up his position in the organ console.

The Pope disappeared into the shadows at the back of the choir, where he would probably remain until it was time to dispense the Sacred Host, and Aiden's thoughts returned to more personal concerns. He was still wondering about making a scene, disrupting the Mass to such an extent he would get himself evicted. If a thousand people saw him led away before the assassination attempt, it would be hard to argue later that he was the assassin. Hard, but not impossible. His prints would still be on the murder weapon, and it could be argued that he had found a way to reenter the building. It hardly mattered if they found his body inside or outside the cathedral, he would still be dead, and so would Father Winkler.

His best hope of survival was to figure out what Eissen's real plan was—but it was a big ask. What puzzled Aiden most was why Eissen was so determined to kill Winkler in the first place. Even if Aiden took the rap for killing him, there was bound to be a major inquiry into how it had been permitted to happen. It did not seem likely that Eissen would risk his reputation, and probably his job, to kill an eighty-eight-year-old paedophile who was going to die pretty soon anyway. Besides, the whole paedophile story seemed deeply flawed to Aiden. The current Pope was heading a campaign against child abuse among the clergy—he had even allowed one of his closest deputies to be indicted—and he must know of the allegations against Winkler. He would hardly block an attempt to have him prosecuted for them, no matter how powerful the priest's protectors were. Yet he was apparently willing to include him among those receiving the Eucharist from his own hands.

The other question that troubled Aiden was why Eissen was so insistent on the priest being killed at the altar rail. He could see over the heads of the congregation to where Winkler was seated in his wheelchair. It was about thirty metres away—well within range of a handgun like the Glock. He looked up to the vertical louvres where the organ pipes should have been. Maybe the angle was wrong, but it didn't look like it from where Aiden was standing. So what other reason could there be for the delay?

And then it hit him.

The priest wasn't the target. Eissen was planning to kill the Pope.

Even as the thought entered his mind, Aiden rejected it as impossible. Ludicrous. And yet . . . No one was in a better position to kill the Pope than members of his own security detail. It would not be the first time a bodyguard had turned his gun on the man or woman he was supposed to be guarding.

Aiden glanced along the aisle to where his neighbour was stationed, on the other side of the door that led to the transept and the organ console—the door Aiden was supposed to take at the start of the Offertory. But what would happen if he went sooner than that? What if he went now?

He thought about it for a few seconds longer, but it was one of those occasions where the more you thought about it, the less likely you were to do it. He crossed the small distance between them.

The man looked at him in astonishment. 'I need to have a pee,' said Aiden. He did not know the Italian for this, but it did not matter, as long as he said something.

He strode to the door that led to the transept. It opened inwards. To his relief the transept was as empty as Eissen had said it would be. The stairs leading to the organ console were on his left, the door to the street straight ahead. He stepped to one side and waited. As he had hoped, the other man was only seconds behind him.

He glared at Aiden and said something in Italian that sounded like an oath, but he kept his voice low as if he did not want to make a scene. Then Aiden pushed the door shut and hit him just above the left ear, his fist wrapped around the heavy metal buckle he had brought with him from the farmhouse.

He fell back against the wall and Aiden hit him again and watched him slide to the floor. He did not think there was much chance of him getting up in a hurry. There was no obvious means of locking the door, but he propped the recumbent figure against it in the hope it would cause a few seconds' delay if anyone else tried to follow him. But no one did.

He found the man's gun in a shoulder holster under his jacket. It was a Glock 19 with a silencer, presumably for silencing Aiden when the time came. He checked it was loaded, cocked it, and made his way up the stairs to the organ console.

Aiden checked the door carefully. It appeared to open inward, away from him, and again there was no sign of a lock. He held the Glock close to his face, pointing to the ceiling, and opened the door.

Eissen was sitting on the organ stool with his back to the keyboard and his eye pressed to a gap in the wooden slats that opened onto the choir of the cathedral. He looked round in surprise. Aiden was more than a little surprised himself. He had not expected Eissen to do the shooting himself, but there was a gun very like the one he had given Aiden in the farmhouse resting across his knees. His hand moved towards it.

'No,' Aiden instructed him sharply. 'Put your hands above your head and stand up, facing me.'

He had no idea what he would have done if Eissen had obeyed this instruction. Marched him out of the cathedral at gunpoint? And then what?

But he didn't. He threw himself backwards off the chair, bringing the gun up in both hands and pressing the trigger. They both appeared to fire at once. Aiden felt a blow high in his chest and fell back against the door, but he remained standing. Eissen remained on the floor. Aiden steadied his arm for a second shot but there was no need. There was a hole in his head, just above his right eye.

Aiden retreated out onto the landing and took a look down the stairs. The other bodyguard was still lying on the floor in front of the door. No one seemed to be trying to get through it. He stepped back into the organ console and put his eye to one of the gaps between the vertical wooden slats. He had a clear view of the altar rail and the first couple of pews. He could even see Father Winkler in his wheelchair. Everyone in his line of sight was looking towards whatever was happening at the altar. No one was looking up towards where he was standing.

Only then did he attend to his wound. He laid the gun down on the keyboard of the organ and felt inside his jacket. There was a lot of blood but it was not pulsing out. He did not think the bullet had pierced an artery. He eased the jacket off his right shoulder and squinted down at the wound, bracing himself for what he might see. But the bullet appeared to have entered just below his shoulder. It was bad but not fatal, possibly not even crippling. The most immediate problem was the blood.

He looked at Eissen again. There was no need to feel for a pulse. The bullet had left a small hole just above his right eye and there was a spreading pool of dark blood on the floor—with more on the wall behind him. Aiden saw that he was wearing gloves, white cotton gloves like those worn by lab assistants. He pulled them off and put one of them on his left hand, using the other to wipe his fingerprints off Eissen's gun. He took out the magazine and wiped that, too, then placed the gun back in Eissen's hand.

Finally, he reached into Eissen's jacket and found his wallet. It contained his ID, various credit cards, and a bundle of euros. Aiden took the euros and put the wallet back. Then he saw the box of tissues on a shelf next to the organ. He took a large handful of them and pressed them against the wound in his shoulder. It was not the best ligature he had ever contrived but it would have to do. Then he took one final look through the slats. The old priest had been wheeled to the altar rails and as Aiden pressed his eye to the gap another figure entered his field of vision and held up the sacred host.

His words carried clearly to Aiden: '*Il corpo di Cristo.*'

Aiden did not stay to watch the rest of the ceremony. Nor did he pause to wipe his prints off the door handle. There was too much of his blood splashed about the little room to hide the fact that he had been here. He descended the stairs and crossed to the door leading to the street. Despite what Eissen had told him, it was bolted at top and bottom, but the bolts slid back easily enough, and it did not require a key. He opened the door cautiously, keeping the gun ready, but there was no guard on the other side. Nor was there a bag with 200,000 euros and his passport and phone, but he had not expected that.

The street was empty. The entire population of Erice was probably in the cathedral. About fifty metres to the right was one of the gates in the old city walls. The Porta Trapani. He remembered the name from the map. On the other side was the ring road around Erice—his escape route—but there was a blue police car blocking the gate with two police officers standing beside it. Italian state police. He thought again about giving himself up, but he was too close to the cathedral. Eissen's men could still pick him up.

He turned in the opposite direction and strode up the narrow, cobbled street, trying not to hurry. He had no clear idea of where he was going, but there must be other gates in the old city walls. If he could reach the ring road he might be able to hitch a lift to Trapani or force someone to take him at gunpoint. He did not know much about Trapani except that it was a port, and if it was a port there must be ferries. There might even be ferries to France. He had a house he could go to in France, not far from Chamonix. He had bought it for the skiing and with the thought that it might make a useful refuge if ever he needed it. If he could make it to Toulon, he could get a bus to Chamonix for about forty euros.

Even as one part of his brain worked out these details, another part told him it was total madness. He was covered in blood. It had soaked the tissues, it had soaked his shirt, and it was pooling above his belt.

Then he realised that he was lost. Not that he had much idea of where he was going anyway, but he had been climbing through the labyrinth of narrow streets, and if he was going to find another gate he had to start going down. He took a turn to the right. This went down, but it was a dead end. He was starting to feel light-headed. He began to retrace his steps and saw someone coming up the hill towards him. It was Danny Zanetti. Who else? He could have used the gun, but to do what? He wasn't going to shoot Danny Zanetti. He wondered vaguely if Danny was going to shoot him. He didn't particularly care anymore.

'Lost again, Aiden?' said Danny. His voice seemed to come from a long way away. 'I think it is better if you let me look after you.'

CHAPTER THIRTY-FIVE

Sanctuary

AIDEN WAS INCLINED TO CONSIDER THAT FROM THE MOMENT OF HIS birth in the backstreets of Belfast the odds had been stacked heavily against him. This presumption had not been greatly modified by fifteen years' service in the Royal Marines. On the other hand, it had taught him that if you cannot change things, you might as well make the best of them, especially if it meant not having to get out of a chair.

Taking a pragmatic view of the situation, things could be a lot worse, he decided, as he sat by the pool of the holiday villa Danny's people had rented for them on the west coast of Sicily and took the top off a bottle of Moretti. The pool was heated but it would have been difficult trying to swim in it with one arm in a sling and his chest swathed in bandages. It was nice to sit in the midday sunshine, though, and have a beer.

'Here's to you, mate,' he said, reaching sideways to clink the bottle against the glass of Campari spritz, which was his companion's preferred tipple. 'I reckon I owe you one.'

A look of stunned disbelief. 'One what? A beer?'

'That was a joke,' Aiden said. 'It's called irony.'

He had explained irony to Danny once, during an idle moment in the Hindu Kush, but he didn't really get it. He owed Danny a lot more than a beer and they both knew it.

After guiding him through the streets of Erice to the temporary refuge of a bus shelter on the ring road, Danny had summoned backup and an ambulance. Then, after a short stay in hospital, Aiden had been removed under heavy guard to their present location.

It would be fair to say that he was impressed—and not just by the house and the pool. He had only a vague idea how Danny had extricated him from what he had the grace to admit was a difficult situation. Something to do with complex issues of national security that warranted AISI supervision. But Danny had warned him that if he did not cooperate fully with the investigation—or as he put it more succinctly, 'if you fuck with us'—he would have no compunction in handing him over to people who would make him a lot less comfortable than he was at present.

'You mean there won't be a pool?' Aiden looked concerned.

'There may be a pool,' Danny told him, 'but it will be full of shit. Like you.'

Aiden perceived that his friend was not in the best of spirits.

'What's the problem?' he enquired.

Danny's main problem, beside Aiden, was with the Vatican.

'They are saying Eissen had maybe just found the gun,' he said.

'What, like just before I came in?'

'They are saying he was just making a final check, in case they missed something. Maybe he found the pistol hidden in the organ console. Then you arrive.'

'Bollocks.' Aiden expressed an informed opinion. 'Who are these people?'

'Some are in the Swiss Guard. Others are senior members of the Curia.'

Aiden thought about it. 'So how did I get in the cathedral in the first place? How did I get to be part of the security detail?'

'Naturally, we have asked them this.'

'And what do they say?'

'Nothing. So far. But I guess they are working on it.'

'And what about the guy whose gun I took?'

'He claims to be suffering from amnesia, due to the knock on the head that you gave him.'

'Oh, for God's sake. Have you spoken to him?'

But so far Danny had been unable to get near the man. He was working on it, he said, but he had a lot of obstacles to overcome. It would save a lot of embarrassment for the Italian government, he said, if they accepted the version of events coming out of the Vatican.

'Does the Pope believe all this shit?' Aiden wanted to know.

'I have not spoken to the Holy Father personally. I suspect he has his doubts, but it would be helpful if we could find something to increase them.'

'Like what?'

'This farmhouse they took you. We need to find it. So—think. When they drove you from Palermo, you think they took the autostrada, yes? But for how long?'

'I don't know. I was asleep.'

'You were asleep?'

'Some of the time. Can't have been much more than an hour or so.'

'Did they not give you anything to eat?'

It had been another myth of their service in Afghanistan that if you did not give Aiden something to eat, he fell asleep.

'I was conserving my energy,' said Aiden. 'Trying not to worry. I woke up when we came off the motorway.'

'And then what?'

Aiden thought back. 'We started going uphill. There were a lot of bends.'

'So, a road with many bends, going uphill. In Sicily. That narrows it down a bit.'

'I had a fucking sack over my head.'

'And the farmhouse?'

Aiden thought some more. 'There were hens. And dogs. And maybe sheep. Or goats. Something with bells on.' Danny closed his eyes. 'For God's sake, Danny, they didn't give me the run of the place.'

Danny sighed. 'What about the sun? Do you remember where the sun was?'

'Apart from in the sky, you mean?'

Danny did mean that.

Aiden remembered the sundial he had made on the floor.

'The room I was in was facing south, I do know that. And there was a range of hills. I remember seeing them from the window, the one time I got a chance to look out. I might be able to remember the formation if I saw some pictures, but you know, one hill in Sicily looks pretty much like another. To someone who isn't Sicilian, anyway.'

'And on the drive to Erice?'

'Well, they put the sack back on. All I know it was mostly downhill.'

'With lots of bends?'

'With lots of bends.'

'And the sun?'

'The sun was on my left.'

'You are sure of this?'

'I was sitting in the back of the car, on the left side, and the sun was on the left side of my face. Yeah, I'm pretty sure.'

'So if you are right, you are travelling south. So this place, it is probably thirty or forty miles to the northeast of Erice.'

'Why not northwest?'

'Because to the west is only the sea.' He stood up.

'What are you going to do?'

'Get some satellite shots of the country northeast of Erice. Then we see what *you* can do.'

There were hundreds of them. And they all looked pretty much the same. Same hills, same valleys, same farmhouses. It took three hours before Aiden found something. The outbuildings, the hills, the track leading to it. They zoomed in as close as they could.

'I think this could be it,' he said.

'You are sure.'

'I'm not sure, but I think that's the hen house. If it's the right place there'll be a bullet hole in the hen feeder.'

They raided the place at dawn the next morning. The men who had snatched Aiden were still there—third-rate mafiosi, Danny told him, with nowhere else to go and fewer brain cells, he said, than the hens that had led him to them. They even found weapons used in the attack on the Jesuits, plans and photographs of Erice cathedral—and forensic evidence, not only of Aiden's presence, but also Eissen's.

Two night later, after he'd had the results from forensics, Danny cooked up a feast for them both. Spaghetti marinari with shellfish brought up from the market in Trapani, followed by fish and chips in Aiden's honour using a tuna steak instead of cod. Aiden would have preferred cod but he kept this to himself. They washed it down with two bottles of a local white wine—Catarratto Bianco—which Danny declared was almost as good as the wines of the Veneto, and finished off with fresh canolli and grappa.

'So, that's it then,' said Aiden. 'All over. A couple of Swiss Guards and a gang of third-rate mafiosi in the hills of Sicily.'

'You think?' Danny looked at him. Aiden did not think this at all, but he wanted to hear what Danny thought. 'Is just beginning, my friend. Now we go for the rest of them.'

His people had sent samples of Eissen's DNA to the police in Berlin and Long Island. They heard back from America the following day. Hairs, fibres, even a thumbprint that had previously been deemed irrelevant. Eissen's apartment in the Vatican had been searched without, apparently, coming up with anything of significance, but it had revealed his ownership of a villa on the coast at Santa Marinella and this had proved far more fruitful.

Danny brought up the pictures on his phone. Weaponry, old and new, military and religious regalia, tall conical hoods that could have belonged to members of the Inquisition or the Ku Klux Klan, and an emblem featuring a black cross on a white background.

'*Die Reigenfolge des schwarzen Kreuzes*,' pronounced Danny in awful German. 'A symbol of the old Prussian army. In English, the Order of the Black Cross. The Vatican is playing it down, in public at least. Just historical memorabilia, they say, but in private maybe is different.'

'So—this Order of the Black Cross . . .' Aiden was thinking of the paintings on the walls of the bunker in Berlin where he had met with Irma Ulbrecht. 'Is it still active?'

'Very much. They have a mission, these boys. To fight the forces of darkness. People like you, Aiden.'

'And the current Pope.'

Danny was scratching his beard, not usually a good sign. 'Well, this is your idea, Aiden. There is no evidence that the Pope was ever a target.'

'So you think it was the old priest?'

'They tried to kill him before, remember.'

He left Aiden to brood on this, but an hour or so later he was back with more news.

'Just heard from our IT people,' he said. 'Eissen hacked into your brother's computer. Or got someone to do it for him. It was on his laptop. He knew what your brother was doing and how much he knew and who his informants were—including Father Winkler and Irma Ulbrecht.'

'But how did he get on to Michael in the first place?' Aiden wanted to know.

'We don't know for sure. But your brother put in a request to interview Cardinal Emerson Seeburg four weeks before he died. The request was in Eissen's files.'

'The guy in the picture with Eissen?'

'That guy. The head of the Holy Office.'

'Why would Michael want to interview Seeburg?'

'We do not know. Whatever it was, the request was denied. But Eissen was very close to Seeburg—he was his security chief at the Holy Office before he took his present job.'

'Means fuck all,' was Aiden's considered opinion.

Danny agreed.

But what all this meant to Aiden personally was that instead of being the chief suspect in two murder inquiries, he was now chief witness for the prosecution, though there was little chance, Danny thought, of there ever being a trial. It was in the interests of both the Vatican and the Italian government to keep the crimes of Eissen and his former colleagues out of the public domain. However, Aiden would still be required to clear up a few things with officers of the Berlin police who would be flying down to interview him.

This might lead to charges, Danny cautioned him—'Apparently, blowing up a houseboat is a crime in Germany,' he remarked dryly—and Aiden would be advised to have a lawyer present. Aiden was almost past caring. Perhaps it was the trauma of being shot, but he felt a deep sense of anti-climax. There were so many questions still unanswered.

'Sometimes is the way,' said Danny when Aiden complained to him about this. 'Shit happen.'

'*Happens*,' Aiden corrected him idly. 'Shit being singular.' He thought about it. 'But I suppose it could be plural.'

'You could teach English,' Danny suggested, 'when you come out of jail.'

They were silent for a while, but Danny was obviously brooding over similar questions. 'It is like with the attack on the Jesuit centre,' he confided to Aiden. 'Why would Eissen take the risk? And use these pigshit mafiosi who fuck it up for him?'

'Local knowledge?' Aiden suggested. 'Didn't want to use his own people? You got nothing from the old priest?'

'Nothing that makes any sense. But there is a limit to how much we can interrogate a man in his late eighties who just has a stroke.'

'Nothing on these papers that Bechmann is supposed to have brought from Berlin?'

Danny shook his head wearily. 'It is bad enough to try to figure out what happens today. This is seventy-three years ago. The people I am speaking to, they are saying: "What is in these papers that can matter so much? Now, after so many years? It is all history." I am starting to agree with them.'

Aiden had finished his beer. 'Any more of these in the fridge?'

'Help yourself.' Danny gestured with his head in the direction of the kitchen.

Aiden lifted his arm. The one with the sling. 'I'm wounded, mate. Can't hardly move.'

Danny sighed, but he heaved his bulk out of the chair and came back in a few minutes with a bottle of Moretti for Aiden and a Campari spritz for himself.

'Another thing I don't understand,' Aiden began. 'If these papers come to light—and they are damaging to the Church, even today—it will be because the Pope has opened up the Secret Archives, right?'

'I guess.'

'So it could be seen as the Pope's fault. He lost control of the narrative. Why would that bother Seeburg? Or Eissen? It makes their case for them. He is the wrong man for the job.'

They drank in silence. More questions they could not answer.

The next day Danny left for Rome. He had things to do, he said, people to see. He would be back before the German police came.

While he was away the weather took a turn for the worse. There was snow on the top of the hills, though it didn't reach Aiden on the coast. He retreated from the pool and lit a fire in the hearth and continued his convalescence in an armchair with a Montalbano novel. He was half asleep with a couple of empty beer bottles at his feet when Danny arrived back from Rome, announcing himself from the doorway of the living room.

'Here he is. The man of action. Is where you find him these days. On the front line. Oh, he needs another beer. I fetch him another beer. But look, fat boy, I bring you a friend.'

Aiden twisted round in the chair. It was Hannah.

'I hear you've been in the wars,' she said. 'How you feeling?'

'I'm fine,' said Aiden. 'How about you?' He thought she looked tired. He'd heard they'd picked her up from the hotel and were holding her somewhere safe. 'I hope they've been treating you okay.'

'Not as well as they seem to be treating you,' she said looking about her.

'You need to get someone to half kill you first,' Aiden said.

'Shut up whining and wait to hear what she has to say,' said Danny. 'It was there all the time, staring you in the face. Tell him,' he instructed her.

'We were looking for the wrong thing,' said Hannah. 'It wasn't the papers. It was the man.'

Chapter Thirty-Six

The Sins of the Father

'Danny asked me to look through Michael's notes,' Hannah began. 'The ones they found on Eissen's desktop. To see if I could make any sense of them.'

Aiden raised a brow at Danny, who shrugged.

'Michael wrote in a kind of code or shorthand,' Hannah explained. 'It takes some figuring out. Y0 is Year Zero. H is Hitler. FB is the *Fuhrerbunker* . . . And there are references to Nostromo and Ash.'

'For any reason in particular?' Aiden asked dryly.

'I think it was just his way. You have to know where he was coming from.' This was perhaps not the most sensitive thing to say to his brother. 'How much do you know about *Alien*?' His expression did not alter. 'The movie.'

This is where it all started, she thought. At the job interview.

'I've seen it,' he said. 'A long time ago. What about it?'

'Well, Michael had a thing about it. *Nostromo* was a spaceship, on its way back to earth with a crew of seven—and the ship's cat. Ash was the science officer, but he was really an android.' Aiden was staring at her in that way he had when he was having serious doubts about her sanity, or his for choosing her as his researcher. She carried on regardless. 'Anyway, they get a distress call and pick up this alien that hatches out of an egg and constantly mutates, like a virus. It kills the crew one by one until only Ripley is left—that's Lieutenant Ripley, the second in command—and the ship's cat. Ripley escapes in the shuttle, *Narcissus*, with the cat, Jonesy.'

'What?'

'That was the name of the cat. Jonesy.'

He nodded, but still with that look of a rabbit caught in the headlights.

'Only then she finds she's got the alien aboard. She manages to expel it into space, but not before it plants its seed—probably in the cat.'

Aiden dragged his eyes away to see how Danny was taking this. Danny shrugged.

'Michael used *Alien* as an analogy for Fascism, or Nazis,' Hannah went on. 'It's like a virus. Always mutating. Finding new hosts. By the end of the war it had killed seventy-five million people. Europe was in ruins. But it seemed to have burned itself out. Hitler was trapped in his bunker with a few other Nazis. Then he gets this idea about the Vatican papers, so he sends Hanna Reitsch off with Heinrich Bechmann in this little plane they've hidden near the Brandenburg Gate. Michael would have loved that. Like Ripley in the shuttle, not knowing she's got the alien with her.'

'The alien being Bechmann?'

'No.' Hannah frowned as if he hadn't been paying enough attention, or she hadn't explained it well enough. Probably a bit of both. 'The alien is Fascism. Bechmann is the host. Nazi zealot, SS officer, Hitler's personal bodyguard. And a war criminal guilty of at least three major massacres. As hosts go, they don't come much better than that—for this particular virus. He was the perfect carrier. Michael must have thought he'd found the Holy Grail—' she frowned. 'That's probably the wrong analogy. But then he finds that Bechmann was killed—within a week of Hitler. In Merano.'

'How?'

'You know how,' said Hannah, a little irritated. 'He was shot by the partisans at *Schlossraben*.'

'I mean how did Michael find out? He didn't speak to Hugo, so far as we know.'

'No, but we know he spoke to Father Winkler and Monsignore Abruzzo. Either one of them could have told him. So, his main antagonist is dead. Kaput. End of story. Except that Michael starts to wonder why Bechmann went to Merano in the first place. He didn't know about the Vatican papers at the time. That was what Irma was going to tell him when he came to Berlin. But what he did know, or found out from his informants, was that in the later stages of the war the Bishop of Merano was harbouring German prisoners of war. In his own palace. He saw it as his Christian duty. And there were rumours he was helping Nazis, too. Nazi officials, SS men, real war criminals. Getting forged documents for them and helping to smuggle them out of Europe. There was a major investigation after the war by the Allies, but they couldn't find any evidence against him—except in one case. A German POW Michael calls Otto. And he was as much an enemy of the Nazis as the Allies were.'

She paused to make sure they were paying attention. They were sitting around the table in the kitchen. Danny had opened a bottle of red and produced a dish of anchovies and one of olives. It was growing dark but they hadn't switched on the lights. If they looked, they could see the sun sinking over the mountains, painting the snow with a red hue, but they didn't look much. They were paying attention.

'Otto was an officer in the Wehrmacht who was caught up in the plot to kill Hitler,' Hannah went on. 'He was sent to Ebensee concentration camp in Austria, where they worked prisoners to death—digging tunnels in the mountains for all the weapons factories they were going to build there. But by then the war was coming to an end, the SS guards had all deserted, and the *Volkssturm* took over. Old men and boys from the Hitler Youth. They didn't know what to do. All the prisoners were dying. Otto and some of the others managed to escape from a work detail. A few days later Otto was picked up by the partisans, trying to make his way over the mountains into Italy. He had the camp tattoo on his wrist, so they took him into Merano and handed him over to the bishop. He was more dead than alive, but he was hidden in the Bishop's Palace and given medical attention.'

She paused again to see if Aiden had guessed.

He nodded but she didn't think he had. She switched on her laptop.

'Michael knew about Otto from *Bonds of Blood*. He even used a picture of him when he was in the Afrika Korps.' She turned the computer round so Aiden could see it. 'I must have seen it when I first read the book at my mother's house, but it didn't mean anything to me at the time. Even with the caption.' She gave Aiden a moment to read it, but said it anyway. 'Otto von Seeburg.'

He had lost that rabbit in the headlights look. He did not look totally enlightened, but he was getting there.

'When the war ended the bishop's people fixed him up with documentation in his own name, and got him a job as a translator with the Allied Commission for Italy. Then he met an American nurse, married her, and went to live in Michigan, where they raised a family. Three boys and a girl. In the early seventies the youngest boy, Emerson, expressed the wish to become a priest. He was sent to a seminary in Rome and his father gave him an introduction to Marcus Senner, who was now a cardinal. Okay? Senner took him under his wing and he shot up the church hierarchy and eventually became a cardinal himself. Cardinal Emerson Seeburg.' She showed Aiden the picture. 'The bookies' favourite for next Pope.'

'And Michael knew this?'

'Almost certainly, but I don't think he was that interested. Not at first. Otto was one of the good guys. Part of the German resistance. A war hero. In fact, I think Michael had begun to lose interest in the whole project. I think that's why he brought me in, to do all the boring bits while he tried to find something with a bit more oomph.' She saw Aiden's pained expression and almost laughed. 'Don't worry, I don't mind, it happens all the time. It's what a researcher does. Michael wanted something like the list of companies who used slave labour in *The Murder Factory*. Something that would make a major splash and promote the book. But just after we met, I think he found something. That's why he sounded so excited.'

'When?'

'When he called me at my mother's place and asked me to come over to Long Island.' Hannah was searching for something else on the laptop. 'It was probably just a routine check. We found a reference to it in his emails.'

The email they had overlooked, with the receipt for $25 *for the reproduction of inboard Federal passenger arrival records for ships and airplanes 1941–1950.*

But Hannah was looking for a different one now. She showed him on the screen. The immigration documents for when von Seeburg and his new wife arrived in New York in 1947.

'But this came after Michael was dead,' Aiden objected.

'No. That was the receipt. They sent him this *before* he died. It was on Eissen's laptop. It's probably what got him killed.'

There was a photograph with the documents. Aiden looked at it and then at her. 'That's not Seeburg,' he said.

'No. It isn't.'

'So who is it?'

Hannah showed him the pictures she had found of Heinrich Bechmann.

'Fuck me,' said Aiden faintly.

'And this is Cardinal Emerson Seeburg,' said Hannah. 'Different uniform, same look. His father's son.'

Aiden was looking at the pictures, shaking his head.

'How did they do it?'

'I don't know, but it's not that difficult to guess. Otto was either dead or dying. They dressed him up in Bechmann's uniform, hung an ID round his neck, and drove him to *Schlossraben.* The partisans did the rest.'

'When you say "they" . . . ?'

'Well, I don't suppose it was the bishop himself. Probably his secretary. Maybe a couple of people they could rely on. And the boy, of course, Johann Winkler. We know he was there.'

'And Winkler never spoke about it?'

'No. Not to me, certainly. I had an idea he was holding something back. We'll probably never know for sure.'

'Why would he hold it back?'

'I don't know. Maybe he really didn't know what was going on. I think he probably found out later, but he was—compromised. He would have felt loyal to the Church and to Senner.'

'Why would Senner do this? For Hitler's number one bodyguard, a mass murderer for the SS?'

'He wanted those documents. He certainly didn't want the Communists getting hold of them. And Bechmann was offering him a deal.'

'Why didn't he just take them?'

'Maybe because Bechmann was holed up with the SS in *Schlossraben*.'

'But what Bechmann asked for was insane,' Aiden protested. 'To set up a meeting with the Pope. To get him to talk to the Allies. There was no way the Pope was going to agree to that, and even if he did, what influence did he have over Roosevelt and Churchill?'

'You're missing the point,' Hannah said.

'Oh. Go on then. What's the point?'

'Hitler died on April 30th. The news was all over the world by the time Bechmann reached Merano. CBS and the BBC put it out on May 1st, 1945. The Germans were about to surrender. Unconditionally. There was nothing for Bechmann to save. Except himself. A new identity, a ticket to South America, and enough money to get by. Maybe a bit more than that. And in return he'd hand over the Vatican papers.'

'You reckon?' Aiden sounded doubtful, but she could see he was thinking about it.

'There may not have been much in them, but why take the risk? And there might have been quite a lot the Vatican would like to keep quiet. They certainly didn't want Bechmann selling them to the Communists. Or the highest bidder.'

Aiden was looking at the pictures again.

'What about the real Otto? Didn't anyone ever miss him after the war? Or ask questions about him? Didn't he have family back in Germany, friends, army comrades?'

'I think they were all dead. After the plot to kill Hitler, the SS went berserk. Even by their usual standards. They killed everyone they could find who had the slightest connection with the plot to kill Hitler. Otto's parents died in Buchenwald. His two brothers had died earlier, on the Eastern Front, fighting the Russians.'

'And you found all this on Eissen's desktop?' Aiden was looking at Danny.

Danny nodded. 'It took a while, but yes.'

'How long had they been hacking into Michael's computer?'

'About two months before he died.'

'So they knew everything he knew?'

'Well, everything he had on computer. There was a record of his conversation with Winkler a week before the attack on the Jesuit centre. A Skype call. A couple of emails. Eissen must have decided he had to plug the leak. Silence the last witness—make it look like a terrorist attack. But they failed on both counts. So he went for your brother.'

Aiden sat there for a minute or so looking at the screen of the laptop. It was almost dark now but no one moved to put the lights on.

'Do you think Seeburg knew?' said Aiden. 'The cardinal?'

'We don't know. We're working on it.'

'Have you asked him?'

'Not yet.' Danny paused a moment. 'I thought it might be better coming from you.'

CHAPTER THIRTY-SEVEN

The Island of the Dead

THEY MET IN VENICE, AT THE BIENNALE. SEEBURG WAS THERE IN A private capacity, because of his interest in art, it was said, but he was still a prince of the Church of Rome. He sent his own launch to pick Aiden up from the jetty on the Giudecca Canal—the Canal of the Jesuits—with a bodyguard who patted him down before he let him aboard, but it was a fairly cursory pat. Aiden had clearance, at the highest level, even from the Vatican.

The cardinal was in the small saloon, seated at a small writing desk strewn with papers. He wore his red tonsure, with a black cape, also trimmed with red. He looked like a Hollywood movie star playing a cardinal.

'I thought we better try and sort this out,' he said, in the soft Michigan accent that sounded so good on television. 'Between ourselves.' Maybe a bit croakier than usual, as if he might be recovering from a cold. Or perhaps he'd done a lot of talking lately. Trying to talk his way out of the unholy mess he was in. He looked like he might be feeling the strain a little. Aiden could just about see the resemblance to Bechmann. The angel with metal wings. Perhaps all it needed was a different uniform.

The documents Danny had sent him were on the table—and the photographs. Seeburg picked up one of them and studied it for a moment, as if seeing it for the first time, though he'd had a month now to familiarise himself with them.

'All this was on Eissen's computer?' he asked, though it was not really a question. He must already know this.

'So I've been told.'

The cardinal looked at him for a moment. It was hard to read his expression. Then he nodded.

'Do you know what made your brother so interested?'

'He was in one of Michael's books. Two in fact. He must have wondered if you were related. It's not a common name, is it? Seeburg. A small town in East Prussia. Poland now. Zybork, the Poles call it.'

He heard himself going on, trying to shake off that sense of what? Reverence? He'd never spoken to a cardinal before. Never even met one. Your Eminence, he was supposed to call him. Aiden still had that little boy in him, who was made to go to confession every Saturday, that mixture of defiance and fear, and that was with a mere priest. But now the roles were reversed. He hoped.

The launch moved away from the jetty and they weaved past the *vaporettos* coming in and out of the Fondamenta Nuove.

'And how did he know who this man was?'

The cardinal was looking at the picture of Heinrich Bechmann on the immigration documents.

'I'm not sure he did, right away, but he was getting close. That's what got him killed.'

'I hope you're not suggesting I had anything to do with that.' He gave Aiden a hard stare and Aiden gazed evenly back. He would not let himself be cowed by a priest, not now, no matter how eminent he was. In the end, it was the cardinal who looked away. Back at the documents and photographs scattered on his desk. The nightmare of history spread out before him. 'I know I have to take some responsibility for all of this. And I have. But believe me, I had no idea what Eissen was up to. Or what he hoped to achieve by it.'

What Eissen had hoped to achieve was the election of Seeburg to the papacy, even if it meant getting rid of the present Pope first. Eissen and those who were behind him. Aiden wondered if Seeburg knew that. He felt the boat pick up speed. They were moving out into the lagoon, out of the ruck of traffic around Venice.

'Where are we going?' he asked.

'The Isola di San Michele. The Island of the Dead. You ever been there?' Aiden shook his head. 'I want to lay a wreath on one of the graves. Then perhaps, we can walk for a while—and talk. In the meantime, if you will forgive me, I would like to take the air.'

The Island of Saint Michael had been turned into a cemetery at the time of Napoleon: a hygienic alternative to the overcrowded, medieval graveyards of Venice. It was still in use and they walked along one of the footpaths, followed at a slight distance by the bodyguard, carrying the wreath. Aiden wondered if he was from the Swiss Guard.

The cardinal stopped at one of the graves. The inscription was in German, but Aiden did not require a translator. It was the grave of Marcus Senner, Cardinal-Bishop of Merano. Born 1895, died 1981. There was an angel guarding it. A white angel.

'I don't know why he chose Venice,' Seeburg was saying. 'He was born in the South Tyrol, you'd think he'd want to go back there. To the mountains. But no, he came here. Perhaps he'd read Thomas Mann.'

But Aiden hadn't. He hadn't the faintest idea what Seeburg was talking about. Hannah would have known.

The bodyguard brought up the wreath. Seeburg took it and placed it against the stone, then stood back a little to make the sign of the cross and close his eyes in prayer. When he had finished, they walked on—in silence at first, their footsteps crunching on the gravel. There was no one else about, but Aiden sensed the bodyguard following them, a discreet distance behind.

'My father would never talk about the war. You can understand why. I didn't know about any of this until Marcus told me, here in Venice, when he was dying. What really happened at Merano at the end of the war.'

He was silent for a moment, either because he was remembering what Senner had told him or was censoring it in his head before he spoke. 'It wasn't a confession, as such, or I wouldn't be talking to you now, but he probably felt he needed to explain himself, especially to me.' He looked sideways at Aiden. 'You know about the SS men at *Schlossraben*—the SS *Einsatzgruppen*?'

'I've been there,' Aiden nodded. 'I've seen their graves.'

'You've been there?' He seemed to be thinking about this. 'For any reason in particular?'

This seemed an odd question to ask. According to Danny he knew the whole story.

'I'd heard about Bechmann, and the papers he brought out of Berlin. But I didn't know where he went after that. Not at the time.'

'Right. The papers from Berlin.' He nodded grimly to himself. 'Marcus didn't even know what was in them, but whatever it was, he didn't want them falling into the wrong hands. The stuff about the death camps was just coming out. There were pictures of the piled-up corpses, the gas ovens. Any hint of complicity with that—or what the Vatican knew about it—even to remind people of the deal they'd made with the Nazis back in thirty-three ... Marcus knew what it would mean. Italy was ready to fall to the Communists—so was most of Europe. The Church was one of the few remaining obstacles. Stalin and the Reds would use anything they could that would appear to link the Vatican with the Nazis. This would be a gift from the gods. Or the devil. So, he agreed. Bechmann wanted a new identity—so Marcus gave him one.' He glanced at Aiden again with what was almost a sigh. 'As you know.'

Aiden nodded. 'What I don't know is how Otto died.'

'Ah. Right. You think they had him shot?' He shook his head. 'No, no, no. Marcus would never have handed Otto over to the Communists if he was still alive. He died of pneumonia. In the Bishop's Palace. He never recovered from what happened to him at Ebensee—and that walk across the Alps. That's what Marcus told me, and I don't think he'd lie about it—not when he was dying himself.'

'So, they put Bechmann's uniform on him and drove him to *Schlossraben*—and dumped him with the other bodies.'

'Well, they gave them a Christian burial as it happens, though that was largely because of Otto, of course. They couldn't very well bury him by himself and chuck the others in the cesspit.'

'We did wonder,' said Aiden.

They walked on.

Aiden broke the silence. 'Did you ever ask your father about any of this?'

'By the time I found out, my father was no longer with us. He died two years before Marcus did.'

They had walked in a large circle and were almost back where they had started from. They could see the landing stage where the launch awaited them among the *vaporettos* going backwards and forwards between the islands. A funeral boat was coming in, followed by a small flotilla of motorboats with the mourners.

The cardinal regarded him with a bland smile. 'So, is there anything else you want to know?'

'The Black Cross?'

'Ah, yes. The Black Cross.' He looked away again towards the funeral boats. 'Well, there's not much I can tell you about that, nothing you don't already know. Certainly, that your friends know, in the AISI. Madness.' He shook his head. 'Utter madness. But I knew nothing of it. And now it's a job for whoever takes over from me—in the Holy Office.'

He had resigned, as of yesterday. It had been in the news. No explanation given. The bloggers were already saying he had been forced out—by the left-wing Pope and his allies.

He looked at Aiden again, a frank open gaze that might have been convincing if Aiden had been more open to being convinced. 'I had no knowledge of what Eissen was up to—not an inkling—not until I met your friend Colonel Zanetti in Rome.'

'But everything Eissen did was for you.'

'Was it?' He shook his head as if in sorrow and turned away, walking on. After a moment Aiden followed. The mourners had disembarked and were crossing the path in front of them. They looked at the red-tonsured figure in surprise. He stopped and made the sign of the cross and they all bowed reverently.

'Eissen's loyalty was obsessive, psychotic,' said the cardinal as they stood there, waiting for the cortege to file slowly past. 'But let's face it, my position was of some value to him, and the people behind him. That might have come into his calculations.'

'Who are we talking about here?'

They had been going round in circles all this time, but at last they were here.

'Eissen wasn't alone in this,' Aiden pressed him. 'He had money behind him.'

'You mean those who would make me Pope?' The thin smile again. *A smile like the silver plate on a coffin.* Another expression Aiden recalled, but from where? Not Danny certainly. It was Michael, of course, talking about some long dead statesman. 'The moneylenders in the Temple. I don't know who they were. I could probably make an informed guess, but—that doesn't count as evidence. And why would I?' He turned to engage Aiden directly again. 'Or are we plea-bargaining here?'

'With me?'

'With the people who sent you. They wouldn't do anything about them, you know, even if they had proof. They wouldn't put them in jail, whatever they're telling you. The people they're interested in, they're untouchable. By any legal means.'

He gave Aiden a look that might have been significant, but he didn't get it at the time, only later, when he thought about it.

'If you could make an informed guess, then,' he said, 'who do you *think* they are, these people?'

The cortege had passed. They walked on.

'It really doesn't matter. It's over now. It died with Eissen. There may have been some people who thought I'd make a better Pope than . . . the present Holy Father. A Pope more amenable to their way of thinking. They were wrong about that, as a matter of fact. I'm nobody's puppet. But we'll never know, will we? I've become a liability. It's no longer feasible, what they had in mind. If it ever was. We have the Pope we have, and I hope he'll live a long time.'

Aiden wondered if he meant that. They seemed to have reached a dead end—in both their walk and their talk. They were at the water's edge, staring back across the lagoon towards Venice in its distant haze. There was another funeral barge coming in. Aiden's time was up. He wondered what it had achieved, from Seeburg's point of view as well as his own.

But then the cardinal started talking again, softly, as if to himself.

'I loved my father. He was a good father. You might even say he was a good man, in his later years. Good Catholic. Went to Mass on Sundays and Saint's Days, joined the Knights of Columbus. It made him very proud, my becoming a priest. If he'd known I was going to be made cardinal, head of the Holy Office . . . the son of Hitler's bodyguard.'

He lifted his head and looked directly at Aiden, a look of defiance in his eyes, or was it appeal? 'They weren't monsters, you know, these people, even though they did monstrous things. They didn't have horns and fangs. They were quite ordinary people, most of them, family men, joined clubs— played football, tennis, paid their taxes, went to church, sang hymns, sang "Silent Night" at Christmas with tears in their eyes. They were just—misled—most of them. Misled or deluded. Probably both.'

Aiden remembered Hannah telling him about Irma's exhibition in the lobby of the Schutzstaffel Museum, all those photographs of 'ordinary people.'

'So why don't you say that?' he asked. 'Forgive them, for they know not what they do.'

A brief flash of the silver plate on the coffin. 'Yes, that would go down well. Don't you think? He didn't just murder Jews, you know, and Russians, my father. You know about Dunkirk? And the crossroads at Baugnez? All those murdered GIs lying in the snow. I don't think people would be that forgiving, do you? That they'd be perfectly happy to see his son crowned as the next Pope.'

It sounded like the last word on the subject. But he couldn't leave it there.

'There was something else Marcus told me, you know, about my father. About an incident in Rome, in 1943. The SS were rounding up the Jews—they wanted to send them off before the Allies arrived, to the death camps—and there were these schoolgirls, from the Jewish High School, they had them lined up in the street, ready to load into the trucks, but a crowd had gathered. They were screaming at the SS, leave them alone, let them go, blocking the street. You'd have expected my father to fire on them, from what we know about him at that stage in his life. But he didn't. He let the girls go. No one knows why. But whatever it was, he let them go. That single act of redemption. It meant a lot to Marcus, that.'

It wasn't enough, Aiden thought, but he let it pass.

'I have to go on to the airport,' Seeburg said. 'But it is easy for you to get a *vaporetto* from here.' He held out his hand. 'Well, I am glad we have had this conversation . . .' It was curved slightly, the fingers pointing down, not straight forward as if for a handshake. Aiden wondered for a moment if he was expected to kiss his ring. Fuck that, he thought. But then he saw the edge of the paper Seeburg was holding in his palm. He bent down to kiss the ring and the paper changed hands.

'Fucking priests,' Aiden said aloud. He was watching the launch heading out across the gulf, back towards Venice.

'Say three Hail Marys and make an Act of Contrition,' said Danny.

'Me or him?'

'I think he knows it will take more than that as far as he is concerned. And as for you . . .'

'Did you get it all?'

'For what it is worth.' Danny held out a hand. 'Give.'

For a moment Aiden thought he meant the paper. He nearly gave it to him. Then he realised and pulled out the wire.

'He probably knew,' he said.

'You think?' Danny made sure it was no longer transmitting. 'Is that why he had nothing to say?'

'He doesn't think you'd do anything with it anyway,' Aiden said.

'I heard what he said.'

'Is he right?'

A slight lift of the shoulders. 'I do what I can. I cannot speak for the politicians. Or even my own bosses.'

'So what will you do—keep it in the files, in case he's the next Pope? So you've got something on him.'

'He will never be Pope,' Danny said firmly. 'Not now. You heard what he said—he is a—what was the word?'

'Liability,' said Aiden. But he was not sure it was true. Times changed, people changed, at least in their opinions. One day Heinrich

Bechmann might become a hero again. It might not be that far away. They walked back along the jetty to where Danny had left his own boat with the sound team.

'So—can we drop you off somewhere?'

'No, Danny, just leave me on the Isle of the Dead.'

Danny laughed. 'I wish. But no, that was a joke. We go back to Venice. Book in the Baglioni. Have a few Bellini.'

Aiden took this as a joke, too. Unless Danny had a better expense account than most policemen.

'Or is there anywhere else you would like to go? Anyone waiting for you?'

Aiden wondered if he meant Hannah. He shook his head.

'Nowhere,' he said. 'No one. Come on, I'll buy you a beer. But not in the Baglioni.'

CHAPTER THIRTY-EIGHT

A German Soldier

AIDEN GAVE HANNAH THE SLIP OF PAPER AND WATCHED HER FACE AS she looked at the list.

'What is it?' she said.

'A list of names,' he said.

'I can see that. But who are they?'

'Four of them are businessmen. At least they call themselves that. One is a media baron. Two are politicians. The other runs a blog. They are all immensely rich and they are all members of the neo-Right. There are other names for them. One of the more polite is Dark Money.'

They were sitting in a pavement café in Merano, where he'd met her off the train from Milan. No snow this time. It was early May and hot for the time of year. Hannah wore a hat—a wide-brimmed sennit hat with a scarf tied round the brim—and a summer dress and sandals. She looked like a tourist.

She passed the paper back to Aiden. 'So what are they to you?'

'Seeburg gave the list to me,' Aiden told her. 'When we met in Venice.'

'Did he say why?'

'No. He knew I would be wired. But he knew I'd make an informed guess.' He used the cardinal's own words. 'They're the people who were behind Eissen. And Seeburg's bid for Pope.'

He kept his voice low, though there was no one sitting near enough to hear him. They were in that hiatus between morning coffee and lunch.

'When you say—*behind* . . . ?'

'Or maybe above. Pulling the strings. The way puppet masters always do. They put up the money, they put on the show. But they stay behind the scenes.'

'Very good,' she said, rolling her eyes. 'So what?'

'Maybe it's time they paid a bit more.'

'You're going to blackmail them?' He looked pained. 'Kill them?'

'I told you. I don't kill people. Not unless they're trying to kill me.'

'They might. If they got wind of this.'

'That's not the way they operate. According to Danny.'

'Have you shown him that?' She meant the paper with the names.

'Not yet.'

'Not yet? It's been two months.'

'I'm thinking about it.'

'Oh well, take your time.'

'Seeburg said they were untouchable,' Aiden said. 'By any legal means.'

'So—what's the alternative? Given you've ruled out killing them?'

'I'm thinking about it.'

'Oh, well let me know when you . . .'

'Look, we know how these people operate. They fund other people to do their dirty work for them. Research institutes, journalists and politicians, trolls and nutcases . . .'

'Swiss Guards.'

'Well, Eissen for sure. Seeburg's pretty pissed off with them at the moment because they've dropped him, but he says he's got no evidence, and if he has, he's not prepared to pass it on to anyone else.'

'So—where does that leave you?'

'Michael left me some money. Quite a bit. Royalties from the books. Other stuff. I think he'd have liked me to carry on with what he was doing.'

'What—writing history books?'

'Very funny. I was thinking of something a bit more direct.'

She looked at him suspiciously. 'Like what?'

'Finding out stuff.'

'About the people on the list?'

'Why not? It's the way *they* work.' He was looking at her in a way she didn't like. 'Only I'd need some help.'

'No way. God, Aiden, after what I've just been through.'

'What's that?'

She looked at him as if she couldn't believe this. 'I mean, it might be normal for you, but . . .'

'You came out of it all right, didn't you? Look at you. Not a mark on you.'

She put her hand up to her brow and massaged it gently, closing her eyes.

'Well, think about it,' he said. He signalled a waiter to pay the bill. 'We better get moving.'

They stood at the graveside. Seven of them, not counting Bruno the dog. Aiden and Hannah, Danny, Hugo with Karl-Luca and his wife Anna—and Father Johann Winkler. Danny had told him what was happening, and he had insisted on being here. He wanted to see things done right, he said, presumably having seen them done wrong, seventy-three years ago. Danny had made the arrangements. He seemed quite fond of the old priest. He sat in a wheelchair which Karl-Luca pushed for him, but otherwise he looked well, for eighty-nine. Eighty-nine was not so old these days, he said to Hugo. Death would have to wait a little longer. He wore a Panama hat against the sun, and he seemed glad to be here, back in his own Heimat, even on so solemn an occasion. The twin giants of Hohe Weisse and Hohe Wilde peering benignly down on them from a perfect sky. Even the *Schloss* looked a little less menacing than when Hannah and Aiden had first seen it in the snow after their trip from Berlin.

Hugo had done everything the way they wanted. The old grave had been dug up and the body moved to a new site, close to Hugo's own family. It was still bare earth, of course, though they had planted bulbs, Hugo said, including the cornflower Otto would have seen in the fields of the family home in East Prussia. It was the nearest thing the old Prussian state had to a national flower, he said, the same colour as the uniform he would have worn on formal occasions. The gravestone was new, too, and very white among the weathered stones that surrounded it. On it was the name Otto von Seeburg and the dates 1917–1945. There had been some discussion about an epitaph. 'Died for the Fatherland' had been proposed—and rejected. In the end they had gone for Hannah's suggestion. *Ein Deutscher Soldat, fur den Frieden gestorben.*

A German soldier, who died for Peace.

There was a small picture of him under glass with a wrought-iron frame—the same picture that Michael had used in *Bonds of Blood* showing a young Wehrmacht officer, smiling for the camera. And a red candle in a small lantern, in the Austrian tradition. Hugo gave Aiden a box of matches and asked him to light it.

'We will keep it burning,' he said. 'But you must light it the first time. One soldier for another.'

Father Winkler said a brief prayer in German, and then they began to make their way back to the terrace where Anna had prepared lunch. The priest stayed a while longer, sitting in his chair at the side of the grave, with Karl-Luca standing at a respectful distance behind him. Hannah paused and watched from the edge of the cemetery, wondering what thoughts were passing through his head and if he was remembering what had happened when they first buried him here. He had hardly said a word to her since she arrived, hardly meeting her eyes. Perhaps he felt guilty after their last meeting, for what he had not said then. More likely, he could not remember what he had said, or who she even was. But then he signalled Karl-Luca, who began to push the wheelchair towards them, and for some reason she stayed standing there until he reached her. Then he looked at her directly and she saw that he knew perfectly well who she was.

'I am sorry,' he said to her in English when the chair drew level.

'Sorry for what?' she said.

'That I could not tell you, what happened here that day.'

Could not or would not, she thought, but did not say.

'All those years of loyalty to Mother Church,' he said. 'It is difficult to change the habits of a lifetime. But I was wrong. I am sorry. Mea culpa, mea maxima culpa.'

He raised his hand again in what might have been a blessing or a farewell and Karl-Luca pushed him on.

Aiden had stopped to wait for her.

'What was that about?' he said.

'How would I know?' she said. 'I'm not a Catholic.'

'Have you thought about it?' he said.

She was confused for a moment, but then she realised what he meant.

'I'd have to be out of my mind,' she said.

It was the first time she had seen him smile, she thought. A real smile and not the ghost of one. Except in the picture Danny had showed her, from a long time ago, when he was still in the Marines.

'I'll take that as a yes, then,' he said.

THE END

Afterword

Truth and Fiction

THIS IS A WORK OF FICTION WITH CHARACTERS THAT ARE MOSTLY OF my own invention, but the historical element is based on a true story, or rather several true stories, and they include a number of people who existed in real life.

One of them is the German aviatrix Hanna Reitsch, who flew into Berlin in the closing days of the war when the Red Army was closing in on the last remnants of Nazi resistance. She was always clear about why she flew *into* the besieged city—it was to die at the side of her Fuhrer—but then he persuaded her to fly out again. Why? This has been the subject of much speculation by historians, but although Reitsch was captured by US forces in Austria and interrogated by a captain in the OSS (the forerunner of the CIA), she either wouldn't say, or what she did say was heavily redacted.

The Russians were convinced for a time that she had taken Hitler with her. Even when they conceded that Hitler probably was dead (they had found the charred remains of his supposed body outside the *Fuhrerbunker*), they continued to believe that before he died, he had given Reitsch certain documents that would persuade the Allies that it was in their interests to negotiate a separate peace from the Soviets.

What were these documents? Again, this is all speculation. But in the prewar period a number of deals were struck between the Nazi regime and foreign governments and international organisations—deals which enabled the regime to maintain power within Germany and then go on to conquer most of Europe.

During the bombing of Berlin, most of the Nazi archives were moved to Potsdam for safekeeping, but there is a suspicion that Hitler kept some of the most important documents with him in the *Fuhrerbunker* or sent for them in the last days of the war. Either way, they would have fallen into the hands of the Russians, who presumably still have them—*unless* Hanna Reitsch took them with her when she flew out again.

Some of these documents concern the deals that were struck between the Nazi regime and the Catholic Church under Pope Pius XII. The significance of these deals has long been a source of controversy, and to tackle the issue once and for all Pope Francis recently decided to open the relevant Vatican archives—formerly known as the Secret Archives—to a number of researchers and historians. This decision generated a storm of criticism from within the Church and among neo-Right groups who were opposed to any investigation of this nature and whose opposition to the present Pope had led them to call for his removal from office.

It is these true stories that form the basis for the novel, and I had the advantage of working as director on a couple of documentaries—one for the BBC and another for the British Channel 4—which covered some of the historical events that are included in it.

Perhaps the most dramatic was the discovery of what remains of the bunker complex under the Potsdamer Platz in the centre of Berlin. In real life this was photographed by the Berlin authorities and then filled with sand to prevent it becoming a shrine for neo-Nazis. But the photographs still exist showing the murals much as I've described them in the novel. The character of Irma Ulbrecht, however, and the idea of turning the bunker into a museum is pure fiction and there is no such thing as the Schutzstaffel Museum, though there are plenty of other such warning museums throughout modern Germany.

In the course of making the Channel 4 documentary, we filmed at a medieval castle, near the spa town of Merano in the South Tyrol. Now a hotel, the castle was used during WW2 as a distribution centre for counterfeit currency forged in the concentration camp of Sachsenhausen, north of Berlin, and despatched in regular shipments throughout the war. The original intention was to scatter the forged notes widely over Britain in the hope it would destroy confidence in the official currency and cause financial chaos. This had worked for the British in Revolutionary France and even in the US at the time of the Independence War. But the men behind the idea decided the notes were too good to throw away, even in a bid to win the war for the Nazis. Instead, they used them to purchase things of real value—works of art, jewellery, property, and shares in some of the world's largest multinational companies—and in the final stages of the war, they were used to purchase a false identity and safe passage out of Europe for certain SS officers and Nazi war criminals.

There is strong evidence that these deals involved agents of the Vatican, representatives of the Swiss Red Cross, members of the Allied intelligence services, and even Zionist groups. I was shown copies of some of these forged documents and photographs taken days after the German surrender of SS men, still in uniform and carrying sidearms, sitting at pavement cafés in Merano with a number of civilians and men in US or British army uniform while an American MP directed traffic.

Ironically, while this was going on, others were hunting down these men, sometimes legally, sometimes not. In Israel—on a farm in Galilee—I met a man in his late nineties who had been based in Italy at the end of the war, with the Jewish Brigade of the British Army. In the weeks following the Nazi surrender he said that he and his comrades would go out at night, with the tacit permission of their officers, to seek their own form of justice on SS prisoners of war.

'You mean you killed them?' I said.

'Well, we did not send them to South America,' he said.

However, the castle I have called *Schlossraben* is an invention, and the members of the von Stahlberg family are pure fiction and bear no resemblance to anyone, living or dead.

So this, in a roundabout way, is to say thank you to the people who told me these stories and who planted the idea for the novel in my mind, particularly the image of the embryonic alien that clamps its tentacles round John Hurt's face and then comes bursting out of